HAVE YOU EVER KNOWN someone with nine lives? Like that daredevil who broke seven bones in his body last summer but somehow led his team in goals this lacrosse season. Or the two-faced girl who sat next to you in geometry—even though she cheated on tests and back-stabbed her friends, the bitch always landed gracefully on her feet. *Mrow.*

Relationships can have nine lives, too—how about the boyfriend you fought and made up with for two years straight? Or the conniving BFF you forgave again and again? She was never truly dead to you, was she? But maybe it would be better if she *was.*

Four pretty girls from Rosewood find themselves faced with an old frenemy they thought had gone up in flames— literally. But they should know by now that nothing in Rosewood is ever really over. In fact, some long-lost bes-ties live on to get exactly what they want.

Revenge.

BOOKS BY SARA SHEPARD

Pretty Little Liars
Flawless
Perfect
Unbelievable
Wicked
Killer
Heartless
Wanted
Twisted
Ruthless
Stunning

Pretty Little Secrets

The Lying Game
Never Have I Ever
Two Truths and a Lie

Twisted

A PRETTY LITTLE LIARS NOVEL

SARA SHEPARD

HARPER TEEN

An Imprint of HarperCollinsPublishers

HarperTeen is an imprint of HarperCollins Publishers.

alloyentertainment
Produced by Alloy Entertainment
151 West 26th Street, New York, NY 10001

Library of Congress Cataloging-in-Publication Data
Shepard, Sara, 1977–
    Twisted / Sara Shepard. – 1st ed.
        p.   cm. – (Pretty little liars ; #9)
    Summary: Now seniors in high school, Spencer, Emily, Hanna, and Aria's friend-
ship has been torn apart by new lies and stress, but they are drawn back together when
anonymous messages threatening to reveal their secrets resume.
    ISBN 978-0-06-208102-5
    [1. Friendship–Fiction.   2. Secrets–Fiction.   3. Conduct of life–Fiction.   4. High
schools–Fiction.   5. Schools–Fiction.   6. Mystery and detective stories.]   I. Title.
PZ7.S54324Twi 2011   2011019360
[Fic]–dc23   CIP
                                                                             AC

Design by Liz Dresner

14 15 16   CG/RRDC   10 9 8 7 6
❖
First paperback edition, 2012

To all the Pretty Little Liars readers and fans

Before you embark on a journey of revenge, dig two graves.

—CONFUCIUS

SOME FRIENDSHIPS NEVER DIE

Have you ever known someone with nine lives? Like that daredevil who broke seven bones in his body last summer but somehow led his team in goals this lacrosse season. Or the two-faced girl who sat next to you in geometry—even though she cheated on tests and backstabbed her friends, the bitch always landed gracefully on her feet. *Mrow.*

Relationships can have nine lives, too—how about the boyfriend you fought and made up with for two years straight? Or the conniving BFF you forgave again and again? She was never truly dead to you, was she? But maybe it would be better if she *was*.

Four pretty girls from Rosewood find themselves faced with an old frenemy they thought had gone up in flames—literally. But they should know by now that nothing in Rosewood is ever really over. In fact, some long-lost besties live on to get exactly what they want.

Revenge.

✦ ✦ ✦

"Last one off the cliff buys dinner!" Spencer Hastings double-knotted the strings of her Ralph Lauren bikini and scampered to the edge of the rocks overlooking the most beautiful turquoise ocean she'd ever seen. That was saying a lot, considering the Hastings family had been to practically every island in the Caribbean, even the tiny ones that required a private plane to reach.

"Right behind you!" Aria Montgomery called, kicking off her Havaianas flip-flops and winding her long, blue-black hair into a bun. She didn't bother taking off the bracelets on each arm or the feather earrings dangling from her earlobes.

"Out of my way!" Hanna Marin smoothed her hands over her narrow hips—well, *hopefully* they were still narrow after the massive plate of fried clams she'd eaten at the welcome-to-Jamaica fish fry that afternoon.

Emily Fields pulled up the rear, leaving her T-shirt on a large, flat rock. As she reached the edge and peered down, a wave of wooziness hit her. She halted in her tracks and covered her mouth until the feeling passed.

The girls jumped off the cliff and hit the warm, tropical water at exactly the same time. They surfaced, giggling—they'd *all* won and lost!—and staring at the The Cliffs, the Jamaican resort high above their heads. The pink stucco building, which housed the rooms, yoga studio, dance club, and spa, towered into the clouds, and several people loitered on their shaded balconies or swilled cocktails on the deck. Palm trees swayed, and island birds cawed. The faintest tinkling of a steel drum rendition of Bob Marley's "Redemption Song" floated through the air.

"Paradise," Spencer whispered. The others murmured in agreement.

This was the ideal spring break retreat, the complete opposite of Rosewood, Pennsylvania, where the four girls lived. Sure, the Philadelphia suburb was like a picture-postcard, resplendent with thick, lush woods, expansive mansions, idyllic horse trails, quaint old barns, and crumbling seventeenth-century estates, but after what had happened just a few months before, the girls needed a change of scenery. They needed to forget that Alison DiLaurentis, the girl they used to admire and adore, the girl everyone wanted to be, had almost killed them.

Forgetting was impossible, though. Even though two months had passed since it happened, the memories haunted them, visions rising up like ghosts. Like how Alison took their hands and told each of them she wasn't her twin sister, Courtney, as her parents had claimed, but their best friend back from the grave. Or how Ali invited them into her family's Poconos house, saying it would be the perfect reunion. How, shortly after they'd arrived, Ali led them to an upstairs bedroom and begged them to let her hypnotize them just like she had done the night she disappeared in seventh grade. Then she slammed the door, locked it from the outside, and slid a note underneath telling them exactly who she was . . . and who she wasn't.

Her name was Ali, all right. But it turned out they

hadn't been friends with the *real* Ali at all. The girl who wrote that note at the Poconos house wasn't the same girl who'd plucked Spencer, Aria, Emily, and Hanna out of obscurity at the Rosewood Charity Drive at the beginning of sixth grade. Nor was she the girl with whom they'd swapped outfits, gossiped, competed, and crushed on for a year and a half. That had been Courtney all along, posing as Ali, stepping into her life shortly after sixth grade began. *This* Ali, the *real* Ali, was a stranger. A girl who hated them with every ounce of her being. A girl who was A, the evil text-messager who'd killed Ian Thomas, burned down the woods behind Spencer's house, got the girls arrested, murdered Jenna Cavanaugh for knowing too much, and killed her twin sister Courtney—*their* Ali—the fateful night of the girls' seventh-grade sleepover. And she planned on offing them next.

As soon as the girls read the last horrible sentence of the letter, their noses twitched with the scent of smoke—the real Ali had doused the house in gas and lit a match. They'd escaped just in time, but Ali hadn't been as lucky. When the cabin exploded, Ali was still inside.

Or *was* she? There were lots of rumors that she'd made it out alive. The whole story was public now, including the twin switch, and even though she was a cold-blooded killer, some people were still fascinated with the real Ali all the same. There had been claims of Ali sightings in Denver, or Minneapolis, or Palm Springs. The girls tried not to think of that, though. They had to move on. They had nothing to fear anymore.

Two figures appeared at the top of the cliff. One was Noel Kahn, Aria's boyfriend; the other was Mike Montgomery, her brother and Hanna's boyfriend. The girls paddled for the steps carved into the rock.

Noel handed Aria a big fluffy towel that had THE CLIFFS, NEGRIL, JAMAICA stitched at the bottom in red thread. "You're so sexy in that bikini."

"Yeah, right." Aria ducked her head and stared at her pale limbs. Certainly not as hot as the blond goddesses just down the beach who'd spent the whole day rubbing tanning oil on their long arms and legs. Had she caught Noel checking them out, or was that just her jealous paranoia getting the best of her?

"I'm serious." Noel pinched Aria's butt. "I'm holding you to skinny-dipping on this trip. And when we go to Iceland, we're getting naked in those geothermal pools."

Aria blushed.

Noel elbowed her. "You *are* excited about Iceland, aren't you?"

"Of course!" Noel had surprised Aria with tickets for her, himself, Hanna, and Mike to go to Iceland this summer—all expenses paid by the über-rich Kahn family. Aria certainly couldn't say no—she'd spent an idyllic three years in Iceland after Ali, *their* Ali, vanished. But she felt a strange resistance about the trip, an eerie premonition that she shouldn't go. Why, she wasn't sure.

After the girls slipped on their sarongs, beach dresses,

and, in Emily's case, an oversized Urban Outfitters tee with the words MERCI BEAUCOUP printed across the front, Noel and Mike led them to a table at the tropical rooftop restaurant. Tons of other kids also on spring break stood at the bar, flirting and doing shots. A knot of girls in minidresses and high, strappy heels giggled in a corner. Tall, sunburned guys in board shorts, snug-fitting polos, and sockless Pumas clinked beer bottles and talked sports. The air had an electric pulse, sparkling with the promise of illicit hookups, drunken memories, and late-night swims in the resort's saltwater pool.

The air throbbed with something else, too, something the four girls noticed instantly. Excitement, certainly . . . but also a hint of danger. It felt like one of those nights that could go either wonderfully right . . . or terribly wrong.

Noel stood. "Drinks? What do we want?"

"Red Stripe," Hanna answered. Spencer and Aria nodded in agreement.

"Emily?" Noel turned to her.

"Just a ginger ale," Emily said.

Spencer touched her arm. "Are you okay?" Emily wasn't a big partier, but it was weird that she wasn't splurging even a little on vacation.

Emily pressed her hand to her mouth. Then she rose clumsily from the table and wheeled toward the small bathroom in the corner. "I just have to . . ."

Everyone watched as she wove around the kids on the

dance floor and shoved hurriedly through the pink bath-room door. Mike winced. "Is it Montezuma's revenge?"

"I don't know . . ." Aria said. They'd been careful not to drink tap water here. But Emily hadn't been herself since the fire. She'd been in love with Ali. To have the girl she thought was her best friend and longtime crush return, break her heart, and try to kill her must have been doubly devastating.

Hanna's cell phone buzzed, breaking the silence. She pulled it out of her straw beach bag and groaned. "Well, it's official. My dad's running for Senate. This dork on his campaign staff is already asking to meet with me when I get back."

"Really?" Aria looped her arm around Hanna's shoul-ders. "Hanna, that's amazing!"

"If he wins, you'll be a First Daughter!" Spencer said. "You'll be in the society magazines!"

Mike skootched his chair closer to Hanna. "Can I be your personal Secret Service agent?"

Hanna reached for a handful of plantain chips from a bowl on the table and shoved them into her mouth. "I won't be the First Daughter. *Kate* will." Her dad's step-daughter and new wife were his true family now. Hanna and her mother were the rejects.

As Aria playfully slapped Hanna's hand, the bracelets on her wrist rattled. "You're better than she is, and you know it."

Hanna rolled her eyes dismissively, though she was

grateful to Aria for trying to cheer her up. That was the one good thing that had come out of the Ali disaster: The four of them were best friends again, their bond even stronger than it was in seventh grade. They'd vowed to remain friends forever. Nothing would ever come between them again.

Noel returned with the drinks, and everyone clinked glasses and said "Yeah, *mon!*" in faux-Jamaican accents. Emily staggered back from the bathroom, still looking seasick, but smiled cheerfully as she sipped her ginger ale.

After dinner, Noel and Mike wandered over to an air hockey table in the corner and began to play. The DJ cranked up the music, and Alicia Keys blasted over the stereo. Several people writhed on the dance floor. A boy with wavy brown hair and a buff physique caught Spencer's eye and beckoned her to join him.

Aria nudged her. "Go for it, Spence!"

Spencer turned away, blushing. "*Uch*, skeevy!"

"He looks like the perfect Andrew cure," Hanna urged. Andrew Campbell, Spencer's boyfriend, had broken up with her a month ago—apparently, Spencer's ordeal with Ali and A was "just too intense" for him to handle. *Wuss.*

Spencer gazed at the guy on the dance floor again. Admittedly, he was cute in his long khaki shorts and lace-less boat shoes. Then she spied the insignia on his polo. PRINCETON CREW. Princeton was her top-choice school.

Hanna brightened, noticing the polo, too. "Spence! It's a sign! You guys could end up being dorm mates!"

Spencer looked away. "It's not like I'm going to get in."

The girls exchanged a surprised glance. "Of course you will," Emily said quietly.

Spencer reached for her beer and took a hearty swig, ignoring their inquisitive stares. The truth was, she'd let her schoolwork go in the past few months—wouldn't anyone, after their supposed BFF tried to kill them? The last time she checked with her guidance counselor about her class rank, she'd slipped to twenty-seventh place. No one ranked that low ever got into an Ivy.

"I'd rather hang out with you guys," Spencer said. She didn't want to think about school on vacation.

Aria, Emily, and Hanna shrugged, then raised their glasses once more. "To us," Aria said.

"To friendship," Hanna agreed.

Each of the girls let their minds go to a Zen-like place, and for the first time in days they didn't automatically think of their horrible past. No A notes blinked in their minds. Rosewood felt like it was in a different solar system.

The DJ put on an old Madonna song, and Spencer rose from her seat. "Let's dance, guys."

The others started to jump up, too, but Emily grabbed Spencer's arm tightly, pulling her back down. "Don't move."

"What?" Spencer stared at her. "Why?"

Emily's eyes were saucers, her gaze fixed on something by the spiral staircase. "*Look.*"

The girls turned and squinted. A thin blond girl in a

bright yellow sundress had appeared on the landing. She had striking blue eyes, pink-lined lips, and a scar over her right eyebrow. Even from where they were sitting they could make out more scars on her body: puckered skin on her arms, lacerations on her neck, withered flesh on her bare legs. But despite the scars, she radiated beauty and confidence.

"What is it?" Aria murmured.

"Do you know her?" Spencer asked.

"Can't you see?" Emily whispered, her voice quivering. "Isn't it obvious?"

"What are we supposed to be looking at?" Aria said softly, worriedly.

"That girl." Emily turned to them, her face pale, her lips bloodless. "It's . . . *Ali*."

TEN MONTHS LATER

1

PRETTY LITTLE PARTY

A pudgy caterer with impeccably manicured hands thrust a tray of steaming, gooey cheese into Spencer Hastings's face. "Baked Brie?"

Spencer selected a cracker and took a big bite. *Delicious.* It wasn't every day that a caterer served her baked Brie in her very own kitchen, but on this particular Saturday night, her mother was throwing a party to welcome a new family to the neighborhood. Mrs. Hastings hadn't been in the mood to play hostess the last few months, but she'd had a burst of social enthusiasm.

As if on cue, Veronica Hastings bustled into the room in a cloud of Chanel No. 5, fastening dangling earrings to her earlobes and sliding a large diamond ring onto her right finger. The ring was a recent purchase—her mother had exchanged every piece of jewelry Spencer's dad had ever bought her for all-new baubles. Her ash-blond hair hung straight and smooth to her chin, her eyes looked wide and huge thanks to expertly applied makeup, and she wore a fitted black sheath dress that showed off her Pilates-toned arms.

"Spencer, your friend's here to work coat check," Mrs. Hastings said hurriedly as she put a couple of stray dishes from the sink into the dishwasher and gave the island yet another spray with Fantastik, even though she'd had a team scour the house only an hour before. "Maybe you should see if she needs anything."

"Who?" Spencer wrinkled her nose. She hadn't asked anyone to work tonight's event. Usually her mom hired students from Hollis College, the university down the road, to do it.

Mrs. Hastings let out an impatient sigh and checked her flawless reflection in the stainless steel refrigerator door. "Emily Fields. I've set her up by the study."

Spencer stiffened. Emily was here? *She* certainly hadn't invited her.

She couldn't remember the last time she'd spoken to Emily—it had to be months. But her mother—and the rest of the world—still thought they were close friends. The *People* magazine cover was to blame—it hit newsstands shortly after the Real Ali tried to kill them and featured Spencer, Emily, Aria, and Hanna entangled in a four-girl hug. VERY PRETTY, BUT DEFINITELY NOT LIARS, the headline said. Recently, a reporter called the Hastings house to request a reunion interview with Spencer—the anniversary of that terrible night in the Poconos was next Saturday, and the public wanted to know how the girls were doing a year later. Spencer had declined. She was sure the others had, too.

"Spence?"

Spencer whirled around. Mrs. Hastings was gone, but Spencer's older sister, Melissa, stood in her place, her body wrapped in a chic gray belted raincoat. A pair of skinny black pants from J. Crew covered her long legs.

"Hey." Melissa reached out and gave Spencer a big hug, and Spencer got a huge whiff of—what else?—Chanel No. 5. Melissa was a mommy clone, but Spencer tried not to hold it against her.

"It's so good to see you!" Melissa crooned as if she were a long-lost aunt who hadn't seen Spencer since she was a toddler, even though they'd gone skiing at Bachelor Gulch, Colorado, two months ago.

Then, someone stepped out from behind her. "Hi, Spencer," said the man to Melissa's right. He looked odd in a jacket, tie, and khaki pants with perfectly ironed creases in the legs; Spencer was used to seeing him in a Rosewood Police Department uniform with a gun on his belt. Darren—aka Officer Wilden—had been the lead detective in the Alison DiLaurentis murder investigation. He'd questioned Spencer about the missing Ali—who had actually been *Courtney*—countless times.

"H-Hey," Spencer said as Wilden wound his fingers around Melissa's. The two of them had been dating for almost a year now, but it still seemed like a crazy match. If Melissa and Wilden registered profiles on eHarmony, the service wouldn't connect them up in a trillion years.

In a previous life, Wilden had been the bad boy of Rosewood Day, the private school in town everyone attended—the kid who wrote dirty messages on the bathroom walls and smoked joints in full view of the gym teacher. Melissa, on the other hand, was the do-gooder valedictorian and Homecoming queen whose idea of getting drunk was eating half an Irish Cream liqueur truffle. Spencer also knew that Wilden grew up in an Amish community in Lancaster, Pennsylvania, but ran away as a teenager. Had he shared *that* juicy piece of gossip with her sister yet?

"I saw Emily when I came in," Wilden said. "Are you guys going to watch that crazy made-for-TV movie next weekend?"

"Uh . . ." Spencer pretended to straighten her blouse, not wanting to answer the question. Wilden was referring to *Pretty Little Killer*, a cheesy cable docu-drama retelling the story of the real Ali's return, rampage as A, and death. In a parallel life, the four of them *would* probably watch the movie together, analyzing the girls who'd been chosen to play them, groaning over inaccurate dialogue, and wincing at Ali's insanity.

But not now. After Jamaica, their friendship began to disintegrate. Nowadays, Spencer couldn't even be in the same room with any of her old friends without feeling antsy and flushed.

"What are you guys doing here?" Spencer asked, steering the conversation away from the past. "Not that I *mind*, of course." She shot Melissa a kind smile. The sisters had had their issues in the past, but they'd tried to put all of that behind them after the fire last year.

"Oh, we're just stopping by to grab a couple of boxes I left behind in my old room," Melissa said. "Then we're off to Kitchens and Beyond. Did I tell you? I'm redoing my kitchen again! I want it to have a more Mediterranean theme. And Darren's moving in with me!"

Spencer raised an eyebrow at Wilden. "What about your job in Rosewood?" Melissa lived in a luxuriously renovated townhouse on Rittenhouse Square in Philadelphia, a gift from their parents for graduating from Penn. "That's going to be a long commute from Philly every day."

Wilden grinned. "I resigned from the police force last month. Melissa got me a job working security at the Philadelphia Museum of Art. I'll get to run up those marble stairs like Rocky every day."

"*And* protect valuable paintings," Melissa reminded him.

"Oh." Wilden tugged at his collar. "Yeah. Right."

"So who's this party for, anyway?" Wilden grabbed two glasses from the granite-topped kitchen island and poured himself and Melissa some pinot noir.

Spencer shrugged and gazed into the living room. "A new family that moved into the house across the street. I guess Mom's trying to make a good impression."

Wilden straightened. "The Cavanaugh house? Someone bought that place?"

Melissa clucked her tongue. "They must have gotten

an amazing deal. I wouldn't live there if they gave it to me for free."

"I guess they're trying to wipe the slate clean," Spencer mumbled.

"Well, cheers to that." Melissa tipped the glass to her mouth.

Spencer stared at the streaky patterns in the travertine floor tile. It *was* pretty crazy that someone bought the Cavanaughs' old place—both Cavanaugh children had died while living there. Toby committed suicide shortly after he'd returned to Rosewood from reform school. Jenna had been strangled and thrown into a ditch behind the house . . . by Ali—the *real* Ali.

"So, Spencer." Wilden turned to her again. "You've been keeping a secret."

Spencer's head jerked up, her blood pressure jumping. "E-excuse me?" Wilden had a detective's instincts. Could he tell she was hiding something? Surely he didn't know about Jamaica. No one could know about that for as long as she lived.

"You got into Princeton!" Wilden cried. "Congratulations!"

Air slowly filled Spencer's lungs again. "Oh. Yeah. I found out about a month ago."

"I couldn't help bragging to him, Spence." Melissa beamed. "I hope you don't mind."

"And early decision, too." Wilden's eyebrows rose. "Amazing!"

"Thanks." But Spencer's skin felt prickly, like she'd spent too much time in the sun. It had taken a Herculean effort to claw her way back to the top of the class rankings and secure a spot at Princeton. She wasn't exactly proud of everything she'd done, but she'd made it.

Mrs. Hastings burst back into the kitchen and clapped her hands on Spencer and Melissa's shoulders. "Why aren't you two circulating? I've been talking about my brilliant daughters for the past ten minutes! I want to show you off!"

"Mom," Spencer whined, though secretly she felt happy that her mom was proud of *both* of them, not just Melissa.

Mrs. Hastings just steered Spencer toward the door. Luckily, Mrs. Norwood, a woman Spencer's mother regularly played tennis with, blocked their way. When she spied Mrs. Hastings, her eyes popped. She grabbed Mrs. Hastings's wrists. "Veronica! I've been dying to talk to you! Well played, darling!"

"I'm sorry?" Mrs. Hastings stopped and offered her a broad, fake smile.

Mrs. Norwood lowered her chin coyly and winked. "Don't pretend nothing's going on! I know about Nicholas Pennythistle! Quite a catch!"

Mrs. Hastings went pale. "O-oh." Her eyes flitted to her two daughters. "Uh, I haven't exactly told—"

"Who's Nicholas Pennythistle?" Melissa interrupted, her voice sharp.

"A *catch*?" Spencer repeated.

Mrs. Norwood instantly realized her gaffe and backed into the living room. Mrs. Hastings faced her daughters. A vein protruded prominently in her neck. "Um, Darren, would you excuse us for a moment?"

Wilden nodded and headed into the main room. Mrs. Hastings sank onto one of the barstools and sighed. "Look, I was going to tell you this evening after everyone left. I'm dating someone new. His name is Nicholas Pennythistle, and I think it's serious. I'd like you to meet him."

Spencer's mouth dropped. "Isn't it a little soon?" How could her mom be dating again? The divorce had only been finalized a few months ago. Before Christmas, she was still moping around the house in sweats and slippers.

Mrs. Hastings sniffed defensively. "No, it's not too soon, Spencer."

"Does Dad know?" Spencer saw her father practically every weekend, the two of them attending art exhibits and watching documentaries in his new Old City penthouse. Recently, Spencer had noticed hints of a woman in her dad's apartment—an extra toothbrush in his bathroom, a bottle of pinot grigio in the fridge—and figured he was seeing someone. It had all felt way too soon. But now her mom was seeing someone, too. Ironically, Spencer was the only person in her family not dating.

"Yes, your father knows." Mrs. Hastings sounded exasperated. "I told him yesterday."

A waitress stepped back into the kitchen. Mrs. Hastings

stuck her glass out for more champagne. "I'd like you girls to have dinner at the Goshen Inn with Nicholas, myself, and his children tomorrow night, so clear your schedules. And wear something nice."

"Children?" Spencer squeaked. This was getting worse and worse. She pictured spending the evening with two small brats with big ringlet curls and a penchant for torturing small animals.

"Zachary is eighteen, and Amelia is fifteen," Mrs. Hastings answered crisply.

"Well, I think it's wonderful, Mom," Melissa said, beaming brightly. "Of course you should move on! Good for you!"

Spencer knew she should say something to that effect, too, but nothing came to her. She was the one who'd exposed their father's past affair with Ali's mother, and that Ali and Courtney were Spencer and Melissa's half siblings. It wasn't like she'd meant to—A made her.

"Now mingle, girls! It's a party!" Mrs. Hastings grabbed Melissa and Spencer's arms and shoved them into the living room.

Spencer staggered into the space, which had filled up with people from the neighborhood, the country club, and the Rosewood Day parents' association. A bunch of kids Spencer had known since kindergarten gathered by the big bay window on the side of the house, not-so-secretly sipping glasses of champagne. Naomi Zeigler shrieked as Mason Byers tickled her. Sean Ackard was deep in conversation with Gemma Curran. But Spencer didn't feel like speaking to any of them.

Instead, she walked toward the bar—she might as well get a drink for this—and instantly her heel caught on the lip of the carpet. Her legs went out from under her, and suddenly she was airborne. She reached out for one of the heavy oil paintings on the wall and steadied herself before she did a nose-plant to the floor, but several heads turned and stared right at her.

Emily caught Spencer's eye before Spencer could look away. She offered Spencer the most tentative of waves. Spencer turned back for the kitchen. They were *not* talking right now. Or ever.

The temperature in the kitchen felt even hotter than it had been a moment before. The mingling smells of fried appetizers and pungent foreign cheeses made Spencer woozy. She bent over the island, taking deep breaths. When she looked into the living room again, Emily's eyes were lowered. *Good.*

But someone else was staring at her instead. Wilden had clearly seen the silent exchange with Emily. Spencer could almost see the gears in the ex-detective's head turning: What could have caused their picture-perfect, magazine-cover friendship to crash and burn?

Spencer slammed the kitchen door shut and retreated to the basement, bringing a bottle of champagne with her. *Too bad, Wilden.* That was a secret neither he nor anyone else would ever know.

FURS, FRIENDS, AND FAR-OFF GIGGLES

"Please don't use a wire hanger," a silver-haired matron said gruffly as she stripped off a Burberry trench and hefted it into Emily Fields's arms. Then, without even a thank you, the woman glided toward the center of the Hastings' living room and helped herself to a canapé. *Snob.*

Emily hung the coat, which smelled like a mix of eau de toilette, cigarettes, and wet dog, on a hanger, affixed a coat check tag to it, and placed it gently in the large oak closet in Mr. Hastings's study. Spencer's two Labradoodles, Rufus and Beatrice, panted behind the doggie gate, frustrated that they were cordoned off for the party. Emily patted both their heads, and they wagged their tails. At least *they* were happy to see her.

When she returned to her perch at the coat check table, she looked cautiously around the room. Spencer had slipped back into the kitchen and hadn't come out again. Emily wasn't sure whether to be relieved or disappointed.

The Hastings house was the same as ever: Old paintings of relatives hung in the foyer, fussy French chairs and couches sat in the living room, and heavy gilded curtains covered the windows. Back in sixth and seventh grades, Emily, Spencer, Ali, and the others had pretended this room was a chamber in Versailles. Ali and Spencer used to fight over who got to be Marie Antoinette; Emily was usually relegated to a lady-in-waiting. Once, as Marie, Ali made Emily give her a foot massage. "You know you love it," she teased.

Despair rolled over Emily like a strong ocean wave. It was painful to think about the past. If only she could box up those memories, mail them to the South Pole, and be free of them for good.

"You're slouching," hissed a voice.

Emily looked up. Her mother stood in front of her, her brow wrinkled and the corners of her lips crumpled into a scowl. She wore a blue dress that hit at an unattractive spot between her knees and her calves, and she carried a fake-snakeskin bag under her arm like it was a loaf of French bread.

"And smile," Mrs. Fields added. "You look miserable."

Emily shrugged. What was she supposed to do, grin like a maniac? Burst into song? "This job isn't exactly fun," she pointed out.

Mrs. Fields's nostrils flared. "Mrs. Hastings was very

nice to give you this opportunity. Please don't quit this like you quit everything else."

Ouch. Emily hid behind a curtain of reddish-blond hair. "I'm not going to quit."

"Just do your job, then. Make some money. Lord knows every bit counts."

Mrs. Fields marched away, putting on a friendly face for the neighbors. Emily slumped in the chair, fighting back tears. *Don't quit this like you quit everything else.* Her mom had been furious when Emily walked off the swim team last June without any explanation, spending the summer in Philadelphia instead. Emily hadn't rejoined the Rosewood Day team in the fall, either. In the world of competitive swimming, missing a couple of months spelled trouble, especially during college scholarship time. Missing two seasons equaled doom.

Her parents were devastated. *Don't you realize we can't pay for college if you don't get a scholarship? Don't you realize you're throwing your future away?*

Emily didn't know how to answer them. There was no way she could tell them why she'd quit the team. Not for as long as she lived.

She'd finally rejoined her old club team a couple of weeks ago and hoped that a college scout might take pity on her and give her a last-minute spot. A recruiter from the University of Arizona had been interested in her last year, and Emily had clung to the notion that he would still want her for the team. But earlier today, she'd had to let go of that dream, too.

Pulling her phone from her bag, she once again checked the rejection email that had come in from the scout. *Sorry to say . . . just not enough room . . . good luck.* Looking at the words, Emily's stomach swirled.

Suddenly, the room smelled pungently of roasted garlic and cinnamon Altoids. The string quartet sawing away in the corner sounded hideously out of tune. The walls closed in around Emily's sides. What was she going to do next year? Get a job and live at home? Go to community college? She had to get out of Rosewood—if she stayed here, the terrible memories would swallow her up until there was nothing left of her.

A tall, black-haired girl near the china cabinet caught her eye. *Aria.*

Emily's heart began to pound. Spencer had acted like she'd seen a ghost when they'd locked eyes, but maybe Aria would be different. As she watched Aria gazing at the knickknacks in the cabinet—acting like the objects in the room mattered more than the people, something she'd always done when she was left alone at parties—Emily was suddenly overtaken by nostalgia. She stepped out from behind the coat-check table and moved toward her old friend. If only she could rush over to Aria and ask her how she was. Tell her what had happened with the swimming scholarship. Solicit a sorely needed hug. If only the four of them hadn't gone to Jamaica together, she could have.

To her surprise, Aria looked up and focused on Emily. Her eyes widened. Her lips pursed.

Emily straightened and offered her a small smile. "H-hey."

Aria flinched. "Hey."

"I can take that for you if you want." Emily gestured to Aria's purple trench coat, which was still knotted tightly around her waist. Emily had been with Aria when she'd bought it at a thrift shop in Philly last year, shortly before they went on spring break together. Spencer and Hanna had told Aria that the coat smelled like an old lady, but Aria bought it anyway.

Aria placed her hands in the coat pockets. "That's okay."

"The coat looks really good on you," Emily added. "Purple has always been your color."

A muscle at Aria's jaw twitched. She looked like she wanted to say something, but closed her mouth tightly. Then her eyes brightened at something across the room. Noel Kahn, her boyfriend, swooped over to Aria and wrapped his arms around her. "I was looking for you."

Aria kissed him hello, then wheeled away without giving Emily another word.

A group of people in the middle of the room burst into laughter. Mr. Kahn, who was staggering as though he'd had too much to drink, started fiddling on the Hastingses' piano, playing the right hand part to the "Blue Danube Waltz." All at once, Emily couldn't bear to watch the party any longer. She tumbled through the front door just before the tears started to fall.

Outside, the air was unseasonably warm for February. She trudged around the side of the house to the Hastingses' backyard, tears rolling silently down her cheeks.

The view in Spencer's backyard was so different now. The historic barn that had stood at the back of the property was gone—Real Ali had burned it down last year. Only scorched, black dirt remained. Emily doubted anything would ever grow in that spot again.

Next door was the DiLaurentises' old house. Maya St. Germain, whom Emily had had a thing with junior year, still lived there, though Emily hardly saw Maya anymore. In the front yard, the Ali Shrine, which had stood for so long after Courtney's—*her* Ali's—death on the DiLaurentises' old curb, was gone, too. The public was still obsessed—the newspapers were already running Alison DiLaurentis Fire Anniversary features, and then there was *Pretty Little Killer*, that awful Alison biopic—but no one wanted to eulogize a murderer.

Thinking about it, Emily slipped her hand into her jeans pocket and felt for the silky tassel she'd carried with her for the past year. Just feeling that it was still there calmed her down.

A small cry rang out, and Emily turned. Just twenty feet away, almost blending into the trunk of the Hastingses' giant oak, stood a teenage girl bouncing a bundled baby. "Shhh," the girl cooed. Then she glanced over at Emily, smiling apologetically. "Sorry. I came out here to keep her quiet, but it's not working."

"It's okay." Emily covertly wiped her eyes. She glanced at the tiny baby. "What's her name?"

"Grace." The girl shifted the baby higher in her arms. "Say hi, Grace."

"Is she . . . *yours*?" The girl looked about Emily's age.

"Oh God, no." The girl laughed. "She's my mom's. But she's inside, schmoozing, so I'm on nanny duty." She shifted for something in the big diaper bag on her shoulder. "Would you mind holding her for a second? I have to get her bottle, but it's way at the bottom."

Emily blinked. She hadn't held a baby in a long time. "Well, okay . . ."

The girl handed Emily the baby, who was swaddled in a pink blanket and smelled like powder. Her little red mouth opened wide and tears dotted her eyes. "It's okay," Emily told her "You can cry. I don't mind."

A wrinkle formed on Grace's tiny brow. She shut her mouth and stared at Emily curiously. Tumultuous feelings rushed through Emily. Her memories pulsed close, ready to break free, but she quickly pushed them down deep.

The girl raised her head from the diaper bag. "Hey! You're a natural. Do you have young brothers or sisters?"

Emily bit her lip. "No, just older ones. But I've done a lot of babysitting."

"It shows." She smiled. "I'm Chloe Roland. My family just moved here from Charlotte."

Emily introduced herself. "Where are you going to school?"

"Rosewood Day. I'm a senior."

Emily smiled. "That's where I go!"

"Do you like it?" Chloe asked, finding the bottle.

Emily handed Grace back. *Did* she like Rosewood Day? So much about the school reminded her of *her* Ali—and of A. Every corner, every room held a memory she'd rather forget. "I don't know," she said, then inadvertently let out a loud sniff.

Chloe squinted into Emily's tear-stained face. "Is everything okay?"

Emily wiped her eyes. Her brain conjured up the words *I'm fine* and *It doesn't matter*, but she couldn't say them. "I just found out I didn't get a college swimming scholarship," she blurted. "My parents can't afford to send me without it. It's my fault, though. I . . . I dropped out of swimming this summer. No team wants me now. I don't know what I'm going to do."

Fresh tears cascaded down Emily's face. Since when did she go around blubbering about her problems to girls she didn't know? "I'm sorry. I'm sure you didn't want to hear that."

Chloe sniffed. "Please. It's more than anyone *else* has said to me at this party. So you swim, huh?"

"Yeah."

Chloe smiled. "My dad's a big donor at the University of North Carolina, his alma mater. He might be able to help."

Emily looked up. "UNC is a great swimming school."

"Maybe I could talk to him about you."

Emily stared at her. "But you don't even know me!"

Chloe shifted Grace higher in her arms. "You seem nice."

Emily peered at Chloe more closely. She had a pleasant round face, sparkling hazel eyes, and long, shiny brown hair the color of a chocolate Pudding Pop. Her eyebrows looked like they hadn't been plucked in a while, she didn't have much makeup on, and Emily was pretty sure she'd seen the dress Chloe was wearing at The Gap. She liked her instantly for not trying so hard.

The front door to the Hastingses' house opened, and a few guests emerged onto the porch. A zing of fear bolted through Emily's chest. *Coat check!*

"I-I have to go," she cried, spinning around. "I'm supposed to be working coat check. I'm probably going to be fired now."

"It was nice to meet you!" Chloe waved, and then made Grace wave, too. "And, hey! If you're that eager for money, want to babysit for us Monday night? My parents don't know anyone yet, and I have a college interview."

Emily paused in the frosty grass. "Where do you live?"

Chloe laughed. "*Right.* That would be helpful, huh?" She pointed across the street. "There."

Emily stared at the large Victorian and swallowed a gasp. Chloe's family had moved into the Cavanaughs' old house.

"Um, sure. Yeah." Emily waved good-bye and sprinted

back toward the house. As she passed by the thick line of shrubs that separated the Hastings property from the DiLaurentises', she heard a high-pitched giggle.

She stopped suddenly. Was someone watching her? Laughing?

The giggling faded into the trees. Emily shuffled up the front walk, trying to shake the sound from her head. She was just hearing things. No one was watching her anymore. Those days were thankfully long, long gone.

Right?

3

JUST ANOTHER PERFECT POLITICAL FAMILY

That same Saturday night, Hanna Marin sat with her boyfriend, Mike Montgomery, in an old glass bottle warehouse turned photography studio in downtown Hollis. The high-ceilinged industrial space was filled with hot lights, multiple cameras, and several different backdrops—a blue cloth, an autumn scene, and a screen covered with a big, waving American flag, which Hanna found unbearably cheesy.

Hanna's father, Tom Marin, stood amid the throng of political advisors, adjusting his tie and mouthing his lines. He was running for U.S. Senate next November, and today he was filming his very first political commercial that would introduce Pennsylvania to just how *senatorial* he was. His new wife, Isabel, stood next to him, fluffing her brown, chin-length hair, smoothing down her red politician's-wife power suit—complete with shoulder pads, *ugh*—and inspecting her orangey skin in a Chanel hand mirror.

"Seriously," Hanna whispered to Mike, who was helping himself to yet another sandwich from the food cart. "Why didn't someone tell Isabel to lay off Mystic Tan? She looks like an Oompa Loompa."

Mike snickered, squeezing Hanna's hand as Hanna's stepsister, Kate, glided past. Unfortunately, Kate wasn't a clone of her mom—she looked like she'd spent the day in the salon getting her chestnut hair highlighted, fake eyelashes glued on, and teeth whitened so she'd look absolutely perfect for her father's big commercial. *Step*father, not that Kate ever made the distinction. And not that Hanna's dad ever did, either.

Then, as if sensing Hanna was thinking nasty thoughts about her, Kate pranced over. "You guys should be helping, you know. There's a ton to do."

Hanna took an apathetic sip from the can of Diet Coke she'd pilfered from the cooler. Kate had taken it upon herself to be her dad's mini assistant like some eager intern on *The West Wing*. "Like what?"

"Like you could help me run my lines," Kate suggested bossily. She reeked of her favorite Jo Malone Fig and Cassis body lotion, which to Hanna smelled like a moldy prune left out in the woods too long. "I have three sentences in the ad, and I want them to be perfect."

"You have lines?" Hanna blurted, and then instantly regretted it. That was exactly what Kate wanted her to say.

As Hanna predicted, Kate's eyes widened with fake sympathy. "Oh, Hanna, you mean you don't have *any*?

I wonder why *that* is?" She whirled around and sauntered back to the set. Her hips swung. Her glossy hair bounced. No doubt there was a huge smile on her face.

Shaking with fury, Hanna grabbed a handful of potato chips from the bowl next to her and shoved them in her mouth. They were sour cream and onion, not her favorite, but she didn't care. Hanna had been warring with her stepsister ever since Kate reentered Hanna's life last year and became one of the most popular girls at Rosewood Day. Kate was still BFFs with Naomi Zeigler and Riley Wolfe, two bitches who'd had it in for Hanna ever since their Ali (aka Courtney) ditched them at the beginning of sixth grade. After Hanna reunited with her old friends, Kate's rise to popularity didn't bother her so much, but now that she, Spencer, Aria, and Emily weren't speaking, Hanna couldn't help but let Kate get to her.

"Forget her." Mike touched Hanna's arm. "She looks like she has an American flag shoved up her butt."

"Thanks," Hanna said flatly, but it wasn't much of a salve.

Today, she just felt . . . diminished. Unnecessary. There was only room for one shining teenage daughter, and that was the girl who'd received three whole sentences to say on camera.

Just then, Mike's cell phone pinged. "It's from Aria," he murmured, texting back. "Want me to tell her hi?"

Hanna turned away, saying nothing. After Jamaica, Aria and Hanna had tried to remain friends, going to

Iceland together because Noel had already bought the tickets. But by the end of that summer, there were just too many bad memories and secrets between them. These days, Hanna tried not to think about her old friends at all. It was easier that way.

A short guy in thick geek-chic glasses, a pink pinstriped shirt, and gray pants clapped his hands, startling Hanna and Mike. "Okay, Tom, we're ready for you." It was Jeremiah, Mr. Marin's number-one campaign advisor—or, as Hanna liked to call him, his bitch boy. Jeremiah was by her dad's side at all hours of the day, doing whatever was needed. Hanna was tempted to make a whip-cracking noise whenever he was around.

Jeremiah bustled about, positioning Hanna's father in front of the blue screen. "We'll do a few voiceovers of you talking about how you're the future of Pennsylvania," he said in a girlish nasal voice. When he ducked his head, Hanna could see the growing bald spot on his crown. "Be sure to talk about all the good community work you've done in the past. And definitely mention your pledge to end teenage drinking."

"Absolutely," Mr. Marin said in a presidential tone.

Hanna and Mike exchanged a look and struggled not to laugh. Ironically, Mr. Marin's cause célèbre was abolishing teenage drinking. Couldn't he have focused on something that didn't have a direct impact on Hanna's life? Darfur, maybe? Better treatment for Wal-Mart employees? What fun would a party be without a keg?

Mr. Marin ran through his lines, sounding robust, trustworthy, and vote-for-me chipper. Isabel and Kate grinned and nudged one another proudly, which made Hanna want to puke. Mike gave his opinion by belching loudly during one of the takes. Hanna adored him for it.

Next, Jeremiah guided Mr. Marin toward the American flag background. "Now let's do the family segment. We'll splice this into the end of the commercial—everyone will see what a good family man you are. And what a gorgeous family you have." He paused to wink at Isabel and Kate, who tittered faux-bashfully.

Family man my ass, Hanna thought. Funny how no one had mentioned that Tom Marin had divorced, moved to Maryland, and forgotten his old wife and daughter for three long years. Interesting, too, that no one had brought up that her dad moved himself, Kate, and Isabel into Hanna's house last year while Hanna's mother took a job overseas, nearly ruining Hanna's life. Thankfully, they'd been kicked out after Hanna's mother returned from Singapore, finding a McMansion in Devon that wasn't nearly as cool as Hanna's house on top of Mt. Kale. But their presence still lingered: Hanna still got whiffs of Kate's Fig and Cassis perfume when she walked down the hall or sank into the couch.

"Okay, family!" The director, a long-haired Spaniard named Sergio, flicked the lights. "Everyone against the flag! Get ready with your lines!"

Kate and Isabel obediently walked into the hot

spotlights and posed next to Mr. Marin. Mike poked Hanna's side. "*Go!*"

Hanna hesitated. It wasn't that she didn't want to be in front of a camera—she'd always fantasized about becoming a famous anchorwoman or a runway model—but she didn't want to be in a commercial with her stepsister like they were a big happy family.

Mike poked her again. "Hanna, *go.*"

"Fine." Hanna groaned, sliding off the table and stomping toward the set.

Several of the directors' assistants turned and stared at her confusedly. "Who are *you?*" Sergio asked, sounding like the hookah-smoking caterpillar in *Alice in Wonderland.*

Hanna laughed uncomfortably. "Uh, I'm Hanna Marin. Tom's *biological* daughter."

Sergio scratched his mop of long curls. "The only family members on my call sheet are Isabel and Kate Randall."

There was a long pause. Several of the assistants exchanged uncomfortable glances. Kate's smile broadened.

"Dad?" Hanna turned to her father. "What's going on?"

Mr. Marin tugged at the microphone one of the assistants had threaded under his jacket. "Well, Hanna, it's just that . . ." He craned his neck and located his assistant.

Swiftly, Jeremiah scuttled over to the set and gave Hanna an exasperated look. "Hanna, we'd prefer if you just watched."

We? "Why?" Hanna squeaked.

"We're just trying to spare you from more nosy press people, Hanna," Mr. Marin said gently. "You were in the limelight a lot last year. I didn't know if you wanted to bring more attention to yourself."

Or maybe *he* didn't want to bring the attention back to her. Hanna narrowed her eyes, realizing her dad was worried about the mistakes she'd made in the past. How she'd gotten caught shoplifting from Tiffany and then stole and wrecked her boyfriend Sean Ackard's car. How the second A—the real Ali—had sent Hanna to The Preserve, a mental institution for troubled teens. And, the cherry on top, some people had believed Hanna and her friends killed Ali—*their* Ali, the girl who'd disappeared in seventh grade.

There was also what had happened in Jamaica, not that Mr. Marin knew about that. Not that anyone would know about that—ever.

Hanna took a big step away, feeling like the floor had dropped out from under her. Her dad didn't want her associated with his campaign. She didn't fit his wholesome family portrait. She was his *old* daughter, his castoff, a scandal-ridden girl he didn't want to remember anymore. Suddenly, an old note from A flashed in her mind: *Even Daddy doesn't love you best!*

Hanna spun on her heel and walked back to Mike. Screw them. She didn't want to be in her father's stupid commercial, anyway. People in politics had bad hair, pasted-on smiles, and horrible fashion sense—except for the Kennedys, of course, but they were the exception that proved the rule. "Let's go," she growled, grabbing her purse from the empty chair.

"But, Hanna . . ." Mike stared at her with round blue eyes.

"Let's. Go."

"Hanna, wait," her father called behind her.

Keep walking, Hanna told herself. *Let him see what he's missing. Don't speak to him ever again.*

Her father called her name once more. "Come on back," he said, his voice dripping with guilt. "There's room for all of us. You can even say a few lines if you'd like. We can give some of Kate's to you."

"What?" Kate shrieked, but someone shushed her.

Hanna turned around and saw her father's eyes pleading with her.

After a moment's frustration, she handed Mike her purse and trudged back to the set. "Tom, I don't think this is a good idea," Jeremiah warned, but Mr. Marin just shrugged him off. When Hanna stepped into the lights, he gave her a big smile, but she didn't smile back. She felt like the loser kid the teacher made everyone play with at recess. Her dad was only asking her back because it made him look like an asshole if he excluded her.

Sergio ran their lines with the family, divvying up Kate's lines between the two daughters. When the camera turned to Hanna, she took a deep breath, cast off the negative vibes around her, and got into character. "Pennsylvania needs a strong leader who works for *you*," she said, trying to look natural, tamping down her wilted hopes. Sergio shot take after take until Hanna's cheeks hurt from smiling so hard. An hour later, it was over.

As soon as the lights dimmed and Sergio declared it was a wrap, Hanna ran over to Mike. "Let's get the hell out of here."

"You were really good, Han," Mike said, jumping off the table.

"He's right," a second voice said.

Hanna looked over. One of Sergio's assistants stood a few feet away, two large black suitcases full of equipment in his hands. He was probably only a few years older than Hanna. His hair was cut in a messy yet artfully arranged way, and he wore snug-fitting jeans, a weathered leather jacket, and a pair of aviator sunglasses, which were propped atop his head. His fawn-colored eyes grazed Hanna up and down as if he approved of what he saw. "Totally poised," he added. "With a ton of presence. You kicked that other girl's ass."

"Uh, thanks." Hanna exchanged a suspicious glance with Mike. Was complimenting the clients part of this dude's job?

The guy rummaged through his pocket and handed her a business card. "You're seriously gorgeous. You could be a high-fashion model if you wanted." He pointed to the card. "I'd love to shoot you for my portfolio. I could even help you pick out some shots for agents. Give me a call if you're interested."

He hefted the suitcases higher and walked out of the studio, his sneakers slapping softly on the dusty wood floor. Hanna stared at the business card he'd given her. *Patrick Lake, Photographer.* On the back was his phone number, website, and Facebook page.

The door to the studio slammed. The rest of the crew packed up. Jeremiah opened the small gray pouch that contained Mr. Marin's campaign petty cash and handed Sergio a wad of bills. Hanna turned Patrick Lake's business card in her hands, suddenly feeling a bit better. When she looked up, Kate was staring at her, her brow wrinkled, her lips pursed. Clearly, she'd heard the exchange between Hanna and Patrick.

How do you like that, bitch? Hanna thought giddily, slipping the business card into her pocket. She may not have won the battle for daddy, but she still might win the pretty-girl war.

4

AND NOW ARRIVING FROM
HELSINKI . . .

"Is your new cologne made of potpourri?" Aria Montgomery whispered to her boyfriend, Noel Kahn, as he swooped in for a kiss.

Noel propped himself up on the couch, looking offended. "I'm wearing Gucci Sport. Like I always do."

Aria took another sniff. She definitely smelled lavender. "I think you accidentally switched it with Grandma's toilet water."

Noel smelled his hands and winced, his soft brown eyes narrowing. "It's the hand soap from the sink. I can't help it that your mom puts girly shit in the bathrooms!" He slithered over to Aria and covered her nose with his hands. "You love it, don't you?"

Aria giggled. It was late Sunday afternoon, and she and Noel were all alone in Aria's mother's house, lying on her couch in the family room. Since her parents' divorce, the room had undergone a bit of a makeover to suit Ella's tastes and adventures. Hindu-god statues from Ella's trip to Bombay last summer lined the shelves, Indian blankets from her stay at an artist's colony in New Mexico this past fall covered the couches and chairs, and tons of green tea-scented candles, the smell of which Aria's father, Byron, had never liked, flickered everywhere. When Aria had crushed on Noel in sixth and seventh grades, she used to daydream about Noel coming over to her house and lying on the couch with her just like this—well, minus the leering looks from the many-armed Ganesh figurine in the corner.

Noel pecked Aria on the lips. Aria grinned and kissed him back, staring at his chiseled face; long, wavy, black hair; and pink lips. He breathed in and kissed her deeper, running his hands up and down the length of her spine. Slowly, he unbuttoned Aria's leopard-print cardigan. "You're so beautiful," he murmured. Then he pulled his T-shirt over his head, tossed it to the floor, and reached for the zipper on Aria's jeans. "We should go to your bedroom."

Aria put her hand over his, stopping him. "Noel, wait."

Noel groaned and rolled off her. "Seriously?"

"I'm sorry," Aria protested, buttoning her sweater again. "It's just . . ."

"Just what?" Noel gripped the edge of the coffee table, his posture suddenly rigid.

Aria stared out the side window, which offered a perfect view of the Chester County woods. She couldn't explain why she'd been so hesitant to have sex with him. They'd been going out for over a year. And it wasn't like she was a prude—she'd lost her virginity to Oskar, a boy in Iceland, when she was sixteen. Last year, she'd hooked up with Ezra Fitz, who happened to be her English teacher. They hadn't slept together, but they probably would have eventually if A hadn't outed them.

So why was she holding back with Noel? Admittedly, it was still mind-boggling that she was dating him at all—Aria's crush on Noel in sixth and seventh grades bordered on the embarrassing. Ali used to tease her about it constantly. "It's probably better you and Noel aren't dating," she'd say. "He's had so many other girlfriends, so much *experience*. And you've had how many boyfriends? Oh right—zero."

Sometimes Aria still got a sense that she wasn't good enough for him—not popular enough, not preppy enough, not the kind of girl who knew which fork to use at dinner or how to maneuver a horse over a jump. She didn't even know the proper *name* for those jumps. Then again, sometimes Aria got the sense Noel wasn't good enough for *her*—like when they'd toured Iceland together this past summer. He'd insisted on only eating at Burger King and paying for cans of Budweiser with U.S. dollars.

She touched Noel's rigid back. "I just want it to be special."

He turned. "You don't think it'd be special?"

"I do, but . . ." Aria shut her eyes. It was so hard to explain.

Noel hunched his shoulders defensively. "You've been so different lately."

Aria frowned. "Since when?"

"Since . . . a while, I guess." Noel slid off the couch and pulled his T-shirt back on. "Is it some other guy? Is there something you're not telling me?"

A chill ran up Aria's spine. She *was* keeping secrets from Noel. Of course he knew about Ali, A, and what had happened in the Poconos—the whole world did. But he didn't know about the unforgivable thing she'd done in Iceland. He didn't know about Jamaica, either, and he'd even been there when it happened—not *there*, of course, but sleeping in a nearby room. Would he still want to be with Aria if he knew any of that?

"Of course it isn't another guy." Aria hugged him from behind. "I just need some more time. Everything's fine, I promise."

"Well, you better watch out," Noel said in a slightly more playful voice. "I'm going to find a slutty freshman to satisfy my needs."

"You wouldn't," Aria threatened, slapping him lightly.

Noel twisted his mouth. "You're right. All the freshman girls are skanks, anyway."

"Not that that's ever stopped you."

Noel turned, buried Aria's head in his armpit, and gave her a noogie. "I hope you count yourself in the skank category, woman!"

Aria squealed. "Stop!" They fell back to the sofa and started kissing again.

"Ahem."

Aria shot up and saw her mother standing in the doorway. Ella's long, black hair was wound on top of her head, and she wore a long, flowing caftan tunic and black leggings. There was a scolding frown on her face. "Hello, Aria," she said evenly. "Hello, Noel."

"H-hey, Ella," Aria said, her face reddening. Despite her mom's liberal attitude about most things, she was still pretty strict about not letting Aria be in the house alone with Noel. Aria hadn't exactly told Ella she and Noel would be here today. "I-I'm sorry," she stammered. "We were just . . . talking. I swear."

"Uh-huh." Ella pursed her boysenberry-stained lips knowingly. Then, with a shake of her head, she padded off to the kitchen. "What are you two doing for dinner?" she asked over her shoulder. "I'm making raw turnip ravioli for Thaddeus and me. You're welcome to stay."

Aria glanced at Noel, who emphatically shook his head. Thaddeus was Ella's boyfriend—they'd met at the art gallery where Ella worked. He was a raw foodist, which meant Ella had become one, too. Aria liked her pasta cooked, thanks very much.

Then, Noel's phone, which was perched on the coffee table, let out a loud foghorn noise.

Noel untangled himself from Aria, checked the screen, and scowled. "Shit. I forgot. I have to pick up someone at the airport in an hour."

"Who?" Aria sat up and pulled her cardigan around her shoulders.

"Just this loser foreign exchange student who's coming for the semester. My parents dropped the bomb on me yesterday after the Hastingses' party. It's going to be so lame."

Aria's jaw dropped. "Why haven't you told me yet? Foreign-exchange students are so interesting!" In fifth grade, a girl named Yuki had come on exchange from Japan, staying with Lanie Iler's family. Most kids thought she was weird, but Aria found Yuki fascinating—she wrote her name in strange characters, folded origami shapes out of her spelling tests, and had the straightest, blackest hair Aria had ever seen.

Noel shoved his feet into his ratty driving loafers. "Are you kidding? It's going to suck. Do you know where he's from? Finland! He's probably going to be such a freak, like one of those guys who wears girls' jeans and plays the recorder."

Aria smiled to herself, remembering how Noel had called her *Finland* the first few weeks after her family had returned from Iceland.

"This dude probably is a huge dork." Noel strode toward the hall.

"Do you want company?" Aria called after him as he stomped down the stairs.

"Nah." Noel waved his hand. "I'll spare you from freak-Finn and his wooden shoes."

That's Holland, Aria wanted to say. She quickly pulled on her coat and slipped on her boots. "Seriously. I don't mind."

Noel chewed on his lip, thinking. "If you insist. But don't say I didn't warn you."

The Philadelphia airport teemed with families hauling suitcases, businessmen running to catch planes, and bedraggled travelers removing their shoes in the security line. The arrivals board said that the plane from Helsinki had just landed. Noel pulled a small cardboard square from his backpack and unfolded it. HUUSKO, it said in large red letters.

"That's his last name," Noel said wearily, staring at the poster as though it were a decree for his execution. "Doesn't it sound like a brand of grannie panties? Or maybe some kind of unidentifiable meat spread?"

Aria giggled. "You're terrible."

Noel plopped morosely on one of the benches by the security gate and stared at the line of people snaking toward the metal detectors. "This is our senior year, Aria. The only time we'll have to just chill before college. The last thing I want is some loser hanging on me. I swear my mom did this to torture me."

Aria made an *mmm* of sympathy. Then, she noticed something on the TV hanging overhead. ANNIVERSARY OF ROSEWOOD MURDERESS'S DEATH, said the yellow-lettered headline on the screen.

A brunette reporter stood in front of the DiLaurentises' old house, the wind blowing her hair around her face. "A year ago this Saturday, Alison DiLaurentis, whose killing spree baffled an entire nation, died in a horrific self-ignited fire in the Pocono Mountains," she announced. "A whole year has passed since the bizarre events, but the town of Rosewood still hasn't recovered."

Images of Jenna Cavanaugh and Ian Thomas, two of Real Ali's victims, flashed on the screen. Then there was the seventh-grade portrait of Courtney DiLaurentis—the girl who'd taken the real Ali's place in sixth grade, the girl whom Real Ali killed during their seventh-grade sleepover. "Many are still puzzled that Ms. DiLaurentis's body was never found in the rubble. Some have speculated Ms. DiLaurentis survived, but experts have claimed that there's no possibility of that."

A shiver ran down Aria's spine.

Noel covered Aria's eyes with his hands. "You shouldn't watch that."

Aria wriggled free. "It's hard not to."

"Have you been thinking about it much?"

"Sort of."

"Do you want to watch the movie together?"

"Oh God, *no*." Aria groaned. Noel was referring to *Pretty Little Killer*, a biopic condensing the events of last year into two TV-ready hours. It was beyond tacky.

Suddenly, an influx of people flowed through the door from immigration. Many were tall, blond, and pale, surely from the Helsinki flight. Noel grumbled. "Here we go." He waved the HUUSKO sign.

Aria peered through the crowd. "What's his first name, anyway?"

"Klaudius?" Noel mumbled. "Something like that."

Older men lugged suitcases past as they spoke on iPhones. Three lanky girls giggled together. A blond family carrying a towheaded child struggled to open a baby stroller. No one looked like a Klaudius.

Then, a voice floated through the crowd of travelers. "Mr. Kahn?"

Aria and Noel stood on their tiptoes, trying to locate the speaker. Just then, Aria noticed a boy with a drawn, elongated face, fleshy lips, zits on his cheeks and forehead, and an Adam's apple that protruded at least an inch from his neck. It was Klaudius, all right. He was even carrying a small instrument case that might just be a recorder. Poor Noel.

"Mr. Kahn?" the voice called again, but the boy Aria thought was Klaudius hadn't opened his mouth.

The crowd parted. A figure in a trapper hat, a down jacket, and fur lined boots emerged. "Hallo! It's you! I am your new exchange! Klaudia Huusko!"

Klaudia. Noel's mouth opened, but no sound came out. Aria stared at the figure in front of them, nearly choking on her gum. Noel's exchange student certainly wasn't a tall, gangly, pock-marked, flute-playing boy. Instead, Klaudia was a girl. A blond-haired, blue-eyed, throaty-voiced, large-breasted, tight-jeans-wearing Scandinavian wet dream.

And she'd be living just down the hall from Noel.

5

MEET THE PENNYTHISTLES

"Spencer." Mrs. Hastings leaned across the restaurant table. "Don't touch the bread. It's rude to start eating before everyone is seated."

Spencer's fingers released the squishy, buttery piece of ciabatta back into the basket. If she died from starvation before the others got here, it would be her mother's fault.

It was Sunday night, and Spencer, Melissa, and her mother were sitting at the Goshen Inn, a stuffy restaurant inside an old 1700s house that had allegedly once been a boarding house for redcoat soldiers. Mrs. Hastings kept clucking about how nice the surroundings were, but Spencer thought the restaurant was as gloomy as a funeral home. It was definitely Colonial Philadelphia chic, with lots of Revolutionary War muskets mounted on the wall, three-cornered hats tucked into window boxes, and candles in old-timey glass lanterns on the tables. And because the clientele looked as old as the décor, the room smelled like an unpleasant mix of musty basement, slightly over-done filet mignon, and Vicks VapoRub.

"What's this Nicholas guy do, anyway?" Spencer folded and refolded the cloth napkin on her lap.

Mrs. Hastings stiffened. "He's Mr. Pennythistle until further notice."

Spencer snickered. *Mr. Pennythistle* sounded like the name of a pornographic clown.

"I know what he does," Melissa volunteered. "I didn't make the connection at the party, but we totally studied him in my entrepreneurs class. He's the biggest real estate developer in the area. The Donald Trump of the Main Line."

Spencer made a face. "So he bulldozes farmland and wildlife sanctuaries to make way for ugly tract homes?"

"He created Applewood, Spence," Melissa gushed happily. "You know, those beautiful carriage houses on the golf course?"

Spencer turned her fork over in her hands, unim-pressed. Whenever she drove around Rosewood, it seemed like a new development was springing up. Apparently it was this Nicholas guy's fault.

"Girls, *shh*." Mrs. Hastings snapped suddenly, her eyes on the doorway. Two people walked toward their table. One was a tall, burly man who looked like he could've been a rugby player in a past life. He had neatly combed graying hair, steel blue eyes, a regal, slanting nose, and the beginnings of jowls. His navy blue blazer and khaki pants looked freshly ironed, and he wore gold cuff links embossed with the tiny initials *NP.* In his hand were three long-stemmed, dethorned, blood-red roses.

A girl of about fifteen was with him. A velvet headband held back her short, curly black hair, and she wore a gray jumper that looked like a chambermaid's uniform. There was a bitter scowl on her face as though she'd been constipated for days.

Mrs. Hastings rose clumsily, bumping her knee on the underside of the table and making their water glasses wobble. "Nicholas! It's so lovely to see you!" She blushed happily as he handed her one of the flowers. Then she gestured around the table. "These are my daughters, Melissa and Spencer."

Melissa stood, too. "So nice to meet you," she said, pumping Nicholas's—er, Mr. Pennythistle's—hand. Spencer said hello, too, though less enthusiastically. Ass-kissing just wasn't her style.

"Very nice to meet you both," Mr. Pennythistle said in a startlingly kind, gentle voice. He handed each of the girls a rose, too. Melissa cooed with delight, but Spencer just twirled it in her fingers suspiciously. There was something about the whole thing that was very *The Bachelor.*

Then Mr. Pennythistle gestured at the girl next to him. "And this is my daughter, Amelia."

Amelia, whose own red rose was peeking out of the top of her ugly messenger bag, shook everyone's hands, though she didn't look very happy about it. "I like your headband," Spencer offered, trying to be magnanimous. Amelia just stared at her blankly, her lips still a tight, straight line, her eyes canvassing Spencer's long blond hair, gray cashmere sweater dress, and black Frye boots. After a moment, she let out a sniff and turned away, as if Spencer was the fashion faux pas, not her.

"Zachary will be along soon," Mr. Pennythistle said as he sat down. "He had an Advanced Placement study group that ran late."

"Understandable." Mrs. Hastings lifted her water glass. She turned to her girls. "Both Zachary and Amelia go to St. Agnes."

The ice cube Spencer had been sucking on slipped down her throat. St. Agnes was the snootiest school in the Main Line, so uptight that it made Rosewood Day look like juvie. Spencer had met a girl named Kelsey from St. Agnes this summer, while she was in an accelerated AP program at Penn. At first they'd been best friends, but then . . .

Spencer inspected Amelia carefully. Did Amelia know Kelsey? Had she heard what happened to her?

Then there was a long silence. Spencer's mom kept sighing at her rose, looking around, and smiling awkwardly. Innocuous classical music tinkled softly over the stereo. Mr. Pennythistle politely ordered a Delamain cognac from the waitress. He kept making these irritating little coughs at the back of his throat. *Just spit out your phlegm already,* Spencer wanted to snap.

Finally, Melissa cleared her throat. "This is a lovely restaurant, Mr. Pennythistle."

"Oh, absolutely!" Mrs. Hastings said, clearly grateful someone had broken the ice.

"Really Revolutionary War–esque," Spencer added. "Let's hope the food doesn't date from then, too!"

Mrs. Hastings barked out a fake-laugh, but she stopped as soon as she saw the confused, almost hurt look on her boyfriend's face. Amelia wrinkled her nose as if she'd smelled something rancid in the air. "Oh, Spencer didn't mean it seriously," Mrs. Hastings said quickly. "It was just a joke!"

Mr. Pennythistle tugged at his starched collar. "This has been my favorite restaurant for years. They have an award-winning wine list."

Whoop-de-doo. Spencer glanced around, wishing she could sit with the table of tittering sixty-something ladies in the corner—at least *they* looked fun. She sneaked a peek at Melissa, hoping to commiserate, but Melissa was beaming at Mr. Pennythistle as though he were the Dalai Lama.

After the waitress delivered their drinks, Mr. Pennythistle turned to Spencer. Up close, he had little wrinkles around his eyes and wiry, out-of-control eyebrows. "So you're a senior at Rosewood Day?"

Spencer nodded. "That's right."

"She's *very* involved," Mrs. Hastings bragged. "She's on Varsity field hockey, and she was cast as Lady Macbeth in the senior production of *Macbeth*. Rosewood Day has a top-notch drama program."

Mr. Pennythistle's eyebrow arched at Spencer. "How are your grades this semester?"

The question caught Spencer off guard. *Nosy, aren't we?* "They're . . . fine. But I got into Princeton early decision, so it's not such a big deal this term."

She said *Princeton* with relish—surely that would impress Mr. Pennythistle and his snotty daughter. But Mr. Pennythistle just inched closer. "Princeton doesn't like slackers, you know." His kindly voice turned sharp. "Now isn't the time to rest on your laurels."

Spencer recoiled. What was with the reprimanding tone? Who did he think he was, her father? It was Mr. Hastings who'd told Spencer she should take it easy this semester—she'd worked hard, after all.

Spencer looked to her mother, but she was nodding along. "That's true, Spence. Maybe you shouldn't relax too much."

"I've heard colleges are looking at your final term grades a lot more these days," Melissa agreed. *Traitor*, Spencer thought.

"I've told my son that, too." Mr. Pennythistle opened the restaurant's wine list, which was the size of a dictionary. "He's going to Harvard." He said it in a haughty voice that seemed to say *which is much, much better than Princeton.*

Spencer ducked her head and arranged her fork, knife, and spoon so that they were exactly parallel with one another on the table. Organizing usually made her calm down, but not today.

Then Mr. Pennythistle turned to Melissa. "And I heard you got an MBA at Wharton. You're working for Brice Langley's hedge fund now, right? Impressive."

Melissa, who had tucked her rose behind her ear, blushed. "I got lucky, I guess. Had a really good interview."

"It must have taken more than luck and a good interview," Mr. Pennythistle said admiringly. "Langley only hires the best of the best. You and Amelia have a lot to talk about. She wants to go into finance, too."

Melissa beamed at Amelia, and Her Highness actually smiled back. *Great.* So this was going to be like any other family event Spencer had ever attended: Melissa was the shining star, the golden child, and Spencer was the second-rate freak no one quite knew how to handle.

Well, she'd had enough. Murmuring an excuse, she rose and placed her napkin on the back of her chair. She wove her way to the bathrooms at the bar area at the back of the restaurant.

The women's bathroom, which was painted pink and had an antique brass knob, was locked, so Spencer slumped down on a cushy barstool at the bar to wait. The bartender, a handsome guy in his mid-twenties, swept over and set a Goshen Inn–embossed cocktail napkin in front of her. "What can I get you?"

The gleaming bottles of alcohol behind the bar

winked temptingly. Neither Spencer's mother nor Mr. Pennythistle could see Spencer from this angle. "Um, just coffee," she decided at the last minute, not wanting to push her luck.

The bartender pivoted to the carafe and poured her a cup. As he set it in front of her, she noticed an image on the TV screen. A recent photo of Ali–the *real* Ali, the one who'd tried to kill Spencer and the others–dominated the top right corner. Across the bottom ran a headline that said DILAURENTIS POCONOS FIRE ANNIVERSARY: ROSEWOOD REMINISCES. Spencer shuddered. The last thing she wanted to do was reminisce about Real Ali trying to burn them alive.

A few weeks after it happened, Spencer made a conscious decision to look on the bright side–at least the terrible ordeal was over. They finally had closure, and they could begin the process of forgetting. She'd been the one to propose the Jamaica trip to her friends, even offering to help pay Emily's and Aria's way. "It'll be a way for us to start fresh, forget everything," she urged, spreading the resort brochures across the cafeteria table at lunch. "We need a trip that we can always remember."

Famous last words. They'd never forget the trip–but not in a good way.

Someone groaned a few feet down. Spencer looked over, expecting to see an old codger in the middle of a heart attack, but instead saw a young guy with wavy brown hair, broad shoulders, and the longest eyelashes she'd ever seen.

He glanced at Spencer and gestured to the iPhone in his hand. "You don't know what to do when this thing freezes, do you?"

One corner of Spencer's mouth twisted into a smile. "How do you know I have an iPhone?" she challenged.

The guy lowered his phone and gave her a long, curious once-over. "No offense, but you don't look like the kind of girl who'd walk around with anything but the best and the latest."

"Oh really?" Spencer pressed her hand to her chest, mock-offended. "You shouldn't judge a book by its cover, you know."

The guy stood up and dragged his barstool over to her. Up close, he was even cuter than she'd originally thought: His cheekbones were well defined, his nose ended in a cute bump on the end, and a dimple on his right cheek appeared whenever he smiled. Spencer liked his white, even, square teeth, untucked white-button down, and Converse All-Stars. Messy prepster was her favorite look.

"Okay, truth?" he said. "I asked you because you look like the only person in this place who actually owns a cell phone." He glanced covertly at the aged population around the bar. There was a whole table of old guys in power scooters. One of them even had an oxygen tube under his nose.

Spencer snickered. "Yeah, they're more of a rotary-dial crowd."

"They probably still use the operator to make a call."

He pushed his phone in Spencer's direction. "Seriously, though, do I restart or what?"

"I'm not sure . . ." Spencer stared at the screen. It was frozen on the stream for 610 AM, the local sports station. "Oh, I listen to this all the time!"

The boy looked at her skeptically. "*You* listen to sports radio?"

"It calms me down." Spencer sipped her coffee. "It's nice to hear people talking about sports instead of politics." *Or Alison,* she silently added in her head. "Plus I'm a Phillies fan."

"Did you listen to the World Series?" the guy asked.

Spencer leaned toward him. "I could have *gone* to the World Series. My dad has season tickets."

He frowned. "Why didn't you?"

"I donated them to a charity that helps inner-city kids."

The boy scoffed. "Either you're an extreme do-gooder or you've got a really guilty conscience."

Spencer flinched, then straightened up. "I did it because it looks good on college applications. But if you play your cards right, maybe I'll take you next season."

The guy's eyes twinkled. "Let's hope they make it."

Spencer held his gaze for a moment, her pulse speeding up. He was definitely flirting, and she definitely liked it. She hadn't felt this much of a spark for anyone since she'd broken up with Andrew Campbell last year.

Her companion sipped from his glass of beer. When he set the glass back on the bar, Spencer quickly grabbed a coaster and placed it under it. Then she wiped the edge of the glass with a napkin to keep it from dripping.

The guy watched with amusement. "Do you always tidy glasses of people you don't know?"

"It's a pet peeve," Spencer admitted.

"Everything has to be just so, doesn't it?"

"I like things done my way." Spencer appreciated the double-entendre. Then she stuck out her hand. "I'm Spencer."

He shook, his grip strong. "Zach."

The name resonated in Spencer's mind. She took in his high cheekbones, his cultured way of speaking, and his suddenly familiar steel-blue eyes. "Wait. Zach as in Zachary?"

He curled his lip. "Only my dad calls me that." Then he retracted, suddenly suspicious. "Why do you ask?"

"Because I'm having dinner with you tonight. My mom and your dad are . . ." She opened her palms, too weirded out to say the word *dating*.

It took Zach a moment to digest what she said. "*You're* one of the daughters?"

"Yep."

He stared at her. "Why do you look familiar?"

"I knew Alison DiLaurentis," Spencer admitted, gesturing toward the TV. The story about Ali's death was *still* on the screen. Wasn't there more important news to obsess over?

Zach snapped his fingers. "*Right.* My friends and I thought you were the hot one."

"Really?" Spencer squeaked. Even compared to Hanna?

"Wow." Zach ran his hands through his hair. "This is wild. I really wasn't looking forward to this dinner. I thought the girlfriend's daughters would be . . ."

"Snobbier?" Spencer provided. "Blander?"

"Kind of." Zach smiled guiltily. "But you're . . . cool."

Spencer felt another flutter. "You're not so bad your-self." Then she pointed at his glass of beer, remembering something. "Have you been here the whole time? Your dad said you were at a study group."

Zach ducked his head. "I needed to unwind before I went in there. My dad kind of stresses me out." He raised a brow. "So you've already met him? Is my sister there, too? Are they being enormous douche bags?"

Spencer giggled. "My mom and sister were equally as lame. They were all trying to out-impress one another."

The bartender set Zach's bill face-down on the bar. Spencer noticed that the clock on the wall said 6:45. She'd been gone for almost fifteen minutes. "We should go back, don't you think?"

Zach shut his eyes and groaned. "Do we have to? Let's run away instead. Hide out in Philly. Hop a plane for Paris."

"Or maybe Nice," Spencer suggested.

"The Riviera would work," Zach said excitedly. "My dad has a villa in Cannes. We could hide there."

"I knew there was a reason we met," Spencer teased, shoving Zach playfully on the arm.

Zach shoved her back, letting his hand linger on her skin. He leaned forward and slightly moistened his lips. For a moment, Spencer thought he was going to kiss her.

Her feet barely touched the ground as she waltzed back into the dining room. But as she passed through the archway, something made her turn around. Ali's face flashed on the TV screen again. For a moment, the picture seemed to come to life, grinning at Spencer as though Ali was looking out from inside the small, square box and seeing just what Spencer was up to. Her smile seemed even more sinister than usual.

Zach's comment suddenly rang in her ears. *Either you're an extreme do-gooder or you've got a guilty conscience.* He was right: Last fall, Spencer had donated her World Series tickets because she felt she didn't deserve to go, not after what she'd done. And in the first few moments after she'd gotten into Princeton, she'd considered declining, not sure she deserved that either, until she realized how insane that sounded.

And it was crazy to think that the girl on the screen was anything more than an image, too. Ali was gone for good. Spencer gazed squarely at the TV screen and narrowed her eyes. *Later, bitch.* Then, rolling back her shoulders, she turned and followed Zach to the table.

6

OH, THOSE INSECURE PRETTY GIRLS

"Surprise!" Mike whispered on Monday afternoon as he slid into an auditorium seat next to Hanna. "I got us Tokyo Boy!"

He unveiled a large plastic bag full of sushi rolls. "How did you know?" Hanna cried, grabbing a pair of chopsticks. She hadn't eaten anything at lunch, having deemed everything in the Rosewood Day cafeteria inedible. Her stomach was growling something fierce.

"I *always* know what you want." Mike teased, pushing a lock of black hair out of his eyes.

They ripped into the sushi quietly, wincing at a sophomore rehearsing a song from *West Side Story* on the stage. Normally, study hall was held in a classroom in the oldest wing of Rosewood Day, but a leak had sprung in the ceiling last week, so somehow they'd ended up in the auditorium—at the same time the Rosewood Day junior girls' choir rehearsed. How was anyone supposed to get any homework done amid the horrible singing?

Despite the bad voices, the auditorium was one of Hanna's favorite places at school. A wealthy donor had paid for the place to look as tricked-out as any theater on Broadway, and the seats were plush velvet, the ceilings were high and adorned with ornate plasterwork, and the lighting on the stage definitely made some of the chunkier choir girls look at least five pounds thinner. Back when Hanna was BFFs with Mona Vanderwaal, the two of them used to sneak on the stage after school and flounce around, pretending they were famous actresses in Tony-winning musicals. That was before Mona turned crazy-town and tried to run her over, of course.

Mike skewered a California roll and popped it into his mouth whole. "So. When's your big TV debut?"

Hanna stared at him blankly. "Huh?"

"The commercial for your dad?" Mike reminded her, chewing.

"Oh, that." Hanna ate a bite of wasabi, and her eyes began to water. "I'm sure my lines were edited out immediately."

"That might not be true. You looked great."

On the stage, a bunch of girls were now trying a harmony. It was like listening to a gang of wailing cats. "The commercial is going to be all about my dad, Isabel, and Kate," Hanna mumbled. "That's exactly what my dad wants. His perfect nuclear family."

Mike wiped a piece of rice from his cheek. "He didn't actually say that."

His optimism was getting on Hanna's nerves. How many times had she told Mike about her daddy issues? How many times had he been up close and personal with Kate? That was the thing about guys, though: Sometimes, they had the emotional depth of a flea.

Hanna took a deep breath and stared blankly at the heads of the study hall students in front of them. "The only way I'm going to end up in a commercial is if I do it on my own. Maybe I should call that photographer."

Mike's chopsticks fell to his lap. "That poseur who was drooling all over you at the shoot? Are you serious?"

"His name's Patrick Lake," Hanna said stiffly. He'd said she was amazing on camera, and had badmouthed Kate right in front of her. That part was her favorite.

"Why would you say he's a poseur?" she asked after a moment. "He's totally professional. He wants to take pictures of me and hook me up with a modeling agency." She'd googled Patrick on her iPhone during lunch, gazing at his Flickr photos and Facebook links. On his website, Patrick listed that he'd taken photos for several Main Line magazines as well as a fashion insert for the *Philadelphia Sentinel*. Plus, he shared a first name with Patrick Demarchelier, Hanna's favorite fashion photographer.

"More like professionally sleazy. He doesn't want to turn you into a model, Hanna. He wants to do you."

Hanna's mouth dropped. "You don't think I'm capable of getting signed by a modeling agency?"

"That's not what I said."

"You pretty much did." Hanna angled her body away from Mike, feeling a flush of anger. "So basically, anyone who approaches me just wants to bone me, right? I'm not pretty enough to take seriously."

Mike shut his eyes like he suddenly had a migraine. "Would you listen to yourself? Only pretty girls get hit on—and that's *you*. If you were a dog, he wouldn't be after you. But that dude was nasty. He reminded me of that artist freak who had a thing for Aria on our trip to Iceland."

Hanna stiffened, knowing immediately what artist Mike was talking about—he'd plunked down next to them at a bar in Reykjavik and deemed Aria his new muse. "Let me text Aria," Mike went on, pulling out his phone. "I bet she'll tell you the same thing."

Hanna caught his hand. "You're not texting your sister about this," she blurted. "We're not really friends anymore, okay?"

Mike lowered his phone, not even flinching. "I already figured that out, Hanna," he said evenly. "I just didn't think it would take *you* so long to admit it."

Hanna swallowed, surprised. She'd figured he just hadn't noticed. He probably wanted to know *why* Hanna and Aria weren't speaking, too—but she couldn't tell him that.

Suddenly, Hanna couldn't bear to be in the same room

as Mike. When she stood up and grabbed her bag off the floor, Mike touched her elbow. "Where are you going?"

"Bathroom," Hanna answered haughtily. "Am I *allowed*?"

Mike's eyes turned cold. "You're going to call that photographer, aren't you?"

"Maybe." She tossed her auburn hair over her shoulder.

"Hanna, don't."

"You can't tell me what to do."

Mike crumpled up the Tokyo Boy bag in his hands. "If you do, you can forget about me coming to any more of your dad's campaign events."

Hanna couldn't believe it. Mike had never issued an ultimatum before. The whole time they'd been dating, he'd treated her like a queen. Now, it looked like someone had forgotten his place.

"In that case . . ." Hanna swept into the aisle. "How about we just forget about everything?"

The skin around Mike's mouth slackened. Obviously he'd been bluffing. But before he could protest, Hanna was already out the door.

She marched past the office, the nurse's station, and Steam, the school's upscale coffee bar, which always smelled like burnt coffee beans this time of day, finally stopping at the double doors to the Commons. It had a tiny alcove where you could make a cell phone call without teachers noticing. Hanna dug her phone out of her purse and dialed Patrick's number.

The phone rang three times, and a groggy voice answered. "Patrick?" Hanna said in her most professional-sounding voice. "This is Hanna Marin. We met at my father's photo shoot on Saturday."

"Hanna!" Patrick suddenly sounded much more awake. "I'm so happy you called!"

In less than a minute, everything was arranged: Hanna would meet Patrick in Philadelphia tomorrow after school, and he would take some test shots of her for his portfolio. He sounded perfectly respectable, speaking to her without even the slightest tinge of flirtatiousness. When they hung up, Hanna held the phone between her palms, her heart pounding hard. *Take that, Mike.* Patrick wasn't a skeev. He was going to make Hanna a star.

As she dropped her phone back into her bag, she saw a shadow flicker in the corner. Reflected in the glass door to the Commons was a blond girl. *Ali.*

Hanna whipped around, half expecting to see Ali standing at a locker behind her, but it was only poster of Ali's seventh-grade school picture on the wall. There were smaller pictures of Jenna Cavanaugh and Ian Thomas, and then a larger photo of Real Ali after her return as her dead twin. ALL IT TOOK WAS ONE LIT MATCH, said a headline under the images. Below it were details of the made-for-TV program, *Pretty Little Killer.*

Unbelievable. Even Rosewood Day was in on the hype. Hanna ripped down the poster and balled it up in her hands.

Suddenly, a teasing, familiar voice from Jamaica echoed in her ear: *I feel like I've known you girls forever. But that's impossible, right?* Followed by an eerie giggle.

"No," Hanna whispered, purging the voice from her head. She hadn't heard it in a long time—not since right after they'd returned from the trip. She wasn't about to let the voice—or the guilt—invade her mind again.

A trio of girls clad in North Face jackets and Ugg boots crossed the Commons. An English teacher flitted down the hall with an armful of books. Hanna tore up the photo of Ali until it was in a thousand satisfying pieces. She brushed off her hands into the wastebasket. There. Ali was gone.

Just like the Real Ali. Of that, Hanna was absolutely sure.

7

TOUCHY-FEELY

On Monday evening, Emily pulled her family's Volvo station wagon into the driveway of the Rolands' house and yanked up the emergency brake. Her palms were sweating. She couldn't believe she was about to go into the house where Jenna and Toby had lived.

In the side yard was the stump of what used to be Toby's old tree house, the site of the awful prank that had blinded Jenna. There was the big bay window through which Ali and the others spied on Jenna when they had nothing better to do. Ali was ruthless with Jenna, picking on her high-pitched voice, her pale skin, or how she brought tuna sandwiches to lunch and then had tuna breath for the rest of the day. But unbeknownst to them, Ali and Jenna shared a secret: Jenna knew that Ali had a twin. It was why, in the end, Real Ali had killed her.

Suddenly, the red-painted oak door whipped open, and Chloe appeared. "Hey, Emily, come on in!"

Emily stepped inside tentatively. The house smelled like apples, the walls had been painted deep reds and oranges, and bejeweled Indian tapestries hung on the big space under the stairs. The furniture was a mismatch of Stickley chairs, threadbare sixties-upholstered divans, and a coffee table made out of one large slab of curly maple. It was like walking into a funky junk shop.

She followed Chloe into the back room, which had big floor-to-ceiling doors that opened out onto the patio. "Here's Gracie," Chloe said, pointing to the baby in a swing in the corner. "Gracie, remember your best friend Emily?"

The baby made a cooing noise and went back to chewing on a rubber giraffe. Emily felt something rise up inside her chest, a feeling she wasn't quite ready to face. She pushed it down again. "Hi, Grace. I like your giraffe." She gave it a squeeze, and it squeaked.

"Want to come up to my room for a sec?" Chloe called from the stairs. "I just have to get a couple of things for my interview. Grace will be fine in her swing for a minute."

"Uh, sure." Emily walked through the living room. The grandfather clock in the foyer bonged seven. "Where are your parents?"

Chloe dodged a bunch of boxes in the second floor hall. "Still at work. They're both lawyers—always super busy. Oh, I told my dad about you, by the way. He said he'd help with the scholarship thing. He says UNC is still looking for good swimmers."

"That's *amazing*." Emily wanted to hug Chloe, but she didn't know her well enough yet.

Chloe pushed into her bedroom, which was decorated with posters of famous soccer players. A shirtless David Beckham kicked a ball. Mia Hamm was caught midstride on the field, her abs looking amazing. Chloe picked up a paddle brush from the bureau and ran it through her long hair. "You said you quit swimming this summer, right?"

"Yeah."

"Do you mind if I ask what happened?"

Emily was surprised by the directness of the question. She certainly couldn't tell Chloe the truth. "Oh, I just had some stuff to deal with."

Chloe walked to the window and looked out. "I played soccer until last year, in case you couldn't tell." She gestured around at the posters. "But then, suddenly, I hated it. I couldn't stand going on the field. My dad was, like, 'what's wrong with you? You've loved soccer since you were a little girl!' But I couldn't explain it. I just didn't want to play anymore."

"How are your parents about it now?"

"Better." Chloe opened her closet. Clothes hung neatly on racks, and there were a bunch of old-school board games—Clue, Monopoly, Mousetrap—piled messily on the top shelf. "But it took a long time for them to get there. Some other stuff happened, though, and that put it in perspective."

She shut the closet door again. Suddenly, Emily

noticed faded pencil writing on the wall to the left of the closet. *Jenna.* Lines on the wall demarcated height, date, and age.

Emily sank back down to the bed. This must have been Jenna's room once.

Chloe saw what Emily was looking at and flinched. "Oh. I keep meaning to paint over that."

"So you . . . know?" Emily asked.

Chloe pushed a piece of brown hair away from her mouth. "I argued with my parents about buying this place—I worried there would be a bad vibe here. But they convinced me it would be okay. This is, like, the best neighborhood or something, and they didn't want to pass up the good deal on the house." She pulled the red sweater over her head, then glanced at Emily. "You knew them, right? The kids that lived here?"

"Uh-huh." Emily lowered her eyes.

"I figured." Chloe bit her bottom lip. "I recognize you, actually. But I didn't know if you wanted to talk about it."

Emily swung her feet, not knowing what to say. Of course Chloe recognized her. Everyone did.

"Are you okay?" Chloe asked softly, sinking next to her on the bed. "That stuff with your old friend sounded awful."

Headlights on the street outside cast long shadows across the room. The scent of lavender and hair spray wafted through Emily's nose. *Was* she okay? After she'd said her good-byes, after she'd understood that the Ali they'd reconciled with wasn't the Ali she'd loved, she was as good as she could be. The Ali that had returned was dangerous, psychotic—it was a blessing that she was gone.

But then Jamaica happened.

Emily had been so excited to go. Spencer made the plans, picking The Cliffs resort in Negril and booking them massages, yoga classes, snorkeling trips, and sunset dinners in the caves. It was going to be the perfect escape, an ideal place to slough off all the horrible stuff that had happened. Emily had hoped the tropical air would cure the stomach flu that she hadn't been able to kick, too.

The first afternoon had been perfect—the warm water, the welcoming fish-fry lunch, the soothing sun. But then she'd seen that girl on the stairs of the roof deck that first night.

When the girl stepped in the doorway, her blond hair blowing, her yellow halter dress fluttered around her legs. Emily's vision tunneled. The girl was the only thing she saw. Her oval face, pointed nose, and slightly chunkier frame looked nothing like Ali's, but Emily just . . . *knew*. In the back of her mind, she'd somehow known she and Ali would meet again, and here she was. Alive. Staring straight at her.

She'd turned to her friends. "That's Ali," she whispered.

They just stared at her. "What are you talking about?" Spencer said. "Ali's dead, Em."

"She died in the fire, remember?" Aria urged. She

watched Emily suspiciously, like she worried Emily might make a scene.

"Did she?" Emily thought back to that night in the Poconos, guilt and anxiety rising inside of her. "What if she escaped? No one found her body."

Hanna turned to the girl in yellow. She had moved off the landing and was walking over to the bar. "Em, that looks nothing like her. Maybe you have a fever."

But Emily wasn't going to give up that easily. She watched as the girl ordered a drink, shooting one of the bartenders an I'm-Ali-and-I'm-fabulous smile. How many times had Emily cherished that smile? *Yearned* for it? Her heart sped up even more. "If Ali survived the fire, she would've had reconstructive surgery for the burns," she whispered. "That could be why she looks totally different. And that's why she has those marks on her arms."

"Emily . . ." Aria clutched Emily's hands. "You're making something out of nothing. It's *not* Ali. You have to get over her."

"I *am* over her!" Emily roared.

Emily snapped back to the present, reaching into the pocket of her corduroys and feeling for the silky orange tassel. If anyone ever asked, if anyone recognized it, she would say she'd found it on the lawn of the DiLaurentises' Poconos house after the explosion, even though it wasn't the truth.

Suddenly, Chloe leapt to her feet. "Mom! Dad! What are *you* doing here?"

A young couple appeared in the hall. Chloe's father, an athletic, dark-haired guy with smooth, flawless skin, wore a gray suit and polished leather shoes. Her mother, who had an angular brown bob and wore dark-framed hipster glasses, had on a tight pencil skirt, a shiny pink blouse, and pointy patent-leather heels. There was something edgy about them, like they went to buttoned-up jobs all day but attended indie bands and poetry readings at night. It was a nice change from the stuffy horsey types that overran Rosewood.

"We live here, remember?" Chloe's dad joked. Then he noticed Emily and smiled. "Hello . . . ?"

"Hi, I'm Emily Fields." Emily stepped forward and offered her hand.

"The coat check girl, right?" Mrs. Roland asked, shaking Emily's hand next. She wore a huge diamond ring Emily recognized from the party.

"And the swimmer," Mr. Roland added.

"*And* the babysitter while I go to my Villanova interview," Chloe told them. "She's wonderful with Grace, I promise."

Mr. Roland leaned on the banister. "Actually, Chlo, I don't think we really need a babysitter. We're both in for the night." He turned to Emily. "We'll still pay you for your trouble, of course."

"Oh, that's all right," Emily said quickly. "It was nice to come over." As soon as she said it, she realized it was true. She'd spent the past fall and winter holed up in her room without anyone to talk to. Worrying. Brooding. She felt like she was waking up from a long nap.

"We insist!" Mrs. Roland cried. "Henry, go get your wallet."

Chloe's mom retreated to the master bedroom, and Chloe and her dad started down the stairs. Emily followed them. "What lunch period do you have?" Chloe asked over her shoulder.

"First on Tuesdays and Thursdays, second on Mondays, Wednesdays, and Fridays," Emily answered.

"I have second lunch on Wednesdays and Fridays, too!" Chloe grabbed her coat from the closet. "Want to eat together? If you're not busy, of course."

"I would love that," Emily breathed. Lately, she'd been eating lunch off-campus—seniors were allowed to leave for the hour. But it was awfully lonely.

They made a plan to meet in front of Steam on Wednesday. Then Chloe rushed off to her interview, and Emily faced Mr. Roland again. He had pulled out a sleek leather wallet. "Really. You don't have to pay me."

Mr. Roland waved away her offer. "So Chloe told me about your swimming conundrum. You're serious about competing at the college level?"

"Of course."

He paused on her for a moment, studying her face. "Good. I have a lot of pull at UNC. If you give me your times, I can get in touch with the recruiter. I know they're still looking for kids to fill out the team."

Emily pressed her hand to her chest. "*Thank* you so much."

"It's my pleasure." Mr. Roland handed her a twenty. His piercing blue eyes twinkled. "Is this enough?"

Emily pushed it away. "That's way too much."

"Please." Mr. Roland placed the bill in her hand and closed her fist. Then, as he steered her toward the door, his hand snaked up her arm, slid down her shoulder, and rested on her hip.

Emily stopped walking, her mouth falling open. She wanted to tell Mr. Roland to stop it, but the nerves around her lips felt paralyzed.

Then Mr. Roland moved away and nonchalantly pulled out his BlackBerry. "Well, see you around, Emily. I'll be in touch." He spoke like nothing inappropriate just happened. All of a sudden, Emily wasn't sure. *Had* it?

She staggered out of the house, skidded down the driveway, and leaned against her car. The night was still and cold. The wind gusted, making the tree branches shake. Then, something shifted along at the border of the Hastingses' house and the DiLaurentises' old house. Emily shot up. Was that a person sneaking around? Who?

Beep. Emily jumped. It was her cell phone, buried deep in her bag. She dug it out and looked at the screen. ONE NEW TEXT. Emily blinked in surprise. The sender was Spencer Hastings. She quickly pressed READ.

Meet me in front of Ali's mailbox. I have something for you.

8

YOU'VE GOT MAIL!

Aria sat cross-legged on the floor of her father's den, listening to a podcast called *Find Your Inner Zen* she'd downloaded from Ella's computer. "Envision your third eye," a gravelly voiced man whispered in her ears. "Let your past blow away in the breeze. Be in the moment, *now*."

The past is blowing away in the breeze, Aria repeated silently, willing herself to believe it was true. After Jamaica, she'd listened to tons of relaxation recordings, but none of them did the trick. Maybe she didn't have a third eye. Or maybe the past was just too heavy to blow away.

"*Damn* it!" Her brother, Mike, said next to her, gripping the PlayStation controller. He was playing Gran Turismo, and every time he crashed his Lamborghini Murcielago into a chicane, he swore violently and beat the controller on the couch. *That* certainly wasn't helping Aria find her third eye, either.

"I hope you don't drive like that in real life," Meredith, her father's fiancée, murmured as she passed down the hall. Lola, her baby, was strapped to a BabyBjörn holder that wound around her arms and connected at her lower back. It looked like a torture device.

"Shut up, both of you," Mike snapped.

"Got something on your mind, Speed Racer?" Aria asked.

"No," Mike said agitatedly. "I'm fine."

But Aria knew better—something was definitely up with him. For one thing, Mike had gotten a ride with her this morning instead of waiting for Hanna to pick him up. Then, on her walk from biology to photography, Aria noticed that the little couch in the lobby where Mike and Hanna snuggled between periods was glaringly unoccupied.

When the game ended, Mike laid down his control paddle. "So you've met the Nordic goddess, right?"

Aria glanced up at him warily. "Excuse me?"

Mike rolled his eyes. "*Duh.* Klaudia, which I'm pretty sure is Scandinavian for *sex vixen.*"

"Scandinavian isn't a language." Aria groaned.

Mike reached to the coffee table and took a big handful of Smartfood popcorn from the ceramic bowl. "You have to tell me everything about her. Take a picture of her in the gym showers . . ."

Aria wound her iPod headphone around the device, trying not to overreact. "I don't think she'd appreciate that. And anyway, no one showers after gym."

"They don't?" Mike looked disappointed, and Aria stifled a laugh. Why did every guy have a secret fantasy of a bunch of butt-naked girls frolicking under the school's communal shower spray? Like girls ever *did* that!

"Well, whatever," Mike said, undeterred. "Get invited to Noel's for a sleepover and take pictures there. I bet Klaudia walks around the house naked twenty-four/seven. I heard Finns do that. They're huge sex addicts, too—there's nothing else to do there."

"Mike, ew." Aria threw a piece of popcorn at him. "And what would Hanna think about your new little obsession?"

Mike shrugged and didn't answer.

A-ha. "Did something happen with you and Hanna?" Aria pressed.

Mike started a new race, this time driving a Ferrari. "I couldn't believe it when Klaudia got out of Noel's car this morning," he said. "That dude seriously hit the jackpot. But he's not telling me anything. He's acting like he doesn't even realize Klaudia's a babe, but come on. You'd have to be blind not to want to hit that."

Aria balled up her fists. "Have you forgotten Noel's my boyfriend?"

One of Mike's shoulders rose. "It's not a crime to appreciate the view. It doesn't mean anything's going to happen between them."

Aria slumped back on the couch and stared at the growing crack around the light fixture in the ceiling. This whole Klaudia thing made her feel itchy and unsettled. Klaudia *was* a Nordic sex goddess—she had white-blond hair, full, pouty lips, cornflower blue eyes, and the body of a *Sports Illustrated* swimsuit model. Everyone had stared at her yesterday as they walked through the international terminal toward baggage claim. Several guys looked like they were about to drop to one knee and propose marriage—or, at the very least, a night of wild sex.

As Klaudia had waited for her luggage, Aria poked Noel's side. "Did you know Klaudia was a girl?" Perhaps that was why Noel hadn't wanted Aria to come with him to the airport. Perhaps he'd seen pictures of his new exchange student and wanted a few moments with her to himself.

"Of course not!" Noel seemed sincere. "I'm just as shocked as you are!"

Before Aria could say anything more, Klaudia returned dragging two oversized suitcases on wheels and carrying two duffels on her shoulder. "Oof, I bring so much!" she said with a heavy accent. Aria frowned. She'd met a few Finns during her years in Iceland, and their English was a million times better than Klaudia's. With her throaty voice and bubbleheaded delivery, she sounded like she'd grown up in a Finnish Barbie factory.

Noel and Aria helped Klaudia bring her crap to the car. After they loaded it in, Klaudia gave Aria a polite nod and said thank you. Then she turned to Noel and double-kissed him on the cheek, European-style, saying, "I so happy we roommates!" Instead of correcting Klaudia—over Aria's dead body were they staying in the same room—Noel just blushed and laughed. Like he thought it was funny. Like he wanted it to be true. Suddenly, Aria felt very, very nervous. Maybe she should have slept with him earlier—several *months* earlier. What if Noel got tired of how Aria said *no, no, no* and wanted someone who said *ja, ja, ja*?

Now, Aria shook out her shoulders, letting that memory of the past blow away in the wind. She was just letting her jealous mind run rampant. She'd thought Noel had a thing for Ali—*Real* Ali, the girl who'd returned to Rosewood and tried to kill them—but that hadn't been true. There'd also been that night in Jamaica: Aria had turned her back for one minute during dinner, and suddenly Noel was by the bar with a sexy blond girl all over him. "Jesus," she'd whispered, feeling the old jealous pull in her stomach.

She marched to the bar to break up the flirting, but when Noel's companion turned, Aria found herself staring into the face of the girl Emily had seen in the doorway. The one she'd thought was Ali.

The girl smiled broadly. "Hey, Aria. I'm Tabitha."

A shiver wriggled up Aria's spine. "How do you know my name?"

"Your boyfriend told me." She patted Noel's shoulder playfully. "Don't worry, he's a good boy. Not like the rest of us cheaters."

Aria flinched. Tabitha winked knowingly at Aria, almost as if she knew Aria's life story. Byron had cheated on Ella with Meredith. And Aria had cheated, too—on Sean Ackard with Ezra Fitz. But how could Tabitha know that? Certainly Noel wouldn't have told her. And though a lot of information had come out about Aria in the press, none of the stories mentioned anything about her parents or her affair with Ezra.

Aria stared warily at the burns up and down the girl's arms. Clearly, Tabitha had been through some sort of massive disaster. Something horrible—maybe even a fire. But it didn't mean Emily was right.

Beep.

Aria looked down. It was her Droid phone on the coffee table. When she picked it up and looked at the screen, it said TEXT FROM HANNA MARIN.

Aria frowned. Hanna? They hadn't spoken in months.

She opened the text. *Meet me in front of Ali's old mailbox. It's important.*

Driving down the DiLaurentises' old street still filled Aria with the sense that she was visiting an old graveyard. Mona Vanderwaal's old house stood at the beginning of the road, the windows dark, the doors shut tight, a tipped-over FOR SALE sign in the front yard. The Hastings house was lit up like a birthday cake, but Aria couldn't help glance at the backyard and the decimated woods, which would take years to recover from the fire Real Ali had set. Aria would never forget running frantically through the smoke that January night and coming upon someone trapped under a log. When she'd pulled the girl to safety, she'd realized it was Ali.

But not *their* Ali. Not the Ali who'd chosen them to be her new BFFs. Not the Ali they'd worshipped, resented, and loved. It was Real Ali, who'd been locked up in the Preserve since sixth grade.

Aria shook the memory away as her headlights swept across the DiLaurentises' old driveway. A figure stood at Ali's old mailbox, hopping from one foot to the other in a clear effort to keep warm. Aria pulled to the curb and got out. It wasn't Hanna, though, but Emily. "What are *you* doing here?" Aria asked.

Emily looked just as surprised as Aria was. "Spencer texted me. Did she text you, too?"

"No, Hanna did."

"I did what?"

They turned and saw Hanna stepping out of her Prius, her auburn hair wound into a bun. Aria held up her phone. "You told me to come here."

"No, I didn't." Hanna looked confused. "I'm here because Emily texted *me*."

Emily frowned. "I didn't text you."

A crack sounded behind them, and everyone whipped around. Spencer burst through the bushes that separated her house from the DiLaurentises'. "You told everyone to come, Aria?"

Aria let out an uncomfortable laugh. "I didn't tell *any-one* to come."

"Yeah, you did." Spencer thrust her phone in Aria's face. *Meet me in front of Ali's mailbox. I have something to show you.*

A cloud passed in front of the moon, blotting out the light. The snowdrifts on the lawn glistened eerily, crusted over with ice. Aria exchanged a worried glance with the others. Her stomach twisted with the familiarity of it—this was a look that had passed between them many, many times before.

"I was babysitting down the street." Emily's voice shook. "When I got my text, I looked at Ali's mailbox and saw someone here. I thought it was you, Spencer, since you'd written me the text."

"It wasn't me," Spencer said in a hoarse voice.

The girls stared at one another for a moment. Aria could tell they were all thinking the same thing. The very worst possible thing.

"Okay, ha ha." Spencer spun and faced the DiLaurentises' dark backyard. "Very funny! You can come out now, loser! We're onto you!"

No one answered. Nothing moved in the yard or in the woods beyond. Aria's heart began to pound. It felt like something—or someone—was lurking close by, watching, waiting, preparing to strike. The wind gusted, and Aria suddenly caught a whiff of smoke and gas. It was the same horrible odor she'd smelled the night Ali burned down the woods. The same odor as the night the house had caught fire in the Poconos.

"I'm leaving." Aria reached for her keys. "I'm not in the mood for this."

"Wait!" Emily cried. "What's that?"

Aria turned. A piece of paper stuck out of the DiLaurentises' old mailbox, flapping in the wind.

Emily walked over and pulled it out. "That's not yours!" Hanna hissed. "It's probably just junk mail they forgot to pick up!"

"Junk mail that has our names on it?" Emily waved a white envelope in their faces. Sure enough, it said SPENCER, EMILY, ARIA, AND HANNA on the front in large block letters.

"What the hell?" Spencer whispered, sounding more annoyed than afraid.

Hanna grabbed the envelope from Emily. Everyone gathered close, the closest they'd been to one another in months. Aria inhaled Hanna's sugary Michael Kors perfume. Spencer's silky blond hair brushed against her cheek. Emily's breath smelled like Doublemint gum.

Spencer turned on her iPhone's flashlight app and directed it at the envelope's contents. Inside was a folded-up piece of glossy paper, seemingly ripped from a magazine. When flattened out, it showed the latest photo of Real Ali when she'd returned from the Preserve last year. PRETTY LITTLE KILLER, read the fancy script at the bottom. THIS SATURDAY. 8 P.M.

"The made-for-TV movie," Aria groaned. "Some idiot is messing with us."

"Hold on." Emily pointed to the other item in the envelope. "What's that?"

Hanna pulled it out. It was a postcard. On the front was a gleaming, crystal-blue ocean surrounded by rocky cliffs. On top of the cliffs was a resort with a huge pool, lounge chairs, tiki huts, and a roof deck and restaurant.

Hanna gasped. "Is that . . . ?"

"It can't be," Spencer whispered.

"It *is*." Emily pointed at the pineapple mosaic pattern on the bottom of the pool. "The Cliffs."

Aria stepped back from the postcard as if it were on fire. She hadn't seen an image of The Cliffs in almost a year. She'd deleted every photo from spring break. She'd untagged herself from Mike and Noel's Facebook postings of them on the beach, at dinner, in an ocean kayak, or snorkeling on the reefs. The ones where she was pretending they were having a good time. Hiding the dark, awful truth.

Simply looking at the aerial view made her sick. A memory formed in her mind, sharp and distinct: Tabitha standing there at the bar, smirking at Aria. Looking at her like she knew exactly who she was . . . and exactly what her secrets were.

"Who could have sent this?" Hanna whispered.

"It's just a coincidence," Spencer said forcefully. "Someone's screwing with us." She looked around again for someone hiding in the bushes or giggling on the

DiLaurentises' old porch, but all was silent. It felt like they were the only people outside for miles.

Then Hanna turned the postcard over and squinted hard at the message there. "Oh my God."

"What?" Spencer asked. Hanna didn't answer, just shook her head frantically and passed the postcard to her.

One by one, each girl read the inscription on the back. Spencer covered her eyes. Emily mouthed *no*. When it was Aria's turn, she focused on the capital letters. Her stomach tightened and her mind began to spin.

I hear Jamaica is beautiful this time of year. Too bad the four of you can't EVER go back there.

Missed you! –A

9

TROUBLE IN PARADISE

The words on the postcard blurred before Spencer's eyes. The wind gusted, and tree branches scraped up against the side of the DiLaurentises' old house. It sounded like screams.

"Could this be . . . real?" Emily whispered. The air was so cold that her breath came out in eerie white puffs.

Spencer looked at the card again. She desperately wanted to say that it was a joke, just like the countless other fake A notes they'd received since Ali died. They'd arrived in her mailbox, addressed to Spenser Hastengs or Spancer Histings or, even more amusing, Spencer Montgomery. Most of the notes were innocuous, saying simply *I'm watching you* or *I know your secrets*. Others were notes of sympathy—although, bizarrely, they were still signed *A*. Some notes were more worrisome, pleas for money with threats if their requests weren't met. Spencer had taken those sorts of A notes to the Rosewood police department, and they'd handled them. Done and done.

But this one was different. It referred to something real, something Spencer hadn't dared to think about for an entire year. If the wrong people found out about it, they'd be in more trouble than they could ever dream of. They could kiss their futures good-bye.

"How is this possible?" Hanna whispered. "How could someone know this? No one was around. No one saw what Aria did."

Aria's lips parted slightly. A look of guilt washed across her face.

"What we *all* did," Spencer clarified quickly. "We were all part of it."

Hanna crossed her arms over her chest. "Okay, okay. But no one was there. We made sure."

"That might not be true." Emily's eyes glowed in the iPhone's artificial light.

"Don't even say it," Spencer warned. "It can't be . . . *her*. It can't."

Hanna turned the card over and looked at the picture of the resort again. Her brow furrowed. "Maybe it's not about what we think. Lots of stuff happened in Jamaica. Maybe whoever wrote this could be talking about something else. Like how Noel stole those little bottles of rum from the bar and took them to our room."

"Yeah, like someone really cares about that a whole year later," Aria said sarcastically. "That wouldn't be reason enough that we couldn't ever return to Jamaica. We *know* what this is about."

Everyone fell silent again. A dog barked a few houses down. An icicle chose that exact moment to break from the eaves of the DiLaurentises' garage and smash to the ground, shattering into a billion pieces. They jumped back.

"Should we tell the cops?" Emily whispered.

Spencer looked at her like she was insane. "What do you think?"

"Maybe they wouldn't ask what happened," Emily said. "Maybe we could get around talking about it. If this is someone real, someone who's after us, we have to stop them before someone gets hurt."

"The only person who'd want to hurt us is someone who knows what we did," Aria said in a small voice. "It'll come out if we go to the cops, Emily. You know it."

Emily looked shiftily back and forth. "But, I mean, we aren't even *sure* what happened that night."

"Stop," Spencer interrupted, shutting her eyes. If she even allowed herself to think about this, the remorse and paranoia would rush over her like a strong ocean current, pulling her under, choking her. "Someone is screwing with us, okay?" She grabbed the postcard from Hanna's grip and shoved it into the pocket of her duffel coat. "I'm not going to be jerked around again. We've been through enough already."

"So what are we supposed to do?" Aria threw up her hands.

"We ignore the note," Spencer decided. "We pretend we never got it."

"But someone *knows*, Spencer." Emily's voice was pleading. "What if A goes to the cops?"

"With what evidence?" Spencer stared around at them. "There is none, remember? There's no link to us except for what we remember. *No one* saw. No one even *knew* her. No one was looking for her the rest of the time. Maybe Hanna's right—maybe this is about something else. Or maybe someone has picked up on the fact that we're not as close as we used to be and figured it might've had something to do with Jamaica."

Spencer paused and thought about how Wilden had watched her with curiosity at the party last night. Anyone could have noticed that their friendship had disintegrated. "I'm not going to be bullied by this," she said. "Who's with me?"

The other girls shifted their weight. Emily played with the silver bracelet she'd bought to replace the old string bracelet Ali had made for her. Aria jammed her hands in her pockets and chewed feverishly on her bottom lip.

Then Hanna straightened. "I'm with you. The last thing I need is another A. Being tormented is *so* last year."

"Good." Spencer regarded the others. "What about you guys?"

Emily kicked at a pile of dirty snow at the curb. "I just don't know."

Aria also had an ambivalent look on her face. "It's such a weird coincidence . . ."

Spencer slapped her arms to her sides. "Believe what

you want, but don't drag me into it, okay? Whoever this stupid A is isn't part of my life. If you guys are smart, you won't let it be part of yours, either."

At that, she spun on her heel and walked back toward her house, her shoulders squared and her head held high. It was ridiculous to think that a new A had emerged or that someone knew what they had done. Their secret was locked up tight. Besides, everything was going so well for Spencer right now. She wasn't going to let A ruin her senior year . . . and she *definitely* wasn't going to let A take Princeton away from her.

Her resolve remained steady for about ten more steps. Just as she reached the glowing light of her front porch, a memory flickered, uninvited, to the forefront of her mind: After dinner that first night in Jamaica, Spencer went to use the bathroom. When she exited the stall, a girl was sitting on the counter in front of the mirror, holding a metal flask in her hand. The blonde Emily swore was Ali.

At first, Spencer wanted to backtrack into the stall and slam the door tight. There *was* something odd about her— she had a smirk on her face as if she was in on a huge practical joke.

But before Spencer could escape, the girl smiled at her. "Want some?" She extended the flask toward Spencer. Liquid sloshed in the bottom. "It's this amazing home-made rum an old woman sold me on the drive here. It'll blow your mind."

Music from the steel drum band playing at the bar

vibrated through the thin walls. The smell of fried plantains tickled Spencer's nostrils. Spencer paused a moment. Something about this felt dangerous.

"What, are you scared?" the girl challenged, as if reading Spencer's mind.

Spencer sat up straighter. She grabbed the flask and took a sip. The molasses taste immediately warmed her chest. "That's really good."

"Told ya." The girl took the flask back. "I'm Tabitha."

"Spencer," she replied.

"You were sitting with those people in the corner, right?" Tabitha asked. Spencer nodded. "You're lucky. My friends ditched me. They switched their reservations to The Royal Plantain up the road without telling me. When I tried to get a room there, they were all sold out. It sucks."

"That's terrible," Spencer murmured. "Did you guys get into a fight or something?"

Tabitha shrugged guiltily. "It was over a guy. *You* know something about that, right?"

Spencer blinked. Immediately, she thought of the biggest fight she'd gotten into over a guy. It had been with Ali—their Ali—over Ian Thomas, whom they both liked. The night Ali went missing in seventh grade, Ali stormed out of the barn, and Spencer followed her. Ali spun around and told Spencer that she and Ian were secretly together. The only reason Ian kissed Spencer, she added, was because Ali had told him to—he did everything she wanted. Spencer had pushed Ali—hard.

There was a knowing smile on Tabitha's face like she was referring to that exact story. But there was no way she could know that . . . right? An overhead bulb flickered, and suddenly Spencer noticed that Tabitha's lips turned up at the corners, just like their Ali's. Her wrists were just as thin, and she could just picture those long-fingered, square-palmed hands grappling with Spencer on the path outside her barn.

Tabitha's phone played the Hallelujah chorus, scaring them both. She glanced at the screen, then scampered toward the door. "Sorry, I gotta take this. See you later?"

Before Spencer could answer, the door swung shut. She stayed in the bathroom, staring at her reflection.

She wasn't sure what made her pull out her phone and do a Google search for Jamaican hotels. And she told herself it was just the strong homemade rum that made her heart pound as she perused the resorts nearby The Cliffs. But when Google finished tabulating the results, Spencer began to accept the uneasy feeling in the pit of her stomach. Something was really messed up here.

There wasn't a Royal Plantain resort nearby. In fact, there wasn't a hotel called Royal Plantain—or anything like it—in all of Jamaica. Whoever Tabitha was, she was a liar.

Spencer glanced at her reflection again. She looked like she'd seen a ghost.

Maybe she had.

10

A STAR IS BORN

The next afternoon, after the SEPTA R5 stopped at every possible local station, Hanna finally arrived in Philadelphia. As soon as the metal door slid open she slung her silver studded hobo bag over her shoulder and stepped onto the steel escalator. Two girls in Bryn Mawr College sweatshirts and boot-cut jeans stared at her.

For a moment, Hanna tensed, thinking of the postcard in Ali's old mailbox last night. Then it hit her: They recognized her from the news reports last year. Rude stares happened to Hanna more than she liked.

She stuck her nose in the air, feigning her best aloof celebrity pose. After all, she was going to her very first photo shoot—what were *they* doing in the city? Bargain shopping for knockoffs at Filene's Basement?

A tall figure with a camera around his neck stood outside the station's McDonald's. Hanna's heart leapt. Patrick even *looked* like an up-and-coming photographer—he wore an army-green coat with a fur-lined hood, slim-cut jeans, and polished chukka boots.

Patrick turned and noticed Hanna approaching. He raised the long-lensed digital camera around his neck and pointed it at her. For a second, Hanna wanted to cover her face with her hands, but instead she threw back her shoulders and gave him a big smile. Maybe this was a test, an action shot of a model in the dingy train station, surrounded by overweight tourists with fanny packs.

"You made it," Patrick said as Hanna walked up.

"Did you think I'd bail?" Hanna teased, trying to control her excitement.

He looked her up and down. "Great outfit. You look like a hotter Adriana Lima."

"Thanks." Hanna put her hands on her hips and tilted to the right and left. Damn right it was a great outfit—she'd agonized over the pink frilly dress, motocross jacket, chunky suede booties, and gold-accented bracelets and necklace all morning, trying on a zillion combinations before she found something that hit just the right note. Her bare legs would probably get frostbite, but it would be worth it.

The SEPTA announcer shouted that a train to Trenton had just pulled into the station, and a bunch of people clamored down the stairs. Patrick picked up a canvas bag full of camera gear and strode toward the Sixteenth Street exit. "I'm thinking we'll do a couple outdoor shots around the city. Some classics in front of City Hall and the Liberty Bell. The light's great right now."

"Okay," Hanna answered. Patrick even *sounded* über-professional.

"Then we'll finish up with some indoor photos at my studio in Fishtown. Do you mind all that? It would be amazing for my portfolio. And like I said, I can help you pick out shots for agents."

"It sounds perfect."

As they climbed the stairs, Patrick pressed his arm against Hanna's, pointing out a patch of ice. "Careful."

"Thanks," Hanna said, steering around the ice. Patrick removed his hand as soon as she'd crossed safely.

"So, have you always wanted to be a photographer?" Hanna asked as they headed along Market Street toward City Hall. It was freezing outside, and everyone was walking around with their heads down and their hoods up. Dirty, slushy snow piled at the curbs.

"Ever since I was little," Patrick admitted. "I was that kid who never went anywhere without a disposable camera. Remember those—or are you too young?"

"Of course I remember them," Hanna scoffed. "I'm eighteen—how old are you?"

"Twenty-two," Patrick said, as if that were *so* much older. He gestured to the left, off to another section of the city. "I went to Moore College of Art. Just graduated."

"Did you like it? I'm thinking of going to F.I.T. or Pratt for fashion design." She'd just submitted applications a few weeks ago.

"I loved it." Patrick ducked out of the way of a hot dog

cart that was smack in the middle of the sidewalk. The smell of greasy sausages wafted through the air. "You'll love New York, too—but I bet you won't be going there for school. One of the modeling agencies will sign you. I'm sure of it."

It felt like there were fairies dancing in Hanna's stomach. "What makes you so sure?" she challenged nonchalantly, like she didn't care one way or another.

"When I was in school, I worked as an assistant on a lot of fashion shoots." Patrick paused for a red light. "You've got the unique look editors and designers love."

"Really?" If only Hanna could record what he just said and upload it to her Twitter feed. Or, better yet, post it directly on Kate's Facebook page.

"So how'd you get the gig for my dad's commercial, anyway?" Hanna asked.

Patrick smiled wryly. "I was doing a favor for a friend. Normally I wouldn't touch commercials—especially political ones. I don't really follow politics."

"Me neither," Hanna said, relieved. She wasn't even clear on her father's opinions on the big issues. If he won the election and someone wanted to interview her, well, that's what media coaches were for.

"He seems like a nice guy, though," Patrick shouted over the noise of a passing city bus. "But what's with your sister? She seemed really uptight."

"Stepsister," Hanna corrected him quickly.

"Ah." Patrick grinned at her knowingly, his almost-black eyes crinkling. "I should've guessed you weren't related."

They reached City Hall, and Patrick got to business, directing Hanna to pose in the shadow of the grand archway. "Okay, think 'girl who wants something so badly she can taste it,'" he instructed, pointing the lens at her. "You're hungry, you're yearning, and you'll stop at nothing for your goal. Can you get into that mood?"

Uh, yeah. She was already *in* that mood. She posed against the wall, giving Patrick the most determined stare she could muster.

"Awesome," Patrick said. *Snap. Snap.* "Your eyes look amazing."

Hanna tossed her auburn hair, tilted her chin down, and parted her lips just so. It was a pose she'd made when she, Ali and the others did model shoots in Ali's den. Ali had always told Hanna that face made her look like a plus-sized model on crack, but Patrick snapped away, shouting, "Brilliant!"

After a while, Patrick paused to gaze at the shots in the preview window. "You're amazing. Have you done lots of photo shoots before?"

"Oh, a few." The photo shoot for *People* after the Poconos scandal counted, right?

Patrick squinted into the lens again. "Okay, chin up a bit. Give me sultry."

Hanna tried her best to make her eyes smolder. *Snap. Snap.*

A crowd of tourists gathered and whispered. "What magazine are you shooting for?" a middle-aged woman asked in a reverent voice.

"*Vogue*," Patrick answered without missing a beat. The crowd clucked and oohed; a few people pushed closer to snap photos of Hanna themselves. She felt like a star.

After a few more shots at the Liberty Bell, Patrick suggested they head to his studio. The sun sank low in the sky as they walked back to Fishtown. He bounced up the steps of a pretty brownstone and opened the door for her. "Hope you don't mind stairs."

When Patrick opened the black-painted door on the fourth floor, Hanna let out a loud *ooh!* The studio was a giant room covered in photographs of all shapes and sizes. Three long windows looked out onto the street. A flat-screen Mac glowed in the corner. There was a tiny kitchen off to the right; on the counter were containers of darkroom chemicals. But instead of smelling like the photography classroom at Rosewood Day, the room was fragrant with Hanna's favorite Delirium & Co candle, China Tea.

"Do you live here?" Hanna asked.

"Nah, just work." Patrick dropped his bag on the floor. "I share it with a couple other photographers. Hopefully no one will bother us while we're finishing up."

He put on an old bossa nova CD, arranged a couple of lights, and positioned Hanna on a stool. Instantly, Hanna began to sway back and forth, entranced by the sound of the music. "Good," Patrick murmured. "Move your body. Just like that." *Snap. Snap.*

Hanna unzipped her leather jacket and undulated to the song, her eyes starting to hurt from so much sexy squinting. The lights beamed hotly on her skin, and in an impetuous moment, she flung off her leather jacket to reveal the thin scoop-neck dress underneath.

"Pretty!" Patrick murmured. *Snap. Snap. Snap. Snap.* "Now fling your hair back and forth! Good!"

Hanna did as she was told, making her hair spill over her shoulders and fall seductively into her eyes. A strap of her dress fell off her shoulder, revealing her bra strap, but she didn't pause to fix it. Patrick's high cheekbones and pink, kissable lips were beginning to mesmerize her. She loved how he made her feel like the most beautiful girl on earth. She wished everyone could see this.

Amidst the luscious music, the hot lights, and the glam poses, an unwanted memory floated into Hanna's head. When Ali returned to Rosewood last year and confessed she was really Hanna's long-lost best friend, she'd taken Hanna's hands and told her how beautiful she'd become. "I mean, you're . . . stunning, Han," Ali whispered, her voice full of awe.

It had been the most wonderful thing Hanna had ever heard. Ever since she'd made herself over, she'd dreamed Ali would somehow return from the dead and see how she was no longer the ugly, chubby, hanger-on in Ali's clique.

But in the end, the comment meant nothing. It was just a charade to get Hanna to trust her.

Then, equally unbidden, a second memory popped into her head. In Jamaica, shortly after the girls ate dinner, Hanna wandered to the big telescope that was set up in the corner of the restaurant. It pointed at the sky above the sea; the night was clear and crisp, and the stars looked close enough to reach out and touch.

A cough made Hanna turn around. A blond girl in a yellow dress stood behind her. It was the same girl Emily had pointed out in the doorway. She looked nothing like Ali except for the similar hair color and the naughty glint in her eye, but she leaned forward and gazed at Hanna like she knew her.

"I heard that telescope's awesome." Her breath smelled slightly of rum.

"Um, yeah." Hanna stepped aside. "Want to see?"

The girl peered through the eyepiece, then introduced herself as Tabitha Clark, adding that she was from New Jersey and this was her first night at the resort.

"Mine, too," Hanna said quickly. "It's awesome. We went cliff diving this afternoon. And tomorrow I'm taking a yoga class," she went on, blabbering nervously. Hanna couldn't help but stare at the burns on the girl's arms. What had happened to her?

"You're gorgeous, you know," Tabitha told her suddenly.

Hanna pressed her hand to her chest. "Th-thanks!"

Tabitha cocked her head. "But I bet you weren't *always* gorgeous, were you?"

Hanna frowned. "What's that supposed to mean?"

Tabitha licked her pink lips. "I think you know, don't you?"

The world began to spin. It was possible Tabitha recognized Hanna from the news reports, and there were a lot of things about her that had come out in the press—how Mona had hit her with her car, how she'd gotten caught shoplifting, how all of them swore they'd seen Ian's dead body in the woods. But Hanna's chubby, ugly past had remained a deep, dark secret from the world. No photos of her pre-makeover circulated on the blogs or in gossip mags—Hanna checked religiously. How could Tabitha know about Hanna's ugly duckling past?

When Hanna stared at the girl again, it was as though her features had been completely rearranged. Suddenly, there was more than just an Ali-like sparkle in her eye. Her Cupid-bow lips looked just like Ali's. It was as though Ali's ghost shone through Tabitha's marred skin.

"Hanna?" Patrick's voice cut through the memory.

Hanna blinked, struggling to break free. Tabitha's voice still echoed in her ears. *I bet you weren't always gorgeous, were you?*

Patrick gazed at her uncomfortably. "Um, you might want to . . ." He gestured to her collarbone.

When Hanna looked down, her pink dress had fallen down her chest, and half of her left boob was somehow hanging out of her strapless bra. "Oops." She pulled it up.

Patrick lowered his camera. "You went dead on me. Everything okay?"

The image of Tabitha blazed in Hanna's brain. But she wouldn't think about it. She'd made a promise to herself. She wouldn't let last night's A message open Pandora's box.

Hanna straightened her shoulders and shook out her palms. "Sorry. Everything's perfect now, I promise." The latest Black Eyed Peas song came on next, and she made a twisting motion with her fingers so Patrick would crank up the stereo. "Let's keep going."

And that was exactly what they did.

11

EMILY'S GOT A SWIMFAN

"Ten one hundreds on a minute-thirty, leave on the sixty!" Raymond, the coach of Emily's year-round club team, yelled at a lane from the edge of the pool on Tuesday. Raymond had been Emily's coach ever since she was a kid, and he'd never diverged from his standard uniform of Adidas shower flip-flops and shiny black TYR warm-up suits. He also had the gorilla-thick arm hair of someone who used to regularly shave their arms for swim competitions, and the broad shoulders of a backstroker.

The clock edged to the sixty. Raymond lurched forward. "Ready . . . go!"

Emily pushed off the wall, her body in a tight, dart-like streamline, her legs dolphin-kicking frantically. The water was cool on her skin, and she could hear strains of the oldies station on the radio in the coach's office. Her muscles relaxed as she stroked through the water. It felt good to be swimming again after such a long break.

She did a flip turn at the other wall and pushed off again. The other kids in her lane paddled behind her. All of them were serious swimmers, too, kids who hoped to get scholarships to choice colleges. Some high-school seniors on the team had already been recruited; they proudly brought Raymond their acceptance letters as soon as they got them.

Paddling strongly, Emily tried to let her mind go blank, which Raymond said would help her swim her fastest. But she kept thinking about the postcard in Ali's mailbox. Who sent it? Had someone seen what they did? No one had witnessed what they'd done in Jamaica. There had been no couples kissing on the sand, no faces peering out of windows, no hotel staff cleaning the back deck. Either A had taken a wild guess—or else A was the person Emily feared most.

Emily touched the wall to finish, breathing hard. "Good time, Emily," Raymond said from the edge of the pool. "It's nice to see you back in the water."

"Thanks." Emily wiped her eyes and looked around the natatorium. It, too, hadn't changed since Emily started here as a six-year-old. There were bright yellow bleachers in the corner and a big mural of water polo players. Motivational sayings covered the walls, and gold plaques of pool records lined the hallway just beyond the doors. When Emily was little, she'd ogled the records, hoping to one day break one of them. Last year, she'd broken *three*. But not this year . . .

Raymond's whistle made a short, sharp tweet, and Emily pushed off the wall for one hundred number two. The laps flew by, Emily's arms feeling strong, her turns steady and sure, her times slowly dropping. When the set was over, Emily noticed someone videotaping her from the bleachers. He lowered the camera and met her eyes. It was Mr. Roland.

He strolled over to Emily's lane. "Hey, Emily. Have a sec?"

A swimmer flip-turned right next to Emily, sending a plume of water into the air. Emily shrugged and pushed out of the pool. She felt naked in her tank suit, bare arms, and bare legs, especially next to Mr. Roland's gray wool suit and black loafers. And she still couldn't shrug off the other night. Had he meant to touch her hip, or was it an accident?

Mr. Roland sat down on one end of a bench. Emily grabbed her towel and sat on the other. "I sent your times to the UNC recruiter and coach. His name's Marc Lowry. He asked me to stop by and watch you practice. I hope that's okay." He raised the video camera and smiled sheepishly.

"Uh, it's fine." Emily crossed her arms over her boobs.

"You have really beautiful form." Mr. Roland stared at a paused frame on the video camera. "Lowry's really impressed by your times, too. But he wonders why they're last year's times, not this year's."

"I had to take some time off last summer and this

fall," Emily said uneasily. "I wasn't able to compete with my school team."

A wrinkle formed on Mr. Roland's brow. "And why is that?"

Emily turned away. "Just . . . personal stuff."

"I don't mean to be pushy, but the recruiter is going to ask," Mr. Roland prodded gently.

Emily fiddled with a loose loop on her towel. It was from Junior Swimming Nationals, which she'd competed in last year before she went to Jamaica. Even back then, she'd felt like something was wrong with her. She'd felt shaky in the locker room, then nearly passed out in the folding chair waiting for her heat. Her times had been decent, only one or two tenths of a second slower than her personal bests, but she'd felt exhausted afterward, like someone had filled her arms and legs with sand. That night, she went home and slept for fifteen hours straight.

As time progressed, she felt worse, not better. When she told her mother she was going to take the summer off swimming to do an internship in Philadelphia, Mrs. Fields had looked at her like she'd sprouted a few extra eyeballs. But Emily played the Ali card—she needed a break from Rosewood, too many awful things had happened here—and her mom relented. She'd stayed with her sister Carolyn, who was taking part in a summer program at Penn before she went to Stanford in the fall. She'd entrusted Carolyn with a secret, too, and amazingly Carolyn had kept it. Not happily, though.

When Emily returned to school that next year and told her mom she wasn't up to swimming on the school team, Mrs. Fields had been livid. She'd offered to take Emily to a sports psychologist, but Emily was firm: She wasn't swimming this season. "You have to get over Alison," Mrs. Fields insisted. "This isn't about Alison," Emily answered tearfully. "Then what is it about?" Mrs. Fields demanded.

But Emily couldn't tell her. If she did, her mother would never speak to her again.

Mr. Roland folded his hands in his lap, still waiting for Emily's answer.

Emily cleared her throat. "Can we just leave it that I took a personal leave of absence? I . . . I was stalked by someone I thought was my best friend last year. Maybe you heard about it? Alison DiLaurentis?"

Mr. Roland's eyebrows rose. "That was . . . *you*?"

Emily nodded grimly.

"I'm so sorry. I had no idea. I knew we bought the house where one of the murdered girls lived, but . . ." Mr. Roland pressed his hand to his eyes. "I think that's all you need to say. Lowry will understand."

At least the Ali mess was good for something.

"I'm fully committed to swimming now," Emily promised.

"Good." Mr. Roland stood up. "It looks like you are. If you're game, I can probably have him or someone on his recruiting team up here by this Saturday."

Emily did a mental check of her schedule. "Actually, I have a meet this Saturday."

"All the more reason for him to come." Mr. Roland tapped something into his BlackBerry. "He'll see you in action. It's perfect."

"Thank you so much," Emily gushed. She felt the urge to wrap her arms around Mr. Roland, but resisted.

"Any friend of Chloe's is a friend of mine," Mr. Roland pivoted toward the exit. "It's nice to see her meeting people so quickly. Nice seeing you, Emily."

He tucked his briefcase under his arm and strode around the puddles toward the steamed-over door to the locker rooms. Suddenly, Emily felt a million times better. Whatever she'd thought she'd experienced in the Rolands' house yesterday was all in her head.

Someone sighed behind her, and Emily turned around. Her gaze darted to the long bank of windows that led to the outside. The sun had set, dyeing the sky midnight blue and bathing the landscape in silhouette. And then she saw something next to her Volvo wagon in the parking lot. Was that a *person*? Skulking around, peeking through the passenger-side window?

Another flip turn splashed her legs, and she stepped back from the pool's edge. When she looked out the window again, the sky was suddenly pitch-black, like someone had pulled a curtain over it. Emily couldn't see anything at all.

12

FINN DINING

On Tuesday night, Aria rang the doorbell at the Kahns' house, a redbrick mansion with white columns, a six-car garage, various porticos and turrets, and an eleven-acre backyard that had been the site of many infamous parties. Tonight, the Kahns were hosting another party, although Aria doubted it would feature body shots or illicit hookups in the Kahns' photo booth. It was a traditional Finnish smorgasbord to welcome Klaudia to the U.S., and judging by the number of cars in the long, circular driveway, it looked like the Kahns had invited everyone in Rosewood and several towns beyond.

Mrs. Kahn flung the door open and beamed. "*Tervetuloa*, Aria!" she said jovially. "That's Finnish for welcome!"

"Uh, *tervetuloa*," Aria echoed politely, trying to get the intonation correct . . . and trying not to gawk at Mrs. Kahn's outfit. Normally, Noel's mother was the epitome of horsey couture: Ralph Lauren riding pants, cable-cashmere sweaters, sleek Tod's boots, and diamonds on her fingers and in her ears that were probably worth more than both Aria's parents' houses combined. Today, though, she wore a long red skirt that looked like it was made out of stiff felt, a shirred blouse with puffed sleeves and elaborate embroidery at the neck, and a very colorful peasant vest that featured yet more embroidery and smelled like mothballs. There was a slightly phallic bonnet on her head and black leather lace-up boots on her feet. And they *definitely* weren't the kind featured in the Jimmy Choo window at the King James Mall.

"Isn't my outfit divine?" Mrs. Kahn crowed, spinning so the skirt flared out. "It's the traditional Finnish costume! Have you ever seen anything so colorful? I'm half Finnish, you know. Perhaps my ancestors dressed just like this!"

Aria nodded and smiled dumbly, though she doubted Finns dressed that way unless they absolutely had to. Who wanted to look like a Grimm fairy-tale character?

Then Klaudia stepped into the foyer. "Aria! We're so happy you make it!" Noel was right behind her. Klaudia looped her arm around Noel's shoulders like they were a couple.

"Uh, I wouldn't miss it." Aria stared pointedly at Noel, thinking he'd break from Klaudia and walk across the foyer to join her, his *girlfriend*. But he just stood next to Klaudia with a stupid grin on his face. Klaudia turned and whispered something in Noel's ear. Noel said something back, and they both chuckled.

Prickles rose on Aria's skin. "Is something funny?"

"It's . . . never mind." Noel waved away Aria's question.

Tonight, Klaudia wore a marled sweater dress that was at least two sizes too small. Her blond hair spilled down her back, and she wore wet, glossy lipstick that drew the eye straight to her mouth. Every guy at the party stared at her—including Mr. Shay, the elderly biology teacher at Rosewood Day who Aria had always thought was legally blind.

But then Noel slithered around the knot of adoring male admirers and wrapped his arm around Aria. "I'm glad you're here." It made Aria feel slightly better, especially since Klaudia was watching.

Everyone turned toward the kitchen, which boomed with polka-ish music Aria could only assume was Finnish. The table had a fairy-tale quality to it, too: There were burbling cauldrons, oversized goblets, sausage bursting out of its casing, fish with their heads still on, and gingerbread cookies that looked straight out of *Hansel and Gretel*. A glass pitcher held soured milk. In front of a bubbling Crock-Pot Mrs. Kahn had affixed a label that said MOOSE! The Rosewood residents gathered around the table looked a little bit lost.

"Ooh, delicious!" Klaudia chirped when she reached the table. About ten guys scrambled to help her, as if she were an infant incapable of making her own plate. Mason Byers offered to spoon up Klaudia a bowl of soup. Philip Gregory asked if Klaudia wanted some sausage—*nudge,*

nudge. Preston Wallis and John Dexter, who'd graduated from Rosewood Day but were going to Hollis and
still some of Noel's closest friends, retrieved napkins for
Klaudia and poured her a mug of cider.

The girls were a different story, though. Naomi Zeigler
and Riley Wolfe shot Klaudia dirty looks from the kitchen
island. Lanie Iler, who was standing near Aria in the food
line, leaned over to Phi Templeton, who wasn't nearly as
much of a dork as she used to be when Aria, Ali, and the
others made fun of her in seventh grade, and whispered,
"You know, she's not *that* pretty."

"She's in my English class," Phi answered, rolling her
eyes. "She barely knows how to read English. I thought
people from Europe were, like, fluent."

Aria hid a smirk. She would have thought Razor
scooter–obsessed Phi would be sensitive about making
fun of others.

"If James keeps looking at her, I'm going to kick her
ass," Lanie continued through her teeth, spearing a sausage and plopping it on her plate. James Freed was her
new boyfriend.

Someone tapped Aria on the shoulder and she turned.
Klaudia was right behind her, staring at Aria with her
large, blue eyes. "Hallo, Aria," she said. "I eat you?"

At first, Aria thought she was serious—it was just the
thing a fairy-tale villainess might say. Then Klaudia peered
nervously into the crowd. "So many people, and I only
you know!"

"What a lovely idea!" Mrs. Kahn appeared from out of nowhere and clapped a hand on Aria's shoulder. "You two should definitely eat together! You'll love Aria, Klaudia."

"Oh." Aria fiddled with the bat-wing sleeve of her silk blouse. Wouldn't Klaudia rather eat with her male entourage? But it wasn't like she could say no with Mrs. Kahn standing there.

After spooning a few more bites of vegetarian goulash on her plate, Aria led Klaudia to the bay window seat. They were quiet for a moment, taking in the party. The popular girls from Rosewood Day had moved to the long table in the breakfast nook, still giving Klaudia—and Aria, by association—the evil eye. A nearby cluster of adults Aria didn't recognize were out-boasting one another about where their kids had gotten into college. Through the archway to the living room, Aria caught sight of Spencer and a boy she didn't recognize, but she knew better than to wave.

The postcard haunted her. Today, she was sure she felt someone watching her—even in classes where she sat in the last row of the room, even when alone in a stall in the girls' bathroom. She kept whipping around, heart in her throat, but no one was ever there. During study hall, she'd listened to two meditation tapes in a row, but they'd only gotten her *more* riled up. Even sitting here, in Noel's kitchen, she kept peeking at her cell phone, terrified of a new text.

Could A seriously be back? What if A really knew the horrible thing she'd done?

Aria turned to Klaudia, trying to shake the awful thoughts from her mind. "So how do you like Rosewood Day?"

Klaudia dabbed her mouth with a napkin. "So big. I get much lost! And people give directions, and I'm like . . . oof!" She pretended to wipe sweat off her brow. "My old school in Helsinki? Six rooms! Thirty people in our class! Nothing like this!"

The corners of her mouth turned down as she spoke. She finished the tirade with a shaky titter. Was Klaudia . . . scared? It had never occurred to Aria that such a gorgeous, confident creature could be intimidated by anything. Perhaps she was actually human.

"I know what you mean." Aria swallowed bite of beet and turnip mash. "The high school I went to in Reykjavik only had about a hundred students. I knew everyone within a couple of weeks."

Klaudia lowered her fork. "You did school in Reykjavik?"

"Yeah." Didn't Noel tell Klaudia *anything* about her? "I lived there for almost three years. I loved it."

"I go there!" Klaudia's smile broadened. "For the Iceland Airwaves festival!"

"I went to that, too!" The Iceland Airwaves festival was the first concert Aria had gone to. She'd felt so adult traipsing onto the grounds, passing the hippie tents selling temporary tattoos and dream catchers, and inhaling the smells of exotic vegetarian cuisine and hookah pipes.

During one of the many Icelandic bands' sets, she'd met three boys: Asbjorn, Gunnar, and Jonas, and Jonas had kissed her during the encore. That was when Aria knew moving to Iceland was the best thing that could've ever happened to her.

Klaudia nodded excitedly, her blond hair bouncing. "So much music! My favorite was Metric."

"I saw them in Copenhagen!" Aria said. She would have never pegged Klaudia for a Metric girl. Music was one of those things Aria hadn't been able to talk about with anyone here the way she had in Iceland—all the Typical Rosewoods, as she called them, never ventured to listened to anything not on the iTunes Most Downloaded list.

"I loved! So much—*tanssi!*" She squinted, trying to think of the English word, and then bobbed her head back and forth as though she were dancing.

Then, setting her paper plate on the windowsill, Klaudia pulled out her iPhone and flipped through pictures. "This is Tanja." She pointed at a foxlike Sofia Coppola look-alike. "Best friends. We go to Reykjavik concert together. I miss so much. We text every night."

Klaudia flipped through more photos of her friends, mostly blond girls; her family, a gaunt, makeup-free mother, a tall, rumpled father who she said was an engi-neer, and a younger brother who had messy hair; her house, a modern box that reminded Aria of the house they rented in Reykjavik; and her cat, Mika, which she cradled like a baby in the same way Aria cradled her own cat, Polo. "I miss my Mee-mee so much!" she cried, bringing the picture to her lips and giving the cat a kiss.

Aria giggled. In these pictures, Klaudia didn't look slutty or conniving—she seemed normal. Cool, even. It was possible Aria had judged Klaudia unfairly. Maybe she was overly touchy-feely with Noel because she was uncomfortable in her new surroundings. And maybe she dressed sluttily because she thought all Americans did—if you went by American television, you'd certainly think so. Really, Aria and Klaudia had more in common than Aria originally thought—the Typical Rosewood Girls shunned Klaudia, just like they did Aria. They always blacklisted things they didn't immediately understand.

Klaudia turned to the next photo in the stack, a shot of her friends in ski gear on top of a mountain. "Oh! This is Kalle!" She said it like *Kah-lee*. "We ski every weekend! Who will I ski with now?"

"I'll ski with you," Aria volunteered, surprising herself.

Klaudia's eyes brightened. "You ski?"

"Well, no . . ." Aria forked the remaining goulash on her plate. "Actually, I've never skied in my life."

"I teach you!" Klaudia bounced in her seat. "We go soon! So easy!"

"Okay." Come to think of it, Noel had mentioned that his family was thinking about going on a ski trip for the long weekend at the end of the week. Surely Klaudia would be invited, too. "But I'd like to teach you something in return."

"How about that?" Klaudia pointed at the pink mohair scarf wound around Aria's neck. "Did you *neuloa*?" She rotated her hands around, pantomiming knitting.

Aria inspected the scarf. "Oh, I knitted this years ago. It's not very good."

"No, is beautiful!" Klaudia exclaimed. "Teach me! I make presents for Tanja and Kalle!"

"You want to learn to knit?" Aria repeated. No one, not even Ali or the others, had asked Aria to teach them— it had always been Aria's weird thing. But Klaudia didn't seem to think it was weird.

They arranged to meet on Thursday at a ski supply store so Aria could get proper gear. As they rose to check out the desserts, Aria noticed Noel staring at her from across the room with a surprised smile on his face. Aria waved, and so did Klaudia. "He your boyfriend, right?" Klaudia asked.

"Yeah," Aria answered. "For over a year."

"Ooh, serious!" Klaudia's eyes twinkled. But there was nothing envious about her demeanor.

Mr. Kahn appeared in the doorway. Aria hadn't seen him in weeks. He was always traveling on important business. Now, he was decked out in a brown loincloth, what looked like a bearskin coat, black boots, and a massive horned hat. He looked like Fred Flintstone.

"I'm ready for the feast!" he bellowed, raising a club in his left hand.

Everyone cheered. The Rosewood Day girls in the

corner tittered. Aria and Klaudia exchanged a horrified look. Was he *serious*?

"Save me!" Klaudia whispered, hiding behind Aria.

Aria burst into giggles. "Those horns! And what's with the club?"

"I don't know!" Klaudia held her nose. "And Mrs. Kahn's skirt smell just like *hevonpaskaa*!"

Aria didn't exactly know what the word meant, but just the sound of it made her double over with giggles. She could feel the stares of the bitchy girls across the room, but she didn't care. All at once, she felt so grateful Klaudia was here. For the first time in almost a year, Aria had someone to laugh with again. Someone who really understood her in a way that the Typical Rosewoods couldn't.

For a moment, it even made her forget about A.

13

SEDUCTION AND SECRETS

Spencer stood at the back of the Kahns' smorgasbord line, eyeing the food spread. Some of this crap looked like cat vomit. And who in their right mind drank soured milk?

Two hands grabbed her shoulders. "Surprise," Zach Pennythistle said, waving an uncorked amber-colored bottle in her face. Inside was a greenish liquid that smelled like nail polish remover.

Spencer raised an eyebrow. "What *is* that?"

"Traditional Finnish schnapps." He poured a few slugs into two foam cups from the stack on the table. "I snuck it from the bar cart when no one was looking."

"Bad boy!" Spencer shook her finger at him. "Are you always so deviant?"

"It's why I'm the black sheep of my family," Zach teased, lowering his dark eyes at her, which made Spencer's insides whirl.

She was thrilled Zach had accepted her invitation to

the smorgasbord party tonight. Ever since the dinner at
The Goshen Inn on Sunday, she couldn't stop thinking
of their fun, flirty banter. Even after they'd sat down at
the table with the rest of the family, they'd continued to
shoot one another feisty looks and secret smiles.

They drifted through the living room and set up camp
on the Kahns' stairs. The party was getting raucous, with
a bunch of Rosewood Day kids Irish-jigging to the polka
music in the Kahns' enormous living room and some of
the adults already slurring their words. "I usually don't
peg Harvard boys as the black sheep of their families,"
Spencer said to Zach, picking up on their previous conversation.

Zach sat back, frowning. "Where'd you hear I was
going to Harvard?"

Spencer blinked. "Your dad said so at dinner. Before I
found you at the bar."

"Of course he did." Zach took a long drink of his
schnapps. "To tell you the truth, I'm not entirely sure
Harvard and I are a match made in heaven. I have my eye
on either Berkeley or Columbia. Not that *he* knows that,
of course."

Spencer raised her glass. "Well, here's to getting what
you want."

Zach smiled. "I *always* get what I want," he said
meaningfully, which sent more tingles up her spine.
Something was going to happen between them tonight.
Spencer could just feel it.

"Is that booze?" cried an outraged voice. Zach's sister, Amelia, emerged from around the corner with a plate full of food.

Spencer sighed and shut her eyes. Her mother had been thrilled that she'd invited Zach to the smorgasbord— it would be a good way for the two of them to get to know each other, she said. "In fact, why doesn't Amelia join you, too?" she'd chirped a millisecond later. Before Spencer could protest, Mrs. Hastings was on the phone with Nicholas, extending the invitation to Zach's pinched-faced sister.

Did Amelia even *want* to be here? A hideous scowl had settled over her features as soon as she'd stepped through the Kahns' door. When Mrs. Kahn put on a traditional Finnish folk dance song, Amelia had actually winced and covered her ears.

"Want some?" Zach pushed his cup toward Amelia. "It tastes like peppermint patties, your favorite!"

Amelia moved away, making a face. "No thanks." Her idea of party wear was a striped Brooks Brothers button-down tucked very tightly into a denim pencil skirt that fell to her knees. She looked exactly like Mrs. Ulster, Spencer's substitute Calc II teacher.

Amelia leaned against the banister and glowered at the Rosewood residents. "So are these people your friends?" She said *friends* like she might have said *bedbug-infested mattresses.*

Spencer surveyed the crowd. Most of the Rosewood

Day senior class had been invited, as well as a smattering of the Kahns' society friends. "Well, they all go to my school."

Amelia made a dismissive *uch*. "They seem really lame. Especially the girls."

Spencer flinched. Other than Kelsey, she hadn't hung out with St. Agnes girls in ages. But she had been to a couple of their parties back in middle school; each clique named themselves after a European princess or queen—there were the Queen Sofias of Spain, the Princess Olgas of Greece, and the Charlottes of Monaco, daughter of Princess Carolina. Hello, lameness?

Zach drained the rest of his drink and set his cup on the stairs. "Oh, these girls look like they might have some dirty little secrets up their sleeves."

"How can you tell?" Spencer teased.

"It's all about watching people, noticing what they do. Like when I met you at the restaurant on Sunday—I knew you were in the bar area because you were escaping from someone. Taking a breather."

Spencer gave him a playful slap. "You're such a liar."

Zach crossed his arms over his chest. "Wanna bet? There's this game I sometimes play called She's Not What She Seems. I bet I can suss out more secrets than you can."

Spencer flinched for a moment at the name of the game. For some reason, it reminded her of the postcard they'd received last night. Even though Spencer pretended it didn't matter, flickers of anxiety threatened to ignite inside of her. Could someone know about Jamaica? A lot of people had been staying at the resort—Noel, Mike, that group of kids from California they'd gone surfing with, some party-crazy boys from England, and of course the staff—but Spencer and the others looked up and down the dark beach after everything had happened and hadn't seen a soul. It was like they were the last people on earth. Unless . . .

She shut her eyes and swept the thoughts away. There was no *unless*. And there was no new A. The postcard was just a big coincidence, a lucky guess.

A bunch of girls on the Rosewood Day newspaper staff flitted into the living room with plates of meatballs, potatoes, and sardines. Spencer turned back to Zach. "I'll play your little secrets game. But you realize I know these people, right? I have a home-court advantage."

"Then we have to pick people you don't really know." Zach leaned forward and gazed around the room. He pointed to Mrs. Byers, Mason's mom, who was decked out in head-to-toe Kate Spade. "Know anything about her?"

Amelia, who had been watching them both, groaned. "*Her?* She's as generic as they come! Soccer mom, drives a Lexus. Snore."

Zach clucked his tongue. "That's where you're wrong. She *looks* like your regular upscale suburban housewife, but she likes her boyfriends young."

"What makes you say that?" Spencer asked incredulously.

"Look." Zach pointed at how Mrs. Byers was eagerly filling the cup for Ryan Zeiss, one of Mason's lacrosse teammates. Her hand lingered on Ryan's shoulders for a long time. *Too* long.

"Whoa," Spencer whispered. No wonder Mrs. Byers always volunteered to be the team's travel mom.

Then it was Spencer's turn. She looked around the room, trying to locate her victim. Mrs. Zeigler, Naomi's polished mother, glided across the cheerful black-and-white checkerboard floor. *Bingo.* "She gets secret Botox treatments," Spencer said, pointing.

"Oh puh-leease." Amelia rolled her eyes. "*All* of these women get Botox. Some of the kids probably do, too."

". . . under her arms," Spencer added, remembering how, a few years ago, Mrs. Zeigler always had visible sweat stains on her T-shirts whenever she raised her arms to clap for a field hockey goal. This hockey season, however, those sweat stains had magically disappeared.

"Nice." Zach whistled.

They went around the room, making up more secrets. Zach pointed to Liam Olsen and said he was cheating on his girlfriend, Devon Arliss. Spencer zeroed in on a Goth-looking caterer and said she was a huge Justin Bieber freak and French-kissed his portrait every night. Zach said that Imogen Smith looked like the type who'd secretly had a sexually transmitted disease, and Spencer hypothesized that Beau Baxter, her hot, reclusive costar in *Macbeth,* had affairs with older women. And then Amelia pointed half-heartedly at someone in the crowd. "Well, *she* looks like the type who hooks up with teachers."

Spencer squinted at who she was talking about and almost gasped. It was Aria. After the girls started hanging out again, Aria had told Spencer and the others everything about her affair with Ezra Fitz, her English teacher. How could Amelia know *that*?

Then Amelia turned her beady little pea eyes on Spencer. "So what's *your* secret?"

"Uh . . ." A chill ran up Spencer's spine. Suddenly, Amelia seemed weirdly intuitive, like she already knew. *Jamaica. How I got into Princeton. What I did to Kelsey.* There were definitely a few things Spencer had done she wasn't proud of.

Zach rolled his eyes. "Don't answer her. We all have some secrets we don't want to share—including me."

Shortly after that, Amelia wandered off into the party to talk to a couple of girls she recognized from candy striping. The party devolved into a giant drunken Finnish clog dance, with the cheesy polka music blaring and Aria and the new exchange student girl dancing wildly at the center.

A glass and a half of schnapps later, Spencer and Zach were still playing She Isn't Who She Seems.

"Sean Ackard's a serial masturbator," Spencer posited, pointing.

"That woman in the head-to-toe Gucci buys all her designer clothes on Canal Street in New York," Zach countered.

"Celeste Richards loves the smell of her own farts." Spencer giggled.

"That new Finnish girl is actually a drag queen." Zach wailed.

"Lori, Kendra, and Madison are into orgies!" Spencer cried, referring to the three soloists from masterworks halfheartedly clogging in the corner.

She was laughing so hard tears flowed freely down her cheeks, probably smearing her mascara. She and Zach had moved closer on the steps again, their legs touching, their hands brushing often, their heads occasionally lolling onto one another's shoulders.

Eventually, the party began to break up, and everyone started for home. The two of them collected Amelia and piled back into Zach's car. Spencer took control of Zach's iPod and blasted St. Vincent, singing along to "Actor Out of Work." Amelia sat in the back and sulked.

Zach pulled up to the Hastings curb and yanked up the emergency brake. Spencer turned to him, both sad that the night was ending and jittery because this was the moment she'd waited the entire evening for—the good-night kiss. Surely Zach would get out of the car and walk her to her door—away from his sister.

"You know, we never figured out a wager for your little Secrets game," Spencer said in a silky voice. "And I think I won—I definitely figured out more secrets than you."

Zach raised a brow. "Au contraire. I think I deserve the prize." He leaned closer to her, and Spencer's heart pounded hard.

Amelia groaned loudly and jutted forward from the backseat. "Would you guys stop flirting? You realize we're like one romantic date away from becoming stepsiblings, right? If you two hooked up, that would practically be incest."

Zach stiffened and moved away from Spencer. "Who said anything about hooking up?"

Ouch. Spencer shot Amelia the nastiest glare she could muster. Way to ruin the moment.

When she turned back to Zach, he pecked her politely on the cheek. "Call me. We should do brunch at the Rosewood Country Club. Tons of people have secrets there."

"Uh, absolutely," Spencer said, trying not to sound disappointed.

She walked to the front door, avoiding the patches of snow and ice on the sidewalk. As she fumbled for her keys, her cell phone chimed. She pulled it out, hoping it was a text from Zach. *Can't wait to see you without my sis next time*, perhaps. Or, even better, *I did want to kiss you. I hope I can soon.*

But it was a message from an anonymous sender instead. The schnapps immediately drained from Spencer's head, leaving her feeling instantly sober. She looked around,

searching for two eyes peering through the bushes, a figure moving through the trees. But there was nothing.

She took a deep breath and pressed READ.

Hey Spence. Everyone has secrets, indeed. And guess
what? I know yours. –A

14

BFFS 4-EVR

On Wednesday afternoon, Emily stood in front of Steam. As usual, every stool in the café was taken. Naomi Zeigler, Riley Wolfe, and Kate Randall held court under the big Italian poster of *La Dolce Vita*. Kirsten Cullen and Amanda Williamson stood at the counter and argued over which cupcake they wanted to split.

Students swept down the hall, heading to lunch or their next classes. First, Emily spotted Hanna through the crowd. She had a faraway smile on her face, seemingly oblivious to the people around her. Then, almost a split second later, Spencer rounded the corner, talking loudly to Scott Chin, one of her yearbook coeditors. "I had an amazing time at the Kahns' smorgasbord last night, didn't you?" she said.

And next, possibly because Emily was thinking about her, Aria strutted down the hall, arm in arm with that new exchange student from Finland who was living with Noel Kahn.

Not a single one of them glanced at Emily. The horrible A note in Ali's mailbox seemed a zillion miles from their thoughts. Why couldn't Emily forget about it, too?

"Hey, Emily!"

Chloe emerged through the clot of students. Emily waved. "Hey!"

As Chloe ran toward her, Emily felt a happy rush. This was their first lunch together, but since Emily had visited Chloe on Monday they'd friended one another on Facebook, commented on each other's posts, and had a lengthy IM chat last night before bed, gossiping about people in their classes, teachers to avoid, and the long-standing rumor about how the A/V supply room was where horny couples went to have sex.

Chloe looked Emily up and down, a smirk on her face. "Now, where have I seen that outfit before?" She gestured to Emily's Rosewood Day uniform plaid skirt and white blouse, then fingered her own identical blue blazer. "It's so bizarre to go to a school that enforces uniforms. We look like members of a cult."

"I've had to suffer through it for twelve years," Emily groaned. Then she turned toward the cafeteria. "You ready?"

Chloe nodded, and Emily followed the crowd of kids into the cafeteria, which was rapidly filling up with students. As they walked through the food lines, Emily gave Chloe a brief run-down. "The sushi is good, but don't get the chicken teriyaki—it comes out of a can."

"Got it."

Emily selected a Caesar salad and a package of pretzels and put them on her tray. "The pasta bar is okay, but for some reason only kids in band and orchestra eat pasta. No one else."

"What about soft pretzels?" Chloe pointed at the pretzel rack.

"Pretzels are fine," Emily said vaguely. Actually, the big soft pretzels used to be Ali's signature lunchtime food in seventh grade. Once they became part of Ali's clique, Emily, Aria, and Spencer ate pretzels, too, and lots of girls in their class copied them.

A charred smell wafted out of the kitchen then, reminding Emily of the fire in the Poconos. Even though the flames had reached the tops of the trees, even though the police had sworn over and over that there was no way Ali could have survived the explosion, Emily still had a horrible feeling Ali had gotten away. The very night after it happened, she'd had a dream about finding Ali in the woods beyond her parents' cabin, covered in burns. Ali had opened her eyes and stared straight at her. "You just dug your own grave, Emily," she said laughingly, reaching out to claw Emily with catlike talons.

"You coming?" Chloe called, staring at Emily inquisitively.

Emily looked down. She'd stopped dead in the cafeteria line, lost in thought. "Of course," she said, scurrying through the checkout.

They found a seat by the windows. Pure white snow blanketed the practice fields.

Chloe pulled out her phone and pushed it across the table to Emily. "Look at this picture of Grace. My mom sent it to me this morning."

On the screen was a photo of Grace with Cheerios all over her face. "Adorable," Emily cooed. "You must just want to eat her up every day."

"I do." Chloe beamed. "She's just so pudgy and cute. It's so fun to have a little sister."

"Was she . . . planned?" Emily blurted, surprising herself. She squeezed her eyes shut. "Sorry. That was really nosy."

"Nah, everyone asks it." Chloe took a bite of pretzel. "She was and she wasn't. My parents always wanted me to have a sibling, but it was pretty hard for them to get pregnant again. When Grace came along, they were both stunned. She saved my parents, though—they were having problems before this. Now, everything's great."

"Oh." Emily feigned fascination with a piece of chicken in her salad, not wanting to make eye contact. "What were things like with your parents before Grace?"

"Oh, the usual crap." Chloe stuck a straw into her can of ginger ale. "Bickering, rumors of cheating. My mom is a classic over-sharer, so I heard way more than I should have."

"But everything's good now?" The few bites of salad Emily had eaten felt like lead in her stomach. Mr. Roland's hip-grab floated into her mind again.

Chloe shrugged. "It seems to be."

A figure loomed over them, and Emily looked up. Ben, her old boyfriend from swimming, leered at both of them. "Hey, Emily. Who's your friend?"

Chloe smiled innocently. "Chloe Roland. I'm from North Carolina."

She stuck out her hand, and Ben made a big deal of shaking it. His best friend, Seth Cardiff, sidled up behind him and started to snicker. "You guys look pretty cozy together," Ben teased.

"I'm going to vote you Best Couple," Seth joked.

"Very funny," Emily snapped. "Leave us alone."

Ben looked at Chloe. "You know about her, right? You know what she's into?" He made a humping motion with his hips.

"Go *away*," Emily said through her teeth.

The two boys dissolved into dirty-sounding chuckles and wandered away. Emily stared out the window, her heart raging in her ears.

"What was that about?" Chloe asked.

"He's my ex," Emily said flatly. "He's kind of never forgiven me for something."

"What?"

Emily turned and watched as Ben and Seth bumbled out of the cafeteria, periodically shoving each other into the wall. She hadn't wanted to tell Chloe about her past so soon, but there was no way around it now. "I broke up with him last year to go out with a girl."

A surprised look passed over Chloe's face, but it disappeared fast. "God. I bet it was a huge blow to his manhood, huh?"

"Uh, *yeah*. He tormented me for months." Emily's squinted at Chloe, surprised at her tempered reaction. It was so nice that someone wasn't freaking out for once. "You don't think that's weird that I dated a girl?"

"Hey, if it feels good, go with it." Chloe popped the last of her pretzel into her mouth. "That's my motto. So was this girl special?"

Emily thought of Maya St. Germain, her crush last year, and smiled. "She was at the time. She really helped me figure out what I did and didn't want. But we don't talk much now—she's seeing someone else, a sophomore. She wasn't the love of my life or anything."

That, of course, was Ali—*her* Ali. Was it crazy to still crush on a dead girl? Her Ali still had such a hold on her. And when "Courtney" returned, confessed to Emily that she was her real friend, and kissed Emily passionately on the lips, Emily had been in heaven. Now, even though Emily knew, logically, that her Ali had died the night of the seventh-grade sleepover, she still longed for that girl to return once more.

It made her think of that fateful first night in Jamaica. When Emily was on her way back from the bathroom after yet another puke session, a hand caught her arm. "Hey!" a girl said in a bright, familiar voice.

Emily stared. It was the girl she'd seen earlier, the one she thought was Ali. "H-Hi?"

"I'm Tabitha." The girl thrust out her hand, which was covered in scars. "I saw you watching me from across the room. Do you go to my school?"

"I-I don't think so," Emily squeaked. But she couldn't stop staring. *Did* Tabitha look like Ali, or didn't she?

Tabitha cocked her head. "Want to take a picture? It'll last longer."

Emily wrenched her eyes away. "Sorry. I just feel like I know you from somewhere."

"Maybe you do." Tabitha winked. "Maybe we've met in a past life." A Ke$ha song blared over the stereo. Tabitha's eyes lit up. "I love Ke$ha!" she exclaimed, grabbing Emily's hand harder. "Dance with me!"

Dance with her? It was one thing for this girl to remind Emily of Ali, but now she was acting like her, too. Still, Emily couldn't resist. Feeling hypnotized, she let Tabitha lead her onto the dance floor and spin her around. Halfway through the song, Tabitha stretched out her arm and took a picture of both of them with her phone. She promised to send it to Emily later, but she never did.

A straw wrapper bounced off Emily's nose. Chloe giggled across the table. "Gotcha, space cadet!"

It was enough to break Emily out of her funk. "That's it." She grabbed her own straw and peeled off the wrapper. "You're going down."

She blew the wrapper at Chloe's ear. Chloe retaliated by tossing her napkin at Emily's shoulder. Emily beaned a crouton at Chloe, and Chloe pelted her with an M&M.

It ricocheted off Emily's forehead and disappeared down Imogen Smith's shirt.

Imogen turned around and glowered. James Freed stood at a nearby table and grinned. "I'll search for it, Imogen!" Imogen had some of the biggest boobs in the class.

The cafeteria monitor, an ancient woman named Mary, stormed over to Emily and Chloe. "No throwing food! Am I going to have to separate you two?" Her glasses swung on a chain around her neck. She wore a sweatshirt with kittens on the front.

"Sorry," Emily whispered. Then she and Chloe looked at each other and burst into giggles. It reminded Emily of a feeling she'd had a long time ago, when she, Ali, and the others used to giggle in just this way in just this cafeteria.

Suddenly, she realized what that feeling was: happiness.

15

HANNA MARIN, ROLE MODEL

"Okay, everyone, please find your seats!" Jeremiah
flitted around the back room of Mr. Marin's campaign
headquarters, a large office in a luxury building that
also housed a plastic surgeon, a high-end interior design
firm, and several psychiatrists' offices. His glasses were
askew, and there were bags under his eyes. What Jeremiah
needed, Hanna thought, was a very long day at the spa.

Hanna tried not to get jostled by the staff members,
consultants, and focus group leaders piling into the room.
It was Wednesday evening, and they'd gathered here to
watch the final cut of her dad's commercial.

The elevator dinged and Isabel and Kate swept in, all
broad smiles and glossy hair. Isabel looked orange and ridiculous as usual, but Kate looked fresh and pretty in a coral-colored
Rachel Pally jersey dress and black Kate Spade platform
heels. As soon as she saw Hanna, she shot her a tight, self-
satisfied smile. "Hey, Hanna! Excited to see the final result?"

Hanna rolled her eyes at Kate and her saccharine, rubbing-it-in-your-face enthusiasm. *Yeah, yeah, yeah,* Kate was about to be the star of a political commercial. A few days ago, it might have stung, but not anymore.

"Sure." Hanna pulled the Love Quotes silk scarf she'd bought this afternoon at Otter, her favorite boutique, around her shoulders. All the models on *Full Frontal Fashion* wore diaphanous scarves backstage. "Any exposure is good for my modeling career."

Kate's icy smile drooped. "*What* modeling career?"

"Oh, you didn't know? A photographer discovered me at my dad's taping," Hanna said breezily, as though this were a regular occurrence. "We did a shoot in Philly. It was super high-fashion. He's going to send my portfolio to some New York agents pronto. He's really well-connected."

Kate's eyes shifted back and forth, and her cheeks reddened. She looked like she was about to spontaneously combust. "Oh," she said finally, the word sounding like a belch. "Well, good luck with that." Then she flounced away, her shoulders rigid, her butt cheeks tightly clenched. *Score.*

Hanna's father appeared through the doors, and everyone applauded. He walked to the front of the room and waved his hands to quiet them down. "Thank you all for coming! I can't wait for you to see the commercial. But first, let me introduce some people who helped make it happen . . ."

Then he proceeded to praise about fifty billion people,

from the video editor to his stylist to the lady who cleaned the office. Hanna looked around, hoping Patrick might be here, but Sergio was the only representative from the photo shoot. Her crush on Patrick had blossomed over the last twenty-four hours: She'd sent him several texts during school, and he'd responded immediately, saying her photos were as beautiful as she was. Already, she had visions of the two of them taking New York by storm, the up-and-coming fashion photographer and his supermodel girlfriend.

Hanna's dad then gave a special shout-out to Jeremiah, who bowed humbly. He regaled Isabel with a long-winded thank-you-for-sticking-by-me-through-thick-and-thin serenade. *Gag.* Isabel stood and smiled beatifically, her eyes wet with tears. Hanna could see visible panty lines through her skirt.

The lights dimmed, and the television flipped on. Mr. Marin stood in front of the Rosewood courthouse, looking chic in his blue suit, red-and-white striped tie, and American flag lapel pin. There were shots of him talking to citizens, waving his hands earnestly and eagerly, surveying a building site, and talking to a classroom of kids about the dangers of alcohol. An inspiring orchestral score played, and an announcer confidently insisted that Tom Marin was the right choice for Pennsylvania. *Rah, rah, rah.*

Next was the family scene in front of the waving flag. Hanna inched forward in her chair, surprised to see her own image on the screen. The camera even remained on her for a moment. Had someone made a mistake? Was this not the final cut?

The camera moved to Kate, who spoke her lines overly loudly and directly, as though she were leading a recital of the Pledge of Allegiance. Hanna's own face appeared on the screen once again, startling her anew.

"We all deserve a better life," the Hanna on the screen said, looking straight into the lens, her eyes twinkling, the dimple on her left cheek prominent. She seemed natural and poised. She didn't have a double chin. Her teeth weren't crooked. Her hair was a pretty coppery color, not poop brown. Several people in the audience turned around and gave her big smiles.

The commercial finished with a Tom Marin logo splashed across the screen. When the TV went dark, everyone applauded. Several people jumped up and pounded Hanna's father on the back. A champagne cork popped, and one of Hanna's father's aides poured the liquid into waiting glasses. The rest of the aides went right back to tapping on their BlackBerrys.

"Surprised, Hanna?"

Hanna jumped and looked over. Jeremiah had sidled over and was now staring down his nose at her.

"Yeah, but in a good way," she admitted.

"Well, it wasn't *my* decision," Jeremiah said snootily. "Let's just say I was outvoted."

Two women Hanna didn't recognize bustled around

him and clasped Hanna's arms. Both were in power skirt suits and black high heels. "There you are!" one of them crowed in Hanna's face, her breath smelling like cinnamon Tic Tacs. "Hanna, I'm Pauline Weiss of Weiss Consulting."

"And I'm Tricia McLean of Wright Focus Groups. It's *so* nice to meet you." The other woman pushed a business card into Hanna's hand.

"H-Hi?" Hanna looked at both of them, feeling overwhelmed.

"We ran the focus groups," Pauline explained. She had big teeth and a bulbous mole on her cheek. "And they loved you! You tested so well with Tom's potential voters!"

"You were fresh and real," Tricia continued. She was at least six inches shorter than Pauline and shaped like a bowling ball. "Have you done television work before?"

Hanna blinked hard. "Um, a little." Did the microphones shoved in her face during Ian's murder trial count? What about the reporters who camped out on her doorstep when the press had deemed Hanna and her friends the Pretty Little Liars?

"The public recognized you from *People*," Tricia said. "You caught their attention instantly, which is *great* for a candidate."

"Everyone sympathizes with what you went through last year, Hanna!" Pauline piped up. "You'll bring in the emotional vote."

Hanna stared at the two consultants. "But what about

my . . . mistakes?" she asked, eyeing Jeremiah, who lurked behind them, eavesdropping.

"People said that made you more relatable." Tricia paused to flip through her clipboard. She read straight from a sheet of paper. "'We all have incidents in our past we're not proud of, and the goal is to learn from them and become better people.'"

"The public thinks you're repentant and humbled," Pauline added. "It works especially well with your father's campaign against underage drinking—you're the poster child of what *not* to do. We were even thinking you could do speaking tours to help campaign!"

"Whoa." Hanna sank back into her chair. A poster child? Speaking tours? Were they serious?

Hanna's father appeared behind them. "I guess they told you the news." He draped his arm around her shoulders, and several flashbulbs popped. "It's pretty amazing, huh? It looks like you're a real asset to my team!"

He gave Hanna's shoulders another squeeze. Hanna grinned maniacally, feeling like she was having an out-of-body experience. Was he really saying these things to her? Was he really *grateful* she was his daughter?

"Uh, Dad?"

Kate stood timidly behind the focus-group ladies. "What about my lines? Did the focus groups say anything about me?"

Pauline and Tricia's smiles wavered. "Ah. Yes."

They glanced at each other nervously. Finally, Tricia

spoke. "Well, people seemed to think you were a little . . . wooden. Not quite as relatable, dear."

"With a good media coach you can learn to get more comfortable in front of the camera," Pauline added.

"But I *am* comfortable in front of the camera!" Kate wailed. "*Aren't* I, Dad?"

Everyone nervously bit their lips and averted their eyes, including Hanna's father.

"Why would anyone like *her*?" Kate jabbed a finger at Hanna. "She stole someone's car! She was accused of killing her best friend!"

"Yes, but she *didn't* kill her best friend," Hanna's father said in a scolding voice Hanna had never heard him use with Kate. "There's nothing wrong with needing media coaching, honey. I'm sure after some practice you'll do great."

It was too delicious for words. Kate clamped her mouth shut and stormed away, her chestnut hair flying. Hanna was about to call out a gloating remark—how could she resist?—when her cell phone beeped. She smiled apologetically at the focus group women. "Excuse me."

She stepped out of the conference room and into her father's office, which contained a massive oak desk, a gray safe, and a bulletin board plastered with notes, campaign bumper stickers, and flyers. Maybe the text was from Patrick, saying her portfolio was ready. Or maybe from her adoring public, already telling her how much they loved her.

But instead, the message was from someone

anonymous. Hanna's blood turned to ice. *No.* This couldn't be starting again. Not now.

What happens in Jamaica stays in Jamaica? I don't think so. What will Daddy say? –A

16

WHAT A CUTE LITTLE *PEIKKO* ARIA IS!

"Welcome to Rocky Mountain High!" a tall, scrawny guy in a blue fleece pullover and baggy jeans said to Aria and Klaudia as they strutted through the ski store's fake-snow-decorated double doors. "Is there anything I can help you ladies with today?"

"We're cool," Aria said, strolling past racks and racks of down-filled coats. It was Thursday after school, and Aria and Klaudia were shopping for the Kahns' ski trip to New York this weekend. But now that she was inside the store, which was decorated with posters of skiers and snowboarders spraying up rooster tails and wildly flipping in the air, she wondered if this was really a good idea. Honestly, Aria had always found skiing kind of . . . pointless. You rode a gondola to the top of a big hill, raced down at speeds that could kill you, and then did it over again. And, oh yeah, it was below freezing outside.

"Are you *sure* you don't need some help?" the sales

assistant asked, his eyes fixed on Klaudia. Today, she wore a pink mini dress, gray tights, and furry Uggs that somehow made her legs look shapely and long. Those sorts of boots always made Aria's legs look like tree stumps.

Klaudia looked up from her iPhone, and batted her eyelashes at the sales boy. "Oh! I know how you help. There's a jacket in back on hold for Klaudia Huusko. Can you go get?"

"Klaudia Huusko?" the guy repeated. "Is that you? Where are you from?"

Klaudia grinned at him. "If you get jacket, I tell you."

The guy saluted, spun around, and made a beeline for the back room. Aria gazed at Klaudia. "Did you really order a jacket?"

"No." Klaudia giggled. "But now he leave us alone! He be back there for hours!"

"Nice." Aria gave Klaudia a high five.

"Okay." Klaudia squared her shoulders and steered Aria to the back of the store. She promptly selected a purple down-filled jacket, legging-like black ski pants, matching purple-and-black padded ski gloves, a package of thick Wigwam socks, and orange goggles with a thick strap. Chuckling, she placed the goggles over Aria's eyes, then put a blue pair on her own. "Sexy, *ja*?"

Aria stared at her reflection in the mirror. She looked like a bug. "*Ja*," she agreed. Then she spied a rack of jester hats worn only by the dorkiest band geeks or drama kids at Rosewood Day. "Those are sexier."

"Oh, *ja*," Klaudia said. They galloped over to the rack of hats, trying each one on and making sexy poses in front of the mirror. Each jester hat, felted king crown, and oversized cloche was worse than the last.

"Smile!" Klaudia cried, using her iPhone to snap a picture of Aria in a fleece pointed cap and an orange ski mask that made her look like a burglar.

"Say cheese!" Aria took a photo with her own phone as Klaudia pulled on a wooly hat with bear ears. Amazingly, even *that* made her look cute.

They pulled more and more hats off the racks, taking pictures with long socks on their hands, in lace-up boots that looked like they could battle the frozen tundra, and in fur trapper hats that fell over their eyes. Then, Klaudia pointed at something on a hanger. "Try this. Noel will like."

It was a bright yellow snowsuit with a padded butt. Aria wrinkled her brow. "*Noel* would like that? It'll make me look like a huge banana!"

"He will think you serious ski bunny!" Klaudia insisted.

"But it's . . . yellow," Aria murmured.

"It will bring you together as couple!" Klaudia's eyebrows made a stern *V*. "What you have in common? What you do that's same?"

Hackles rose on the back of Aria's neck. "Did Noel *tell* you that?" An image of the two of them sitting on the Kahns' sectional, swapping relationship stories floated into her mind. Maybe Noel had confessed that he and

Aria were a bit mismatched. Maybe he'd even said Aria was *kooky*, the word Ali always used when she said Noel wouldn't go for Aria in a million years.

Or what if Noel told Klaudia Aria hadn't slept with him yet? *Would* he tell her something like that?

"He tell me nothing." Klaudia pushed her white-blond hair behind her ears. "I just trying to help what I see! Like Dr. Phil!"

Aria stared at a ragged pair of snowshoes mounted on the wall. Klaudia was smiling so genuinely, as if she really thought she was giving good advice. Maybe she was. Aria and Noel *were* pretty different. She attended his home lacrosse games, but she always tuned out halfway through. She never wanted to watch the latest Jason Statham movie with him, and she sometimes found his never-ending my-parents-are-out-of-town-*again* house parties tedious. Noel tried a lot harder with Aria: He went to poetry readings with her, even though he found them intolerable. He tagged along to her favorite ethnic restaurants, although he usually ordered items on the menu most closely related to a hamburger or chicken nuggets. He even supported Aria applying to the Rhode Island School of Design instead of to Duke, where he'd already gotten a lacrosse scholarship.

Maybe Aria hadn't given enough back. Maybe she hadn't been a good girlfriend. The incident in Iceland flashed through her mind again, and she shut her eyes.

"Okay," Aria consented, gathering the snowsuit in her

arms. "I'll try it on. But if it makes my butt look enormous, I'm not buying it."

"Awesome!" Klaudia cried.

Then Klaudia's eyes widened at something across the store. "Be back," she murmured, migrating toward a long black coat with a fur hood that looked almost identical to the one she was wearing. Aria turned to the dressing room, then noticed an iPhone balanced on the hat rack. It had a big Finnish flag on the case.

"Klaudia?" Aria called. The phone had to be hers.

But Klaudia was too busy finding the coat in her size. Aria picked up the phone. It made a chiming sound, startling her. She stabbed the screen to shut it up. A text bubble from Tanja, Klaudia's friend, appeared. The text was in Finnish, but Aria noticed her name in Klaudia's previous message. Huh.

She peered across the store again. Klaudia had tried on a coat and was inspecting herself in the mirror. She looked down at Klaudia's phone. It felt heavy in her hands. She should just turn it off. Friends didn't read other friends' texts.

But as she slipped into the dressing room, her name on the screen haunted her. What were Klaudia and her friend saying about her? Was it good or bad? *Just one peek*, she decided. She moved her finger across the iPhone to unlock it. The text thread between Klaudia and Tanja popped up, blocks and blocks of words with umlauts and *O*s with slashes through them. Aria skimmed the Finnish, spotting Noel's name. Then Noel's again. And then *again*. But maybe that was natural—they *were* living under one roof. Maybe Aria would write about her foreign exchange host, too.

Finally, she found her name at the bottom. *Aria on peikko*, Klaudia wrote.

Peikko? Aria sounded it out in her mouth—*PEE-ko*. It sounded so cute, like a Disney character. What could it mean? Sprightly? Gamine? The best friend ever?

Excited, she scribbled it down on a pad she kept inside her purse. After a moment, she decided to copy Klaudia and Tanja's sentences about Noel, too. Maybe Klaudia had written about one of Noel's cute and slightly embarrassing habits Aria already knew about. It could be something she and Klaudia could laugh about together— *Hey, I accidentally saw your text about Noel. Isn't that crazy that he watches* iCarly *every afternoon?*

"Aria?"

It was Klaudia. Aria peered through the crack in the dressing room door and saw her standing only a few feet away. "Uh, hey," Aria said. The iPhone felt like a grenade in her hands. She quickly hit the home screen button, opened the door of the dressing room, and shoved it out. "I found this on the floor. I didn't want someone to step on it."

"Oh." Klaudia glanced confusedly at Aria, but then just shrugged and slipped it in her pocket. "You try on ski suit?"

"Just getting to it." Aria shut the door again. She stared at her reflection, expecting the guilt to be written on her face, but she looked like she always did—wavy black hair, ice blue eyes, and pointed chin. The urge to find out what *peikko* meant pulsed inside her. Maybe Klaudia could teach her Finnish and the two of them could use it as a secret code against the Typical Rosewoods.

She reached for her own phone in her bag and copied the Finnish texts into Babel Fish. The little wheel spun slowly, processing the results. When a new page appeared, Aria's mouth dropped open.

Noel deserves better, said the English translation of Klaudia's texts. *He is so hot and American sexy and needs real girl.*

Like you? Tanja wrote back. Klaudia replied with a winking smiley.

Aria's stomach burbled. She hadn't just read that. Babel Fish had made a mistake. Swallowing hard, she typed in *Aria on peikko.* The page loaded even slower this time.

"Aria?" Klaudia's voice sounded from the other side of the dressing room. "It look good? You super ski bunny?"

"Uh . . ." Aria glanced frantically at the snowsuit hanging from the hook in the corner. It was so yellow it nearly blinded her. Why *had* Klaudia chosen it for her? Because Noel would appreciate the effort . . . or because it would make her look like a neon-yellow Sasquatch? Because he was a super hot American boy and needed an appropriate girlfriend, not a skiing-hating, artsy freak?

Don't think that way, she told herself. Klaudia had been nice. There had to be another explanation.

But then the latest translated page popped up. Aria read the line slowly, her mouth suddenly bone-dry. Aria is a . . . *troll*.

Aria's hands gripped her phone. *Aria on peikko* meant *Aria is a troll*.

"Is okay?" Klaudia called from outside, her voice still friendly and chipper.

Aria ran her hands down the length of her face and stared at her phone again. Suddenly, it made a loud trumpeting sound, nearly causing her to drop it. NEW TEXT MESSAGE FROM ANONYMOUS, the screen said.

Dizziness overcame her. *Please no*, Aria thought. But when she opened the text, she saw it was exactly what she feared.

Watch out, Aria—I think you have some competition. We both know Noel has a thing for blondes, after all. Mwah! –A

17

DANCE LIKE NO ONE'S WATCHING

"There's a spot!" Spencer bellowed, pointing to an empty space on the side of Walnut Street in downtown Philadelphia.

Zach nodded, wrenched the wheel of his Mercedes to the right, and pulled in neatly behind a dented Ford Explorer. "Am I a genius parallel parker or what?"

"The best," Spencer said.

She peeked at Zach out of the corner of her eye. Tonight, he was wearing fitted dark-denim jeans, a striped Paul Smith button-down, shiny wingtips, and a pair of aviator sunglasses on his head. He'd splashed himself with a spicy, woodsy cologne, and he'd combed his hair off his head so she could see every angle of his fine-boned face. Each moment Spencer spent with Zach, he got cuter and cuter.

And tonight, she had him all to herself.

It was Thursday, a school night, but Zach was sneaking

out to Club Shampoo in Philly to see his favorite DJ spin and asked Spencer to come along. When he'd picked her up earlier this evening, she was thrilled to see Amelia wasn't glaring at her from the front seat. "She had flute practice," Zach said as soon as Spencer opened the door, as if reading her mind. "We're *free!*"

A pulsing bass assaulted Spencer's ears as soon as she stepped out of the car. She straightened her clingy black dress, rotated her ankles in the ultra-high Elizabeth and James heels she'd stolen from Melissa's closet ages ago, and followed Zach toward the group of people waiting behind velvet ropes at the door. As she crossed the slick-with-rain city street to join the line, her cell phone buzzed. She pulled it out of her sequined clutch and stared at the screen.

Aria: I just heard from A. Have you?

The words sent a knife through Spencer's chest. Should she have told the others about her A note?

I'm not paying attention to A, Spencer typed back. *Neither should you.*

Aria replied immediately. *What if A knows?*

A car blared its horn, nearly sideswiping Spencer. She jumped away, still staring at her phone. Should she reply? Should she worry? Or was that exactly what A wanted?

"Spencer?"

When she looked up, Zach was standing at the front of

the line. The bouncer had unclipped the rope and opened the door for him.

"Coming!" Spencer slipped the phone back in her purse. She couldn't deal with A right now.

The music thrummed in Spencer's ears as she ducked into the dark, industrial space. Vague outlines of bodies stood at the bar and gyrated on the dance floor, backlit by neon flashing lights and round, swinging bulbs. Zach was right about Thursday being the night to go out—Shampoo was packed, and the air was humid and sweaty. Four bartenders worked efficiently, pouring drinks so quickly they barely even looked down at what they were doing. Beautiful girls in barely there dresses turned to smile at Zach, but Zach didn't even notice them. His eyes were squarely on Spencer. *Swoon.*

"Two mojitos," Zach told a bartender, using the proper Spanish intonation. Their drinks arrived quickly, and they found a table in the corner. It was almost too loud to speak, so for a while Spencer and Zach just sat and watched the crowd. More girls eyed Zach as they swept by, but Zach acted like they didn't exist. Spencer wondered if everyone assumed the two of them were boyfriend and girlfriend. Maybe they *would* be after tonight.

Finally, Zach leaned so close to Spencer that his lips nearly touched her forehead. "Thanks for coming with me tonight. I needed to blow off some steam—my dad's been relentless lately."

Spencer sipped her mojito, which tasted just like summer. "He's *that* bad?"

One of Zach's shoulders rose. Lights flashed across his face. "He wants us to be little clones of him, doing exactly what he wants at all times. The thing is, I'll never be like him. For so many reasons." This last part he seemed to mutter more to himself than to her.

"Your dad does seem intense." Spencer agreed, thinking about how Mr. Pennythistle grilled her about her grades at the restaurant.

"Intense isn't even the half of it. If I don't go to Harvard like he wants, I'll probably be disowned. I'm supposed to talk to some guy named Douglas when we go to New York this weekend. He's on the Harvard admissions board. But I'm thinking about bailing."

Spencer nodded, catching his reference to traveling to New York for the long holiday weekend. She and her mom were going to New York City, too—Mrs. Hastings and Mr. Pennythistle were attending a gala hosted by one of Mr. Pennythistle's real estate friends. The idea of twenty-four hours in New York with Zach sounded delicious.

"What about your sister?" Spencer moved out of the way as a raucous bachelorette party, complete with penis balloons and a girl in a long, trailing veil, tramped through the narrow space. "Does she have to go to Harvard, too?"

Zach made a face. "My dad's a lot easier on her. She's quiet, demure, always proper—at least around him—so he adores her. But me—everything I do is wrong."

Spencer stared into her glass. She could certainly relate.

"That's the way things used to be with my family, too."

"Yeah? How?"

Spencer shrugged. "Whatever I did wasn't good enough. I'd get cast in the school play, but Melissa would be cast as an extra in a movie being shot nearby. I'd get an A on a test, Melissa would get a perfect score on her SATs."

Zach squinted at her in the dim light. "You guys seemed okay at dinner."

"We're better now—although it'll probably never be perfect. We're too different. And it took going through the Alison DiLaurentis thing together to really change things. Alison almost killed Melissa, too."

It was strange to utter those words so baldly and effortlessly in a public place. The admission seemed to startle Zach, too, because he took a big sip of his drink and stared at her long and hard. "I don't mean to pry about that Alison stuff, but are you okay?"

The door to the club opened, bringing in a whoosh of freezing air. Goose bumps rose on Spencer's bare arms, but it wasn't entirely from the cold. Aria's texts drifted into her mind.

"I'm okay," she said quietly. But as she looked around the club, a spear of despair ripped through her. It was at a place just like this where the girl Spencer thought was Courtney said she was actually Spencer's long-lost best friend. Then, Real Ali admitted that she'd known for a long time that she and Spencer were actually half sisters, but she'd never known how to tell Spencer back when they were friends.

Ali had made so many promises. *We'll start fresh. I'll be the sister you always wanted.* Of course Spencer had fallen for it. She'd longed for a sister who truly cared about her ever since she could remember. Someone with whom she had something in common, someone with whom she'd share secrets and have fun. With Ali last year, she felt like she'd hit the jackpot—until Real Ali revealed her true identity and tried to kill her, that is.

Letting go of the dream had been hard; its dark cloud had followed her everywhere. It stung, even when she saw girls who were obviously sisters giggling together at the bar or renting a two-person kayak. After she'd shared a drink with Tabitha in the bathroom, she returned to their table. Her friends had scattered—Aria was arguing with Noel at the bar, Hanna stood by the telescope on the other side of the restaurant, and Emily was nowhere to be seen. After a while, someone tapped her arm, and she turned. It was Tabitha again.

"Sorry to bug you, but I just have to ask." Tabitha perched on the edge of the table. "Don't you think we look similar?"

Spencer stared at her, a nervous swoop running through her body. "I don't think so."

"Well, *I* do." Tabitha grinned. "I think we look just like long-lost sisters."

Spencer shot to her feet so fast the chair underneath

her tipped over. Tabitha remained where she was, a Cheshire-cat grin on her face. Why would she say that? Could she *know*? The story of Mrs. DiLaurentis's scandalous love affair with Mr. Hastings was something that hadn't been released to the public. Spencer wasn't even sure if the police knew about it.

The rattling sound of a martini shaker startled her from the memory. She glanced around Shampoo. "*Jesus*," she whispered to herself. Hadn't she vowed *not* to think about Jamaica tonight?

The DJ put on a fast, electronic song, and Spencer stood and grabbed Zach's hand. "Let's dance."

Zach raised his eyebrows, looking amused. "Yes, ma'am."

The dance floor was packed with sweaty bodies, but Spencer didn't care. She led Zach to the middle of the room and started to sway. Zach gyrated, too, shutting his eyes and feeling the music with his body. Unlike most guys, who shuffled back and forth like Frankenstein's monster, Zach danced like a pro. He didn't freak when other guys bumped him, either, but just shrugged and went with it. He opened his clear, blue eyes, met Spencer's longing stare, and winked.

Spencer threw her head back and laughed. He was the sexiest guy she'd ever met. The voltage between them was cranked up as high as it could go.

She leaned into his ear. "This is awesome."

"I know," Zach answered. "You're a great dancer."

"So are you."

The beat slowed down, and Zach and Spencer moved closer and closer to one another until their hips touched. Spencer's heart clanged in her chest like the clapper in a bell. When she opened her eyes, all she could see were Zach's beautiful lips. He opened his eyes and gazed at her, too. She moved an inch closer. Zach edged in, too. *Here goes* . . .

Taking a deep breath, Spencer grabbed the back of his neck and planted her lips on Zach's. He smelled like a spicy face cream and tasted like sugar and lime. His lips were stiff for a moment, but then they opened and let her in. Spencer's stomach did somersaults. Electricity snapped off her skin. She raked her hands through Zach's soft hair, wishing they could fall into bed.

But then Zach pulled away. The strobe light danced across his face. He looked confused. Upset. Spencer took a few steps back, too, heat immediately rising to her cheeks. It felt like everyone was looking at her, laughing at her.

Zach grabbed Spencer's arm and pulled her into a sitting area just off the dance floor. He settled down on the plushy velvet couch under billowing canopies. It was the sort of place couples tumbled into to make out, but suddenly the moment felt charged in all the wrong ways.

"I think you've misunderstood," Zach said. "Maybe I've misled you."

"It's fine," Spencer snapped, staring pointedly at the glowing disco ball in the center of the dance floor. "So what is it? Do you have a girlfriend or something? Are you freaked out that our parents are dating?"

"It's not any of that." Zach shut his eyes. "Actually, Spencer . . . I think I'm gay."

Spencer's jaw dropped. She stared at Zach's thick eyebrows and strong shoulders, not believing it. He didn't *look* gay. He liked baseball. And beer. And he'd seemed to like *her*.

"I didn't mean to give you the wrong idea." Zach grabbed Spencer's hands and squeezed them hard. "I've been having so much fun with you, and I don't want anything between us to end. It's just . . . no one knows. Especially not my dad."

The song morphed into a sped-up mix from something by the *Glee* cast, and a bunch of girls screamed. Spencer stared at Zach's soft, slender hands in hers. Something inside her turned over.

"Your secret is safe with me," she said, squeezing his hands hard. The proud, always-gets-what-she-wants girl inside of her still felt disappointed and embarrassed, but she also felt flattered and touched that Zach found her as fun as she found him. If their parents continued dating, maybe Zach would end up being the perfect quasi-sibling Spencer had always wanted. Maybe she should've been searching for a brother instead of a sister all along.

Zach jumped to his feet and pulled Spencer up, too. "Glad we got *that* straightened out. Now where were we?"

Spencer tossed her blond hair over her shoulder. She

felt light and free as she sashayed through the crowd, but a presence behind her made her stop and turn. There, under the glowing EXIT sign, stood a dark, hooded figure staring straight at her.

Spencer stepped back, her heart leaping to her throat. A split second later, the figure had turned away and melted into the crowd—anonymous, undetectable, but still dangerously close.

18

FRIENDS TELL FRIENDS EVERYTHING

The Rolands' SUV was already gone when Emily pulled into the driveway that same Thursday night. When she went to ring the doorbell, she noticed the front door wasn't completely closed. "Hello?" Emily pushed it open and stepped into the foyer. A cartoon was on in the living room. Grace was in her baby swing in the corner, her head lolled to the side and her eyes closed. The Roland parents had sprung a last-minute outing on Chloe, and Emily had offered to help her babysit Grace.

"Emily?" Chloe called from the kitchen. "Is that you?"

"Hey, Chloe!" Emily walked toward her. "I'm so sorry I'm late!"

"It's cool! I'm making nachos!"

Emily passed through the living room into the big, bright kitchen. Boxes of Cheerios, drying bottles, stacks of unopened Pampers, and a container of baby wipes littered the table. A bag of Tostitos and a jar of cheese dip sat on the island along with an open bottle of champagne. Chloe noticed Emily looking at it. "Want a glass?"

Emily glanced at the snoozing baby in the living room. "But what about Grace?" All she could think of were those TV shows featuring police officers hauling drunk babysitters off to jail.

"One glass won't hurt." Chloe's limbs moved loosely as if she'd already had a glass or two before Emily arrived. She poured champagne into two crystal flutes. "And anyway, we need to toast."

"To what?"

"To being friends." Chloe chanced a smile. "It's awesome to come to a new school and immediately bond with someone."

Emily smiled. She'd always been a sucker for cheesy friendship rituals—Best Friends necklaces, secret languages, complicated inside jokes—and it had been so, so long since anyone wanted to share one with her. "One glass," she relented, grabbing the flute.

The girls toasted and sipped. The microwave dinged, and Chloe retrieved the plate of nachos, and they carried the plates, glasses, and bottle of champagne to the living room so they could keep an eye on Grace.

"So where are your parents?" Emily asked after she'd settled on the couch.

"At a romantic dinner." Chloe crunched on a chip. "My mom says they need to rekindle their relationship."

Emily frowned. "I thought you said things were great between them."

"They were . . . but things have been different since we moved here." A faraway look washed over Chloe's face. "I swear it's because of this house. It has bad mojo."

Emily stared blankly at the cover of the large book called *Rome in Pictures* on the coffee table, her heart pumping hard between her ears. "When you mentioned one of your parents cheating, was it your mom or your dad?"

Chloe wiped a blob of cheese from her chin. "My dad. But I never found out if it was true or not." Then she gave Emily a funny look. "Why do you care so much about my parents, anyway?"

"I don't!" Warmth rose to Emily's face. "Or, I mean, I *do*, but . . ." She trailed off.

"We should be talking about *our* relationships, not theirs." Chloe slurred her words a little. "I'll tell you a secret of mine if you tell me one of yours."

"I *already* told mine," Emily said. "Dating the girl? Remember?"

"Yeah, but you didn't give me details." Chloe crossed her arms over her chest, waiting.

Emily traced a large gash in the wooden table with her index finger. "How about you go first?"

"Okay." Chloe tapped her lips, thinking. "I dated someone I wasn't supposed to. My soccer instructor."

"*Really?*" Emily nearly dropped the gooey chip she was holding.

"Yup. His name was Maurizio. He was from Brazil. Everyone had a crush on him, but one night we found ourselves alone in the practice room, and . . ." Chloe shut her eyes. "It was pretty hot."

"Wow." Emily breathed. "Are you still together?"

"No way." Chloe's chandelier-style earrings smacked against her face as she shook her head. "I found out he had a girlfriend in Rio. Apparently she wanted to kick my ass. Honestly, that was the main reason I quit soccer. I couldn't handle being around him."

Emily crunched silently for a moment. Grace, still in her baby swing next to the couch, opened her eyes and sucked gently on her pacifier, unimpressed by the news.

"So." Chloe crossed her legs. "Have you ever had a boyfriend besides that swimming loser? Or did he turn you off guys for good?"

The champagne burned in Emily's stomach. "Um, I had a boyfriend after him—Isaac. But it didn't work out." A pang of sadness overcame her, and she lowered her eyes.

Chloe shifted her weight. "Do you wish it had?"

Grace began to fuss, and Emily stroked her soft, downy head. *That* was a loaded question. "Yes and no, I guess." The next words out of her mouth surprised her. "He wasn't the love of my life, though. Ali was. Well, the girl I knew as Ali in seventh grade was."

Chloe's mouth dropped open. "You and Ali were . . . together?"

Emily took a deep breath. "Not exactly. I had a huge

crush on her. I was devastated when she disappeared. I had this fantasy she was totally fine, and I dreamed about her coming back all the time. And then . . . she *did*."

The whole story spilled out of her, right up until Real Ali kissed her. "But it was all an act," Emily whispered, her eyes filling with tears.

"Oh my God." There were tears in Chloe's eyes, too. "I'm so, so sorry."

For some reason, Chloe's sympathy opened a floodgate inside Emily. And the more Emily's shoulders shook, the more she wasn't entirely sure she was crying *just* because of Ali. Maybe it was because of Jamaica, too. When Tabitha and Emily danced, everything had suddenly felt right, just like the moment when Real Ali kissed her. But then, something on Tabitha's wrist caught Emily's eye. It was a bracelet made of faded blue string.

Emily stopped dead on the dance floor and stared at it. It looked exactly like the bracelet Ali had made for Emily, Spencer, and the others the summer after they'd accidentally blinded Jenna Cavanaugh. Ali had ceremoniously passed around the bracelets, making the girls promise to wear them—and keep the Jenna Thing a secret—until the day they died.

Alarms blared in her head. She took a big step away from Tabitha. There was no way she could've gotten her hands on that bracelet. Unless . . .

Tabitha stopped, too. "What's wrong?" She looked down and realized what Emily was staring at. A bemused smile drifted over her face, as if she knew precisely what made Emily so afraid.

Now, Grace began to cry. Emily gently lifted her out of her swing and cradled her in her arms. "It's okay," she said softly, her voice croaky with tears. Grace's cries turned to muffled whimpers.

"You're so good with her," Chloe said. "It's amazing."

Those few, kind words tore painfully through Emily. She looked up, suddenly unable to hold something inside any longer. "I have to tell you something," she whispered. "I had a baby this summer."

Chloe's hand froze half-extended to her mouth. "*What?*"

"I got pregnant from my last boyfriend, Isaac. And . . . I had a baby girl," Emily repeated, glancing at Grace. The words felt so surreal coming out of her mouth. She hadn't planned on telling anyone, ever. "That's why I didn't swim this fall—I wasn't up to it, afterward. It's why I'm scrambling for a scholarship now."

Chloe ran a hand through her hair. "*Wow,*" she whispered. "Is the baby okay? Are *you* okay?"

"The baby's fine. As for me . . ." Emily shrugged. "I don't know."

Chloe's eyes darted back and forth. "What did your parents think?"

"My parents don't know. I spent the summer in Philly, basically in hiding. My older sister knew, but she hated me for it."

"Did you have anyone to rely on?" Chloe asked, grabbing Emily's shoulder. "A counselor, a doctor, someone you could talk to?"

"Not really." Emily shut her eyes, her chest tight. "I don't really want to talk about it anymore, actually. I'm sorry to burden you with this."

Chloe pulled Emily to her, careful not to squish Grace. "I'm so glad you told me. And I won't say anything, I swear. You can say anything to me, okay? I promise."

"Thanks." Emily's eyes filled with tears again. She buried her head in Chloe's soft hair, which smelled like Nexxus hair spray and a variety of styling gels. Grace snuggled between them, silent and content. It felt so good to hug someone. To *tell* someone. Even more than a BFF necklace or a champagne toast, this felt like the most meaningful friendship ritual of all.

Bang.

Emily opened her eyes with a start. Her mouth felt sticky and swollen.

She was on an unfamiliar couch. Out the windows, she saw the big, distinctive pine trees that lined the center island of the street Ali and Spencer lived on. The room smelled strongly of vanilla soap. She sat up, disoriented.

Footsteps sounded in the kitchen. A cabinet opened and closed. The floorboards creaked, and a figure stepped into the living room and sat down next to Emily. The vanilla odor seemed to multiply. It was Ali. *Her* Ali. Emily was sure of it.

Wordlessly, Ali leaned over Emily, almost like she was going to tickle her like she sometimes did in the middle of the night. A split second later, a pair of lips touched hers. Emily kissed back, fireworks exploding in her stomach.

But Ali's chin felt scratchy, not smooth. Emily opened her eyes, waking up for real.

It was a man's face pressing up against hers, not Ali's. He smelled like cigars, alcohol, and, most prominently, vanilla pudding. His weight was more than double that of Ali's, pressing down on her stomach and flattening her boobs.

Emily jerked away and squealed. The figure backed off, then snapped on a light. The golden bulb showed off Mr. Roland's salt-and-pepper hair. Of course Emily wasn't at the DiLaurentises'—she was still at Chloe's; they'd been babysitting.

"Wake up, sleepyhead," Mr. Roland said. His smile was like a jack-o'-lantern's, all scraggly and mischievous.

Emily cowered behind the couch. "What are you *doing*?"

"Just waking you up." He lunged for her again.

Emily leapt back. "Stop!"

Mr. Roland lowered his eyebrows and looked toward the stairs. "*Shhhh*. My wife is up there."

Emily stared across the room. Not only was Mrs. Roland upstairs, but Chloe was, too. She grabbed her coat from the back of the chair and backed out of the house without even tying her shoes. "Emily, wait!" Mr. Roland whisper-called after her. "Your payment!" But she didn't go back.

It was deathly still outside, the air crackling with coldness. Emily rushed to her car, fell into the driver's seat, and hyperventilated. *It's just a dream,* she chanted to herself. She looked out on the street. *If a car passes in the next ten seconds, it's just a dream.* But it was after midnight; no cars passed.

Beep.

Emily's phone lit up inside her jacket pocket. The seat belt strap went limp in her hands. What if it was Chloe? What if she'd seen? She pulled out the phone. It was something worse: a text from Anonymous. Shaking, she opened the message.

Naughty, naughty! Don't you just love to be bad, Killer?
Xx,
—A

"*Killer?*" Emily whispered, her hands trembling uncontrollably. She looked out onto the dark, empty street. That was Ali's secret name for her. A name very, very few people knew.

19

A PICTURE'S WORTH A THOUSAND TEARS

On Friday morning, after wedging herself into a jam-packed SEPTA train, Hanna huffed and puffed her way up to Patrick's fourth-floor photography studio. He'd sent her a note late last night saying that he wanted to see her ASAP. Luckily, she had the day off school for the long weekend, which meant she didn't even need to come up with an excuse to the front office.

In the light of day, Patrick's building didn't seem nearly as charming as it had the other night. The stairwell smelled like rotten eggs. Someone had left a pair of muddy running shoes outside their door. Behind another apartment, a couple was screaming at each other. The door slammed in the lobby, followed by a high-pitched, tinkling laugh. Hanna whipped around, her heart pounding hard. But no one was there.

She heard Tabitha's voice again, loud and clear: *I bet you weren't always gorgeous, were you?*

Hanna clapped her hands over her ears and scampered to Patrick's floor. Music pumped softly within his studio. She rang the bell, and Patrick flung the door open immediately, almost as if he'd been watching for her through the peephole.

"Miss Hanna!" He grinned, dark hair falling in his eyes.

"Hey." Hanna stepped into the room, taking deep, even breaths. The eerie laugh still echoed in her ears . . . as did A's note from her dad's screening.

"You look beautiful today," Patrick said, standing close to her.

Hanna's insides flipped over. "Thanks," she whispered.

They stood there for a moment, Hanna's heart pounding faster and faster. She was dying to kiss him, but she didn't want to seem like an overeager high-school student. "So, um, where are my photos?" she asked in the most casual voice she could muster.

"Hmm?" Patrick gave her a dazed look.

"You know, those things you took with your camera the other day?" Hanna teased, pantomiming snapping a picture. She was eager to send them to agencies. IMG was her top choice, and then maybe Next or Ford.

"Oh!" Patrick rubbed a hand through his thick hair. "Yes. Of course. I'll go get them."

He wandered off into the next room. *Artists*, Hanna thought with an adoring smile. Always so absent-minded and lost in their own world.

Hanna's phone started to buzz. The call was from Emily.

Sighing, she pressed her ear to the receiver. "What?"

"I've been getting more notes from A," Emily said in a shrill voice. "Have you?"

A horn honked loudly outside. Patrick bumped into something in the other room and let out a loud *shit*. "Um, maybe," Hanna answered.

"Are they about . . ." Emily cleared her throat.

Hanna knew exactly what Emily meant. "Yeah."

"What are we going to do, Hanna? Someone knows!"

Hanna winced. If A knew—really knew . . .

Just then, Patrick emerged from the back room. Hanna gripped the phone with both hands. "I have to go." She stabbed END like she was killing a spider.

"Everything okay?" Patrick asked from the doorway.

Hanna flinched. "Of course." She dropped the phone back into her leather bag and whirled around to face him. Strangely, Patrick wasn't holding anything in his arms. No photos, no digital camera, no leather portfolio, nothing.

Patrick strode over to the leather couch in the corner and plopped down. He patted the seat next to him. "Come sit next to me, Hanna."

The floorboards creaked as Hanna crossed the room. She slid onto the couch, and Patrick scooted over to her. "You're stunning, you know that?"

Hanna's stomach did another flip. She ducked her head bashfully. "I bet you say that to all your subjects."

"No, I don't." He turned Hanna's chin toward him

and stared deeply into her eyes. "To tell you the truth, I'm not that great with girls. It carries over from when I was in high school—I was kind of a loser. And you . . . well, you're like that popular girl I lusted over but couldn't have."

Hanna's insides melted. "I used to be a loser, too," she whispered. "I used to be so ugly I couldn't stand to look at myself in the mirror."

Patrick cupped her face with his hands. "I doubt you were *ever* ugly."

Then, he leaned forward and kissed her. Hanna leaned in, too, giddy with anticipation. But as their lips touched, something felt . . . wrong. The kiss was slimy and frantic. Patrick tasted like wheatgrass, and his hands felt like heavy paws on her body, not gentle and sweet like Mike's had always been. As he eased her down on the couch, an image of Mike flashed in Hanna's mind, and she felt a twinge of longing.

She pushed against Patrick's chest. "Uh, can we look through the shots right now? I'm dying to see your work."

Patrick chuckled lightly. "Let's worry about that later," he said, then buried his face in Hanna's neck.

A sour feeling welled in Hanna's stomach. Patrick's weight pinned her on the couch. "But we can do *this* later too, right?" she said, still trying to sound light and carefree. "Please can I see the photos? *Please?*"

Patrick continued to grope her. All at once, Hanna noticed how his lips made smacking noises. His hair looked oily, and there was a smattering of dandruff on his shoulders. A horrible thought struck her: What if Mike was right about him?

She shot off the couch. "Patrick, I want my photos. Now."

Patrick leaned back and crossed his arms over his chest. With a cruel sneer of his lip, he instantly transformed from a lovestruck photographer into something far more sinister. "So you're nothing but a tease, huh?"

Hanna blinked hard. "I just think we should keep things professional. You asked me to come over to look at my photos. I thought you were going to send them out today."

"Come on, Hanna." Patrick rolled his eyes. "Are you really *that* naïve?"

In a sweeping motion, he leaned down and pulled out a large manila envelope from under the couch. He undid the string fastener and revealed six glossy photos of Hanna. They weren't the shots of her at the Liberty Bell or City Hall, though, but six almost-identical photos of her at his studio. The wind was in her hair, there was a slutty expression on her face, and her dress had fallen down her chest to reveal most of her lacy, strapless bra.

They weren't like the provocative, half-naked Annie Leibovitz *Vanity Fair* photos, either. The lighting was brassy. Certain parts of Hanna were out of focus, and the composition wasn't artful at all. It looked like bad porn.

Hanna flinched, suddenly light-headed. "What *are* these? Where are the others? The good ones?"

"The others don't matter." Patrick's smile grew broader and broader. "*These* are the gold mine. To me, anyway."

Hanna backed away, her heart sinking. "W-what do you mean?"

"C'mon, Hanna. Do I really have to spell it out for you? What would Daddy do if he saw these? If his *competitor* saw these? I have friends in high places. This would make a top story on TMZ. And then . . . *poof!*" Patrick snapped his fingers. "Bye-bye, Senate campaign!"

Hanna's body felt swelteringly hot, then frigidly cold. "You wouldn't!"

"I wouldn't? You don't even *know* me, Hanna."

Hanna wilted against the island, her hopes and dreams leaking out of her like a punctured balloon. Everything he'd said, all his kind praise, had been a ruse. "Please don't show those to anyone. I'll do anything."

Patrick placed his finger on his chin and cast his eyes to the ceiling, like he was pretending to think. "I won't if you come up with ten thousand dollars by the end of this weekend. How about that?"

Hanna's jaw dropped. "I don't have that kind of money!"

"Of course you do, rich girl." Patrick's eyes gleamed. "You just have to be creative about where to look. I want it in cash in a manila envelope. Give it to a guy named Pete who works at the flower stand at Thirtieth Street Station. If you don't, you'll be link of the week. Daddy's little assistant will have to work very hard removing this from the Internet. And I doubt the public will trust a man whose teenage daughter takes off her top for strangers."

Hanna stared at him. Her gaze fell to the photos again. Suddenly, the whole scenario was hideously clear to her. "Y-you're not even a real photographer, are you? You don't have connections in New York. You just said that to set me up! You *lied*!"

Patrick laughed and held up his palms. "You got me." Then he lowered his face to Hanna's. "I guess you're not the only one who's good at lying, Ms. Marin."

Hanna didn't wait to hear another word. She backed away and ran out the door, slamming it hard. The building seemed even more derelict than it had twenty minutes ago. The couple was still arguing downstairs. The tin ceiling looked like it was about to collapse. Four floors down, Hanna thought she heard the faintest giggle yet again, like someone had heard everything.

"That's *it*," Hanna screamed. Whoever this bitch A was, Hanna was going to tackle him or her to the ground and tell them to *shut the hell up*. She raced to the bottom of the stairs, her arms pumping hard, her fingers barely grazing the dilapidated railing.

But once she reached the lobby, it was empty. The front door swung on its hinges, the only indication that someone had just been there. A had gotten away again.

20

NOTHING LIKE THAT FRESH MOUNTAIN AIR

The Kahns' Range Rover, equipped with snow chains and a heavy-duty ski rack, rolled into the circular driveway of the Whippoorwill Lodge on Lenape Mountain. Bellhops and valets in heavy padded jackets rushed to the car and began to remove their baggage from the back. Noel and his two older brothers, Eric and Christopher, jumped out and stretched their legs. Aria followed, nearly wiping out on the icy asphalt. Hello, hadn't the bellhops ever heard of *salt*?

Last but not least, disembarking from the car like a fur-clad princess, was Klaudia. The tip of her nose was adorably pink from the cold and her butt was perfectly round in dark-denim jeggings. Every one of the bellhops turned to gape at her. "Do you need help?" they asked in unison. "Is there anything we can carry for you?"

"You so sweet!" Klaudia trilled, shooting each of them winning smiles that made Aria want to puke.

Aria turned to Noel. "Can we go inside? It's freezing out here." The digital temperature readout on a bank they'd passed had said two degrees Fahrenheit.

Noel chuckled. "This is nothing—wait till you're on top of the mountain!"

"You won't feel cold when you *hiihto!*" Klaudia said to Aria in an excited voice. By now, Aria knew that *hiihto* was Finnish for *ski*. Why couldn't Klaudia just say it in English? It wasn't like it was hard. Three letters long. *Ski.* Figure it out.

Aria shot Klaudia a tight smile and turned away, feeling as rigid and sharp-edged as the icicles that dangled precariously from the roof. This was just about the last place she wanted to be right now, but she was terrified of what might happen if she let Noel out of her sight. Klaudia might get her talons in him—and how could he resist her? After all, his current girlfriend was nothing but a *peikko*.

"Aria?"

Aria blinked and looked up. Noel was calling to her from the lodge door. The Kahn brothers and Klaudia had already gone in.

She followed them into the large lobby. Every surface was paneled in oak, making the room look like a giant sauna. The air smelled like cinnamon and hot chocolate, and people clonked by in heavy ski boots, wooly hats, and oven mitt–sized gloves. Guests lounged on tobacco-colored leather couches and warmed themselves by a blazing fire in the corner. A yellow lab with a red kerchief tied around his neck dozed on a doggie bed next to the big window that looked out on the slopes.

"Nice," Christopher murmured, walking over to the window. Christopher was three years older than Aria and Noel and home from Columbia on a break. He had Noel's same clean-cut, golden features, but there was something hard about him, less endearing.

"Perfect powder," Eric murmured. He was two years older than Noel and went to Hollis—but only as a formality. His real goal in life was to become a ski bum in Montana or a surf instructor in Barbados.

"*Mahtava!*" Klaudia chirped, staring out the window, too. Whatever *that* meant.

Aria looked at the view. The mountain seemed to go straight up at a ninety-degree pitch. Skiers expertly zigzagged down the face. When a boy fell, a cloud of snow billowed in all directions. Aria felt tired just watching them. She eyed the sleeping dog in the corner again. *Lucky.*

The Kahns checked in, and the concierge doled out five room keys, one for each of them—thank God Aria and Klaudia didn't have to share. Once Aria was in her room—which had a king-sized bed with lots of pillows, a tiny kitchenette, and yet another view of the daunting ski mountain—she flopped on the bed and shut her eyes.

Looks like you have some competition, Aria! We both know Noel has a thing for blondes!

A's text was like a bad song stuck in her head. A must

have seen Aria reading Klaudia's iPhone. But *how*? Had A hidden behind a rack of snowsuits? Spied on her through the in-store security camera?

Aria had a sinking feeling the note was right—Noel did have a thing for blondes. He'd loved Ali—and he'd definitely noticed Tabitha. Even after they got back from Jamaica, Noel had made passing references to Tabitha, things like *Hey, didn't that blond girl remind you of someone? There was something about her I couldn't quite put my finger on.*

But even though he asked a lot of questions, he wasn't suspicious. *No* one was.

Until now.

A knock sounded on the door. Aria shot up, nerves jangling. "H-hello?"

"It's me," Noel called from the hallway. "Can I come in?"

Aria unlatched the door. Noel thrust a big basket of tiger lilies, coffee, and snacks in her face. "For you!"

"Thank you!" Aria cried. There was even a stuffed pig in the basket, reminding Aria of her favorite puppet, Pigtunia. But then she stiffened. Didn't guys only give their girlfriends flowers when they felt guilty? "What's the occasion?" she asked.

"I saw it in the gift shop and thought of you." Noel set the basket on the TV bureau and wrapped his arms around her. He smelled like the tea tree oil facial cleanser Aria had bought him for Valentine's Day. "Look, I know skiing isn't really your thing, but I'm so happy you came. This trip wouldn't be the same without you here."

He sounded so genuine and earnest that Aria's suspicions thawed. Klaudia and A were turning her into a crazy person. "I'm happy I came, too," she admitted. "This place is gorgeous."

"*You're* gorgeous." Noel pulled her down on the bed. They started kissing, first tentatively, then more and more passionately. Noel pulled Aria's shirt over her head, and Aria reciprocated. They pressed their bare chests together, feeling each other's warmth. "Mmm," Noel murmured.

They paused for a moment, and then Aria touched Noel's waistband and undid his belt buckle. Noel breathed in, obviously surprised. Next, Aria undid the button on his jeans and pulled them off him. She stared at his muscled legs, grinning. He was wearing the golden retriever–printed boxers she'd picked out for him at J. Crew.

After a moment, she reached for the button on her own jeans. Noel grabbed her hand, his eyes wide. "Are you sure?"

Aria gazed around the small room, from the flat-screen TV to the champagne bucket in the corner to the generic-looking chair and ottoman by the large windows. Now that they were in an unfamiliar setting, she felt less inhibited than normal. Or maybe she just felt compelled to prove to Noel exactly what he meant to her. It might just be the only way to ensure he would remain hers.

"I'm sure," she whispered.

Noel pulled off Aria's jeans the rest of the way. They clung to each other for a while, almost totally unclothed, their lips locked in an embrace. Aria's heart pounded. She was really going to do this. It was time. As Noel rolled on top of her, she kissed him hard.

Knock knock knock.

They both froze, staring at each other with wide eyes. There was silence, and then another knock. "Hello?" Klaudia chirped. "Aria? Noel? You there?"

Aria winced. "You've got to be kidding me."

"Noel?" Klaudia's voice was muffled. "Come on! Time for *hiihto!*"

"Maybe if we be quiet she'll go away," Noel whispered, tracing his finger along Aria's bare collarbone.

But the knocking persisted. "Noel!" Klaudia teased. "I know you in there! We must *hiihto!*"

Finally, Noel groaned, grabbed his jeans from the floor, and slid them back on. "Okay," he called back. "We're coming."

"Oh, goody!" Klaudia said from the other side.

Aria stared at Noel, slack-jawed. "What?" Noel asked, pausing with one pant leg halfway past his knee.

For a moment, Aria was so angry she couldn't speak. "We were sort of in the middle of something. Are you seriously going to drop everything for her?"

Noel's face softened. "We'll have plenty of time alone tonight, when no one will disturb us. And Klaudia's right—the lifts close in a couple hours. We've got to get our *hiihto* on. Aren't you ready for your first ski lesson with her?"

"Actually, no." Aria turned away and hugged a pillow to her chest. Fury pulsed inside her like a second heart. "I don't want Klaudia to teach me anything."

The bed springs squeaked as Noel sat back down. "I thought you guys were friends. Klaudia adores you!"

A bitter chuckle escaped from Aria's lips. "I highly doubt that."

"What do you mean?"

Noel was staring at her with such a puzzled look on his face. Aria thought about the texts Klaudia had written about both of them. Should she tell Noel . . . or would that make her look like a psycho?

"I just don't trust her around you," Aria said. "I see the way she looks at you."

Noel's face fell. "Don't be like that, Aria. I've told you a million times you have no reason to be jealous."

"It's not jealousy," Aria argued. "It's the truth."

Noel pulled his sweatshirt over his head and stuffed his feet into his Timberland boots. "Come on." He extended his hand for her, his tone of voice more distant than it had been just a few minutes before.

Reluctantly, Aria got dressed and followed him out— what other choice did she have? Klaudia was waiting for them in a chair across the hall, already dressed in skin-tight ski pants, a shapely white ski jacket with pink lining, and matching pink hat and gloves. She jumped up when she saw Noel and grabbed his hand. "Ready for *hiihto*?"

"Totally," Noel said jovially. He nudged Aria. "We're both ready."

Klaudia's gaze flickered briefly to Aria. Her irises morphed from dark blue to an inky, venomous black. "Good," she said in a chilling voice. An expression crossed her face that Aria couldn't immediately decipher.

But as Klaudia turned, walked out of the lobby, and promptly hopped on a chair lift without inviting Aria along, Aria got the message loud and clear. Klaudia had heard everything Aria said to Noel in the hotel room. The expression on her face meant *This is war.*

21

SOME STRIPPING AND SOME TEASING

"Okay, kids," Mr. Pennythistle said. "The porters will take your things to your rooms. We'll meet at Smith and Wollensky at eight for dinner."

It was Friday afternoon, and Spencer, her mother, Zach, Amelia, and Mr. Pennythistle had just arrived in the lobby of the Hudson Hotel on Fifty-eighth Street in New York, which had the moody lighting of a nightclub. The air smelled like expensive leather valises. Skinny model-types writhed and sipped cocktails in the various bar areas. A bumbling tourist squinted at a guidebook in the low light. Various languages floated through the cavernous space.

The only reason they were staying at the Hudson and not somewhere genteel like the Waldorf or the Four Seasons was because Mr. Pennythistle did business with the hotelier and got all of their rooms for free. Mr. Donald Trump of the Main Line was apparently a cheap bastard.

Mrs. Hastings gave Spencer, Zach, and Amelia a half-wave and then made a break for the elevator bank to the street—maybe she wasn't a fan of the nightclub-style hotel, either. Mr. Pennythistle followed her. After they were gone, Zach fiddled with his iPhone. "So. What do you guys want to do?"

Spencer rocked back and forth on her heels. She was tempted to ask Zach if he wanted to visit Chelsea, the gay capital of New York City. Or maybe the Meatpacking District—there were some amazing men's shops there.

Accepting that Zach was into guys had been easier than Spencer thought. Now, they could be BFFs and tell each other everything, watch episodes of *The Real Housewives of Beverly Hills*, and argue over Robert Pattinson's hotness. And now that there wasn't any sexual tension between them, Spencer had felt comfortable sleeping on Zach's shoulder on the Amtrak ride here, taking a sip from his Coke, and smacking his butt to tell him his jeans looked awesome.

Unfortunately, they were stuck with Amelia today—Mr. Pennythistle had been very specific about not letting Amelia go off by herself—and Spencer couldn't very well suggest Chelsea in front of her. Amelia looked miserable to be here—*and* particularly dowdy today. While Spencer had chosen a chic outfit of black denim jeggings, a Juicy faux-fur jacket, and Pour la Victoire spike-heel booties, and Zach wore a fitted John Varvatos hooded anorak, dark-wash jeans, and black Converse, Amelia looked like a combination of a fifth grader and a prudish middle-aged woman off to church. She wore a crisp white blouse, a plaid skirt that fell past her knees, black wooly tights, and—*ugh*—Mary Janes. Just being around her brought down Spencer's style quotient.

"We should go to Barneys," Spencer suggested. "Amelia needs a makeover."

Amelia made a face. "Ex-*cuse* me?"

"Oh my God." Zach's eyes gleamed. "That's a fantastic idea."

"I don't need a makeover." Amelia crossed her arms over her chest. "I like my clothes!"

"I'm sorry, but your clothes are awful," Spencer said.

Amelia's eyes zeroed in on Spencer's sky-high heels. "Who made *you* an expert?"

"Christian Louboutin," Spencer said with authority.

"Spencer's right." Zach moved out of the way of a blond Swedish couple pulling two Vuitton bags toward the elevator bank. "You look like you're ready to go to the convent."

"Two to one, you're outnumbered." Spencer grabbed Amelia's hand. "You need a new everything, and Fifth Avenue is just around the corner. Come on."

She dragged Amelia down the escalators. Zach caught Spencer's eye and smiled.

On the street, cabs zoomed and honked. A man noisily pushed a hot dog cart. The Time Warner towers soared overhead, silver and sleek. Spencer adored New York, even though her last visit had been disastrous. She'd met with her surrogate birth mother, who drained her college account, much to A's delight.

As they walked down Fifty-eighth Street, a poster in a travel agent's window caught her eye. *Come to Jamaica and feel all right!*

The blood drained from her head. There, in poster-sized photographs, was The Cliffs: the pool with the pineapple decal on the bottom. The purplish cliffs and turquoise sea. The roof deck and restaurant where they'd met Tabitha. The crow's nest and the long, empty expanse of beach. If Spencer squinted, she could almost make out where they'd stood after everything happened . . .

"Spencer? Is everything okay?"

Zach and Amelia stared at her from a few paces away. Busy pedestrians wove around them with annoyance. Spencer looked at the poster again. A's notes shot through her head like a bullet train. Someone knew. Someone had seen them. Someone might tell.

"Spence?"

The strong scent of burnt soft pretzel from a cart wafted into Spencer's nose. Straightening up, she turned away from the travel agent's window. "I'm fine," she murmured softly, pulling her coat around her and rushing toward them.

If only she could believe that.

Barneys pulsed with rich women comparing leather gloves, girls spritzing Chanel No. 5 on their wrists, and hot men ogling the Kiehl's skin cream display. "This place is divine," Spencer said as she stepped through the revolving doors, inhaling the heady scent of luxury.

"It's just a *store*," Amelia said grumpily.

They had to practically drag Amelia up to the Co-op on 8, which brimmed with thousands of wardrobe options. Amelia looked at everything with distaste. "You're trying things on," Spencer urged. She held up a Diane von Furstenberg dress. "The wrap dress is a style essential," she said in her best personal-shopper voice. "Especially because you're straight up and down. It'll give you a semblance of a waist."

Amelia scowled. "I don't *want* a waist!"

"I guess you never want to have sex, either," Spencer said breezily.

Zach giggled and helped her pull several more dresses off the rack. Amelia eyed him suspiciously. "Why are *you* helping with this? I thought you hated shopping."

Spencer almost opened her mouth to protest—what gay guy hated shopping?—but she refrained. Zach shrugged and bumped Spencer with his hip. "What else am I going to do?"

After choosing several pairs of jeans, various skirts and blouses, and a whole array of dresses, Spencer and Zach led Amelia to the dressing area and shoved her into one of the tiny rooms. "You're going to be transformed," Spencer told her. "I promise."

Amelia groaned, but locked the door behind her.

Spencer and Zach sat on the little couch next to the three-way mirror like anxious parents. The door slowly creaked open, and Amelia stepped out wearing a pair of Rag & Bone skinny jeans, a VPL flutter-sleeve top, and a pair of sleek brown booties with two-inch heels. There was a frightened look on her face, and she took mincing steps in the tottering heels toward the mirror.

"Amelia," Zach gasped.

Spencer leapt to her feet. "You look incredible!"

Amelia opened her mouth to protest, but then shut it again when she saw her reflection. There was no way she couldn't say she looked good: Her legs were long and thin, her butt—who knew she even *had* one?—was round and perky, and the blouse elegantly complemented her skin. "This outfit is . . . nice," she deemed primly.

"It's more than nice!" Zach said.

Amelia gazed at the price tag on the jeans. "It's *really* expensive."

Spencer arched a brow. "I think your dad can handle it."

"Try on more!" Zach cried, shoving her back into the tiny booth.

One by one, Amelia tried on new outfits, her hard, bitchy exterior slowly melting away. She even did a tiny twirl in one of the Diane von Furstenberg dresses. By the sixth outfit, she wasn't even wobbling in the heels. And by the twelfth, Spencer felt so comfortable that Amelia wouldn't run away screaming that she tried on a fitted Alexander Wang cocktail dress she'd picked out for herself.

Sliding it over her head, she reached around to fasten the back but couldn't quite grab the zipper. "Zach?" She poked her head out of the dressing room. "Can you help?"

Zach opened the door farther and stood behind her. Spencer's whole back, including the edge of her red lacy thong, were in full view. Their eyes met in the mirror.

"Thanks for paying attention to my sister," Zach said. "I know she's kind of prissy. But you've really brought her out of her shell."

"I'm happy to help." Spencer smiled. "Makeovers always work wonders."

Zach's eyes remained on hers in the mirror. He still didn't pull up the zipper. Then, slowly, he touched the small of her back with his palm. His warm, smooth hand sent tingles up Spencer's spine. She turned to face him. He moved his arms up and wrapped them around her waist. They stood just inches from one another, so close that Spencer could smell Zach's breath mints. In just seconds, their lips would touch. Thousands of questions swarmed in Spencer's head. *But you said you were . . .* Are *you? . . . What is this . . . ?*

"Guys?"

They shot apart. A pair of snakeskin heels peeked under the curtain. "What are you *doing* in there?" Amelia asked.

"Uh, nothing." Spencer fumbled away from Zach, knocking into a few garments hanging on the wall. She pulled her jeans back on underneath the dress.

At the same time, Zach smoothed down his shirt and exited the room. "I was just helping Spencer zip something up," he murmured to his sister.

Amelia's snakeskin-clad feet turned this way and that. "Is that *all* you were doing?"

A long pause followed. Zach was saved by his ringing phone, and he padded out of the dressing room hallway to take the call. Spencer slumped down on the little bench inside her alcove and stared at her flustered face in the mirror. If only Zach had answered his sister. Spencer would have loved to know if that was all they'd been doing, too.

22

THE BRIDGES OF ROSEWOOD COUNTY

A few hours later that same Friday, just after the sun was sinking past the tree line, Emily pulled into the parking lot of the Rosewood covered bridge. It was about a mile away from Rosewood Day, constructed from Revolutionary War–era stone, and spanned a small creek filled with fish—in the summer, anyway. Now, in dreary February, the frozen creek was silent and deathly still. The pine trees whispered in the wind, sounding like gossiping ghosts. Every so often, Emily heard a crack or a snap far off in the woods. It wasn't exactly somewhere she wanted to be right now. The only reason she'd come was because Chloe wanted to meet her here to talk.

She got out and walked under the bridge, inhaling the scent of wet wood. Just like everything else in Rosewood, the bridge held a sad memory. Emily and Ali visited it once in the late spring of seventh grade, sitting under its shady cover and listening to the creek rushing beneath them. "You know that guy I told you about, Em?" Ali sing-songed happily. She'd often teased Emily about an older guy she was in love with. Later, Emily found out it was Ian Thomas. "I think I'm going to bring him here tonight so we can make out." Ali twisted the string friendship bracelet she'd made for all of them around her wrist and gave Emily a sly, I-know-just-how-badly-I'm-breaking-your-heart smile.

Emily's memory shifted to the friendship bracelet she'd seen on Tabitha's wrist. As soon as she'd spotted it, she'd backed away from her fast. Something was really, really wrong.

The crowd on the dance floor and at the bar was thick, making it almost impossible for Emily to find her friends. She finally located Spencer sitting on top of a remote patio table, staring dazedly at the dark, raging ocean. "I know you're going to tell me I'm crazy," Emily blurted out, "but you have to believe me."

Spencer turned and stared, her blue eyes huge. "She's Ali," Emily persisted. "She *is*. I know she doesn't look like her, but she's wearing Ali's old string bracelet—the one she made for us after the Jenna Thing. It's exactly the same."

Spencer shut her eyes for a good ten seconds. Then she told Emily how Tabitha insinuated that they looked like long-lost sisters. "It was like she *knew* me," she whispered. "It was like . . . she was Ali."

Emily felt a hot sizzle of fear. Just hearing Spencer say it made it all feel even more real and dangerous. She looked around to make sure no one was listening. "What are we going to do? Call the police?"

"How could we prove it?" Spencer chewed on her bottom lip. "She hasn't *done* anything to us."

"*Yet,*" Emily said.

"Besides, everyone thinks Ali's dead," Spencer continued. "If we tell them a dead girl has come back to life, they'll have us committed."

"We have to do *something*." The idea of Ali roaming the same resort they were staying at chilled Emily to the bone.

A car door slammed, and footsteps rang out behind her, breaking Emily from her memory. Chloe appeared in the archway of the bridge. "Hey," Emily called.

"Hey," Chloe answered. Her voice sounded dampened and morose, and Emily's chest tightened. Chloe hadn't explained why she'd wanted to meet her tonight—only that they needed to talk. What if she'd seen her father kiss Emily? What if A had told her? A's note pounded in her head: *Naughty, naughty! You just love to be bad, Killer!*

Chloe made her way to Emily, and they both walked through the covered bridge. For a while, the only sounds were their boots crunching through the thin layer of crushed ice. Chloe pulled out a flashlight from her pocket and shone it on the wooden beams, stonework, and graffiti tags. *Brad + Gina. Kennedy is a bitch. Go Rosewood Sharks.*

Chloe still hadn't said a word. Her silence began to unnerve Emily, so she took a deep breath. "Chloe, I'm really, really sorry."

"*You're* sorry?" Chloe turned around. "*I'm* sorry."

Emily squinted at her. "But I—"

"I had so much to drink last night," Chloe interrupted. "A couple glasses before you came, a couple glasses while you were there . . . the whole night is a blur. I barely remember going to bed. I left the responsibility of Grace up to you."

The cold was beginning to make Emily's feet numb. "Oh," she finally sputtered. "It's okay. Grace was fine." She stepped forward. She had to come clean about Chloe's dad. This wasn't a way to start a friendship, and the last thing Emily wanted was to keep yet *another* secret from someone. "Listen, there's something I need to tell you."

"Wait, let me finish." Chloe raised her palms in a halting gesture. "I was hiding something from you last night. I shouldn't have been drinking. I had a problem with it back in North Carolina—I had these friends who drank all the time, I acted out because of my parents' issues, and I took things too far. One time, I even had to be hospitalized for alcohol poisoning."

"Oh, Chloe!" Emily covered her mouth with her hands. "That's awful!"

A huge burst of steam puffed from Chloe's nostrils. "I know. I was out of control. And yesterday was kind of . . . a relapse. My parents would kill me if they knew—they had me in rehab programs, but I swore I was better and didn't need to go to the meetings anymore. That's why I went to bed last night without telling you—I didn't want them to see me in that condition. You didn't mention the champagne to them, did you?"

"No!" Emily cried. She'd run out of the house before she could say much of anything.

Chloe looked relieved. "Do you know if they saw the bottle in the kitchen trash? I took it out this morning, but I was so scared."

Your dad was way too preoccupied to be hunting around for champagne bottles, Emily thought grimly. And she hadn't seen Mrs. Roland downstairs at all. "I don't think so."

A mound of snow fell off the roof with a wet slap, and both girls turned. Chloe wandered farther into the bridge, and Emily followed her. "So why were you drinking yesterday?" she asked.

Chloe's boots made loud *clonk*s on the ground. She shrugged. "It's hard to move to a different place, I guess. Hard to start over. And things feel so strange here—not quite right. The only really happy thing I've found is you."

Emily blushed. "Thanks. And, you know, if you need someone to talk to about it, I'm here."

"I'm here for you, too." Chloe turned. "I didn't black out what you told me last night—about the baby. We can help each other."

They hugged, squeezing each other tight. When they broke apart, a comfortable silence fell over them. Cars swished by on the highway. More twigs cracked in the woods. For a split second, Emily was sure she saw a dark, humanlike shape darting between the trees, but when her vision adjusted, there was only darkness.

"So what were you going to tell me?" Chloe asked suddenly.

Emily stopped short. "When?"

"Just now, silly." Chloe's voice was playful.

Emily curled her numb toes in her boots. Once again, the pendulum swung in the opposite direction. There was no way she could tell Chloe about what her father did—not with the state she was in. The last thing she wanted was to upset her friend and send her into a downward spiral of destructive drinking. "Oh, it doesn't matter. I guess I'm preoccupied today."

"About swimming?"

Emily looked up questioningly, and Chloe smiled. "You have a big meet tomorrow, right? My dad mentioned that the recruiter's going to be there."

Just the mention of Mr. Roland made a nervous streak shoot through Emily's gut. "Oh, yeah. Right."

"You shouldn't worry," Chloe said. "You're going to be great. And you're going to get that scholarship. I can feel it."

"Thanks." Emily nudged her with her hip. "Why don't you come, too? I'd love the moral support."

Chloe's face fell. "I have to babysit tomorrow."

Then, a sharp bleating sound pierced the air. Chloe pulled out her phone and looked at the screen. "I've gotta go. My mom's actually home in time to make dinner tonight."

They both walked back to their cars. Chloe's headlights flickered as she unlocked the doors. After turning on the engine, she leaned out the window and peered at Emily. "Wanna come over after your swim meet? I'd love to hear how it goes."

"Definitely," Emily said.

Chloe pulled out of the space. Emily remained there for a moment, her hands shoved deep in her pockets. Just as she was about to unlock her door, she noticed something tucked under her windshield wiper. Her boots slipped on the icy ground as she groped toward it and yanked it free.

It was a picture, printed on copier paper, probably originally taken with a camera phone. Two girls danced together, one of them holding her arm out to take the photo. As Emily squinted, she realized she was staring at her own image. She wore a top that said MERCI BEAUCOUP, and her skin looked pale and drawn. Behind her were flaming tiki torches, swaying palms, and a familiar wood bar with a cerulean-tiled backsplash.

Jamaica.

Then Emily looked at the other girl, the one who'd taken the photo. The breath left her body. It was Tabitha. This was the picture she'd snapped during their one and only dance.

Crack. Another twig snapped in the woods. Emily peered at the bridge, her heart pounding.

Then she turned the photo over. There was writing scribbled across the center. It matched the script from the postcard they'd found in Ali's mailbox. Emily's mouth fell open as she read the words.

Is this proof enough? –A

23

WHATEVER MEANS NECESSARY

"There she is!" Mr. Marin opened his arms wide when Hanna stepped into the atrium in the bottom level of the office building where her dad was holding a campaign fund-raising party. "My inspiration! The public's new darling!"

Several guests turned and smiled as Mr. Marin embraced Hanna tightly, squishing her face against his wool suit. "My daughter's been through a lot, but she's a beacon of how people can change. How *Pennsylvania* can change. And how *we* can make that happen."

Finally, he released her, giving Hanna a thrilled grin. Hanna's smile was wobbly at best. In forty-eight hours, her dad might know the truth about her—in more ways than one.

How was she supposed to come up with $10,000? And even if she found a way to pay off Patrick, how could she stop A?

Hanna pulled out her phone and started to type a text to Mike. *You were right about Patrick. I miss you. Please call me.*

As she hit SEND, she noticed someone was bustling up the walk. Hanna narrowed her eyes at the bright blue Rosewood Day Swimming anorak. Was that Emily?

"I'll be back in a sec," she told her dad, who had turned to speak to a man in a tailored black suit. Hanna burst out of the atrium and into the frigid outdoors. Emily's reddish-gold hair was wild around her face, and her clear green eyes looked red-rimmed. "I had to talk to you," Emily said, noticing Hanna. "And you keep hanging up on me, so I figured this was the only way."

"How did you know I'd be here?" Hanna demanded, hands on hips.

Emily rolled her eyes. "You posted it all over Facebook. You'd think with A running loose you'd be a bit more secretive about your whereabouts. Or do you still not believe it's real?"

Hanna turned away. "I don't know what to think."

"So you've gotten notes, too?"

An older couple passed them and pushed through the atrium doors. In the middle of the big room, Hanna's father shook hands and slapped backs. This was way too public of a place to be talking about A. She pulled Emily farther down the path and lowered her voice. "I already told you I've been getting notes."

"Someone knows, Hanna." Emily's voice cracked. "A sent me a photo of me and . . . *her.*"

"What do you mean?"

Emily pulled out the picture and shoved it in Hanna's face. Sure enough, it was from Jamaica. "Who could have gotten this? Who knows?"

"It's her, Hanna. Tabitha. *Ali.*"

"But that's impossible!" Hanna cried. "We—"

Emily cut her off. "All of my notes so far have sounded exactly like something Ali might write. In one of them, she even called me *Killer.*"

Hanna stared into the middle distance. Of course her notes reminded her of Ali. "It's not possible."

"Yes it is," Emily insisted, sounding angry. "And you know it. Think about what happened. What we did. What we saw—or *didn't* see."

Hanna opened her mouth, then shut it again. If she allowed herself to talk or think about Jamaica, Tabitha's awful voice would invade her head again.

But it was already too late. Visions swarmed into Hanna's mind like an invasion of ants at a picnic. That awful night, after Tabitha hinted that she knew Hanna used to be a chubby, ugly loser, Spencer and Emily ran toward her, worry on their faces. "We need to talk," Spencer said. "That girl that Emily saw on the landing? There's something weird about her."

"I know," Hanna said.

They found Aria alone at the bar. She'd met Tabitha, too, she said, but she still didn't believe she was Ali. "It has to be a coincidence," she said.

"It's not," Emily urged.

The three of them dragged Aria up to the room she and Emily were sharing and triple-locked the doors. Then, one by one, each of them shared the eerie, Ali-like experience they'd had with Tabitha. With each tale, Hanna's heart galloped faster and faster.

Aria frowned, still skeptical. "There has to be a logical explanation. How can she know things only Ali knows, say things only Ali says?"

"Because she's Ali," Emily insisted. "She's back. Just . . . different. You saw the scars."

Aria blinked. "So you're saying she *didn't* die in the fire?"

"I guess not." Emily shut her eyes, guilt washing over her again. She swallowed it down. "I guess she escaped from the house."

The room went silent. There was a loud *thump* from one of the upper floors; it sounded like kids were wrestling in their rooms. Aria cleared her throat. "But what about her family? Who's been supporting her? How did she *get* here?"

"Maybe they don't know she's alive," Emily whispered. "Maybe she's gone rogue."

"But if this *is* Ali, she had major reconstructive surgery," Aria pointed out. "You said so yourself, Em. Do you really think she got through *all that* on her own? How did she pay for it?"

"It's Ali we're talking about." Hanna hugged a pillow tight. "I wouldn't put anything past her."

Unspoken questions floated almost palpably through the air: What if Ali had deliberately followed them to Jamaica? What if she was planning to finish the job she'd started in the Poconos? What should they do?

A muffled, scratching sound made them turn. There, on the carpet just inside the door, was a folded-up piece of resort stationery. Someone had clearly just slipped it into the room.

Spencer leapt up and grabbed it. The girls gathered around and read it together. *Hey girls! Meet me on the crow's nest in ten minutes. I want to show you something. Tabitha.*

An Amtrak train across Route 30 clanged past, breaking Hanna from the memory. She pinched the bridge of her nose and looked at Emily. "Do you think Wilden would believe us?"

"I heard he isn't a cop anymore." Emily rubbed her hands up and down her arms, shivering. "And could you see his face if we told him we were being tortured by a dead girl? And anyway, if we tell anyone, A would tell what we did. And we can't have that, Hanna. We *can't.*"

"I know," Hanna said softly, her heart thudding hard.

The door to the atrium whooshed open, bringing with it a rush of party noise. Jeremiah stepped out, spied Hanna, and stormed toward her, his face twisted into a scowl. "What are you doing out here? And who's this?" He glared at Emily like she was a spy.

"A friend," Hanna snapped.

"The friend who wrote *this*?" Jeremiah waved his iPad

in Hanna's face. On the screen was an email message. *Hanna's gotten into all kinds of trouble lately! Better ask her about it before the reporters do.* The sender's return address was a nonsensical jumble of letters and numbers.

"Oh my God," Emily whispered, reading the message over Hanna's shoulder.

Jeremiah eyed her. "Do you know what this is about?"

"No," Emily and Hanna stammered together. Which was the truth, at least for Hanna. She didn't know *which* horrible thing it was about: what happened in Jamaica, or what happened with Patrick.

Jeremiah's nostrils flared. He stuffed the iPad back into his man-purse. The flap gaped, giving Hanna a glimpse of a pack of Marlboro Lights and the gray pouch that contained the campaign's petty cash. "Out with it, Hanna. Do you have anything to tell me?"

"I said no," Hanna answered quickly.

"Are you sure? It's better I know before anyone else does."

"For the last time, *no*."

A roar of laughter rose from the atrium. Jeremiah gave Hanna and Emily another withering glance. "Whatever this is, you'd better clear it up before the press gets wind of it. I *knew* you shouldn't have set foot anywhere near this campaign. If it were up to me, you wouldn't be around at all."

Then he stalked away, marching through the atrium to the elevator at the back of the room. Hanna covered her face with her hands.

Emily touched her shoulder. "Hanna, this is getting worse. If we don't do anything, A's going to ruin your dad's campaign! Not to mention our *lives*! We'll go to jail!"

"We don't know if that note's from A," Hanna mumbled.

"Who else would it be from?"

Hanna watched Jeremiah get into the elevator. The lighted display above the car stopped on the third floor, where Mr. Marin's campaign office was. The gray pouch inside his man-purse suddenly flashed through her mind. She peeked at her phone. Mike hadn't written back. Then she set her jaw grimly. She might not be able to control A, but maybe there was a solution to Patrick.

She smoothed down her hair and looked at Emily. "You should go home. I'll handle this."

Emily wrinkled her nose. "*How?*"

"Just go, okay?" Hanna nudged Emily toward the parking lot. "I'll call you later. Get home safe, okay?"

"But . . ."

Hanna went back into the atrium—she didn't want to hear any more of Emily's protests. Ducking her head, she slithered covertly around the edge of the room. People stood at the buffet line, helping themselves to ostrich burgers and caprese salads. Kate flirted with Joseph, one of Mr. Marin's younger aides. Isabel and Hanna's father were yukking it up with a big donor who'd promised to back him for the election. No one noticed as Hanna slipped through the heavy door to the stairwell.

She climbed three flights, her spiky heels ringing out on the concrete treads. At her dad's floor, she pushed open the door to the hall and spotted Jeremiah's balding head just outside her father's office. He was talking heatedly to someone on his Droid. *Come on, come on*, Hanna urged silently. Finally, Jeremiah hung up, pressed through the double doors, and stabbed the DOWN elevator button.

Hanna flattened herself against the wall and held her breath, praying he wouldn't see her. As Jeremiah waited, he rummaged through his suit pants pockets, pulling out receipts and other little slips of paper. An object clunked to the carpet, but he didn't notice.

Ding. The elevator doors slid open, and Jeremiah stepped inside. As soon as the doors closed, Hanna stepped forward, eyeing the shiny object he'd dropped. It was a silver money clip with the initials *JPO*. Everything was falling into place even better than she'd imagined. She scooped it up with the cuff of her coat sleeve over her fingers and pushed into her father's office.

The room smelled like Jeremiah's overpowering cologne. Red, white, and blue posters that said TOM MARIN, PA SENATOR lined the walls. Someone had left a half-eaten Italian sub in one of the cubicles, and a copy of the *Philadelphia Sentinel* lay facedown on one of the black leather couches in the corner.

Hanna tiptoed to her father's separate quarters. The green banker's lamp was still on. Next to a phone was a Tiffany-framed picture from Mr. Marin and Isabel's wedding. Kate stood in front of the newlyweds, and Hanna stood slightly off to the side, like they hadn't intended for her to be in the photo. She wasn't even looking directly at the camera.

Looking around frantically, she spied a small, gray safe wedged in the corner by the window. She knew she'd seen it the night of the screening; it had to be where Jeremiah deposited the petty cash funds. She darted toward it and crouched down. The safe was the kind used in hotel rooms where you had to punch a four-digit code into a keypad. Looking around, she grabbed a tissue from a box on her dad's desk so she wouldn't leave prints. First, she tried November 4th, the date of next year's election, but two big angry red lights blinked in her face. What about 1-2-3-4? More angry red lights. 1-7-7-6, to be patriotic and Founding Father–esque? Nothing.

Creak. Hanna shot up, staring crazily at the door. Was it Jeremiah, back for his money clip? There were no shadows through the frosted glass, though. Another *creak* sounded from the opposite direction. She whipped around and stared at her reflection in the darkened window. Her eyes were wide and huge, and her face was pale.

"H-hello?" she called out. "I-is someone here?"

Snow fell lightly on the sidewalk out the window. Across the street, a parked car idled, its headlights blazing. A figure sat in shadows in the driver's seat. Was Hanna crazy, or was the person's head arced up toward her father's office, staring right at her?

Taking a deep breath, she crouched down and assessed the safe again. The combination had to be something she knew. The photo from the wedding on her dad's desk caught her eye again. With shaking hands, she punched Isabel's birthday. Red lights. Gulping hard, she typed in her own birthday, December 23. Red lights. She glared at Kate's smiling photo once more, then keyed 0-6-1-9–June 19, Kate's birthday.

Click.

The lights turned green. The barrel released and the door swung open. Hanna was filled with a moment of horrible hurt—of *course* he'd set the combination to Kate's birthday—but she forgot about it when she saw the piles of bills stacked in tall, neat piles. She pulled out a wad and counted it. Three more wads made it ten thousand exactly. There was so much more money in the safe; she wondered if her father would even miss it.

She shoved the cash in her bag and pushed the safe door closed. Then, as the final coup de grace, she dropped Jeremiah's money clip a few inches away.

Her head spun as she stood. The money felt like it weighed a thousand pounds in her bag. She peered out the window again. The car still idled there, the driver motionless in the front seat. Did the person see her? Was it A?

A moment later, the engine revved. And then, noiselessly, the car pulled away, the tire tracks making crisp indents in the otherwise pure dusting of snow.

24

EVERY GUY'S FANTASY

A waitress set a mug of hot chocolate on the table in front of Aria and clucked her tongue. "Wow. You look *cold*."

"You think?" Aria muttered sarcastically, pressing her hands to the warm mug and willing the waitress to go away. Coldness was exactly why Aria was sitting as close to the fire inside the ski lodge as she could—in fact, she'd climb *into* the fire if she could. Outside, as the snow swirled past the huge overhead lights, tons of skiers zoomed down the slopes, not looking chilly in the slightest. Guys slalomed without hats on. Girls snowboarded in Fair Isle sweaters and jeans. Then again, they probably hadn't spent hours on their butt, the cold snow soaking through their supposedly high-tech ski gear straight to their sensitive, non-skier skin. Aria was pretty sure even her eyelids were frostbitten.

The evening had been miserable. After Klaudia took off up the lift without Aria, Noel shrugged. "Maybe you're better off getting a lesson from a real instructor anyway."

Then he deposited Aria at the Ski School and disappeared up the same black diamond slope himself.

Honestly, Aria wasn't sure why she hadn't just called it a day right then and there, but she'd somehow had this notion that skiing might be easy; maybe she could quickly learn and join Noel on the hill. *Right.* The beginner lesson was filled with seven- and eight-year-old children. The instructor, a good-natured Australian guy named Connor who kept assuming Aria was one of the kids' nannies, led them to the bunny slope and taught them how to snowplow. Needless to say, every single one of the kids mastered it way before Aria did. The only time she made it down the bunny slope was when she'd slid down on her butt. Occasionally, she saw Noel and Klaudia swooping by, kicking up lots of snow when they stopped at the bottom of the hill. Neither of them looked in the direction of the bunny slope. Why would they? Why would they want to check to see how the *peikko* was doing?

"There you are!"

Aria looked up just as Noel clomped into the lodge, snow and ice caked on his jacket and ski pants. Klaudia followed him, her cheeks pink and her blond hair still perfectly styled. They both looked breathless and happily exhausted, like they'd just had tons of sex. Aria quickly bit the inside of her cheek and turned away.

Noel's two brothers, Eric and Christopher, staggered in behind them. "You were amazing out there, Klaudia!" Eric cried when he saw her. "How long have you been skiing?"

"Oh, I *hiihto* before I walk!" Klaudia unzipped her coat.

"Did you guys see her on the moguls?" Noel removed his hat and goggles. "She got amazing air. Everyone on the lifts was cheering like we were at the Olympics."

"It was good mountain." Klaudia admitted. "A little easy, maybe, but still fun."

Aria let out a sarcastic snort, which made everyone stop and stare. Noel walked over and sat down in the studded leather chair next to Aria. "Hey."

"Hey." Aria answered in a monotone, staring at her pruned hands. They'd probably never go back to normal.

"Where did you disappear to?" Noel asked. "I kept looking for you on the slopes but didn't see you. I figured we'd meet up on the top of the mountain after Ski School."

Aria wanted to dump the hot chocolate on his head. "Sorry, but Ski School didn't teach me to ski moguls. But I hope you and *Klaudia* had a good time." She hated her tone of voice, but she couldn't hide her feelings any longer.

A crinkle appeared between Noel's eyes. "*You* were the one who didn't want her to give you a lesson. Don't be mad because she went off and did her own thing."

Aria balled up her fists. Of course this was her fault—Klaudia was totally blameless.

"Hey, do you guys know what time it is?" Christopher interrupted. "Hot tub!"

"*Sweet!*" Eric gave his brother a high five.

"I love *poreammeita!*" Klaudia jumped up and down like a kindergartner.

Noel looked at Aria. "What do you say? A soak in the hot tub before dinner? You'll love it. I promise."

Aria stared at the melting marshmallows in her hot chocolate. The sulking, pissed-off girl inside her just wanted to go upstairs, take a long shower, and watch a foreign film on pay-per-view. But she *was* freezing. Maybe a soak in the hot tub would melt away her irritation, too.

Fifteen minutes later, Aria had changed into her bikini and wrapped herself in one of the lodge's terry-cloth bathrobes. She scampered across the freezing outdoor pool deck to the hot tub. Steam rose high into the air. The jets bubbled. The Kahn brothers were already soaking and drinking bottles of beer. When Noel saw Aria, he moved over to make space. She stripped off her robe, shivered in the subzero air, and slipped into the tub next to him. *Ahhh.*

"This is beautiful." Aria tilted her head up to the sky. Tons of stars twinkled brightly. The moon blazed just over the mountain. The glistening, falling snow on the mountain looked like a scene inside a snow globe.

"Told you you'd like it." Noel squeezed her hand.

Eric Kahn leaned back and stretched his arms out on the deck. "I can't wait to hit the slopes tomorrow morning."

"I heard Klaudia say she's really eager to go back out, too," Noel said.

"That girl could really carve," Christopher murmured. "I wonder what *else* she's good at."

The older Kahn brothers snickered crassly. Aria stiffened and stared hard at Noel, daring him to laugh too. Luckily, he didn't.

Then, as if on cue, the door from the hotel opened. A figure appeared in silhouette. "Hallo?" Klaudia's chirpy voice pierced the snowy air.

"Hey!" Eric yelled for Klaudia. "Come on in! The water's awesome!"

Klaudia pranced over to the tub. She wore a similar bathrobe to Aria's, the belt knotted tightly around her waist. Her blond hair spilled over her shoulders. Her bare legs protruded beneath the hem. The Kahn boys watched her, their tongues lolling like dogs. Then, slowly, like she was performing a striptease, Klaudia undid the belt to her robe. It dropped to the floor. She shrugged out of the robe and let it fall, too. Noel gasped. So did Eric. For a moment, Aria's eyes couldn't focus—all she could see was skin, lots of skin, like Klaudia had worn a flesh-colored bikini.

But then she realized. Klaudia wasn't wearing anything at *all*. She was totally and completely naked.

"Holy shit," Christopher blurted emphatically and appreciatively.

"Whoa." Eric groaned softly.

Noel gawked at her, too. Klaudia just stood there like a freaky Finnish exhibitionist, her boobs swinging for the whole world to see. Not a single one of the Kahns told her to cover up. Why would they?

It was just too much. Letting out a pent-up scream, Aria pushed out of the tub, grabbed a towel, and ran for the door, barely feeling the frigid air on her skin or the icy concrete beneath her feet. Once inside, she wrapped the towel around her, staggered toward the elevators, and pressed the call button repeatedly. Of course this would be the one time the elevator decided to stop on every floor.

"Ahem."

Aria jumped and turned. Noel stood in the doorway, steam misting off his half-naked body. There was a trail of wet footprints from where he'd come in. "Where are you going?"

Aria pressed the call button again. "To my room."

"Shouldn't you apologize first?"

She whipped around. "To *who*?"

"Klaudia didn't do anything wrong, Aria."

She gawked at him. "Are you *kidding* me?"

Noel just shrugged.

It felt like a billion blood vessels just burst in Aria's brain. "Okay. *Okay*. Whatever. If you want to have your little foursome with Klaudia, that's fine. But not in front of me, okay? I didn't think I actually had to *watch*."

Finally, the elevator dinged and the doors slid open. Aria marched inside, but Noel pulled her back out. His green eyes were full of hurt. "Aria, Klaudia's crying out there. She didn't realize she was supposed to wear a bathing suit in the hot tub. In Finland, nobody does! Guys go naked in hot tubs. Girls go naked in hot tubs. They're not as prudish about it as we are. You shouldn't have screamed at her—I would think that you of all people would understand the meaning of cultural sensitivity."

Aria wrenched her arm from his. "Cultural sensitivity? Noel, Klaudia showing up naked at the hot tub isn't a cultural thing—it's a *slutty* thing!"

Noel's mouth dropped open. He closed his eyes and shook his head like he didn't believe her. Like he thought she was just being a jealous bitch.

The elevator doors started to slide closed again, but Aria thrust her foot between them and caught them. "Klaudia wants you, Noel," she said icily. "And if you weren't so smitten with her, you'd notice she's being really obvious about it, too."

She stepped inside the elevator doors and pressed down hard on the CLOSE button. Part of her hoped Noel would step inside and ride up with her, but he just stood in the vestibule, blinking at her, his face full of disappointment. With a *whoosh*, the doors closed, and in moments the car swept Aria up to her floor. Where Noel went after that, she didn't know.

And she tried to fool herself into believing she didn't care.

25

ONE BIG HAPPY FAMILY

At 8 P.M. sharp, Spencer, Zach, and Amelia passed under the green-and-white awning of Smith and Wollensky, the upscale steakhouse on Third Avenue, and swished through the brass-handled double doors.

The bar area was six people deep, and everyone was shouting. Businessmen sat at giant oak tables eating rib eyes and juicy burgers the size of their heads. Trophy wives sipped martinis and winked flirtatiously at the white-coated Irish guys pouring goblet-sized glasses of wine behind the bar. The air smelled like testosterone and meat.

"Leave it to my dad to pick somewhere über-masculine," Zach mused in Spencer's ear as a hostess guided them around the crowded dining room to where their parents were waiting. "Do you really think your mom finds this place romantic?"

Spencer doubted it, but she pinched his arm. "Now,

now. We need to be on our best behavior, remember?"

Zach raised a brow. "Actually, I propose we be on our *worst* behavior."

"Oh? What are you thinking?"

"Drinking game." Zach's eyes sparkled. He reached into his bag and showed Spencer the very tip of a stainless steel flask. "It's filled with Absolut Kurant."

"Naughty boy!" Spencer whispered. "I'm in. Here's my rule: Every time my mom fusses over your dad, we take a drink."

"Deal. And every time my dad acts like a big shot, we drink."

Spencer snorted. "We'll be loaded before the food arrives."

Zach raised his eyebrow. "Isn't that the idea?"

Tingles shot up Spencer's back. After their provocative moment in the dressing room, Zach had been even more touchy-feely than ever, brushing his hand up against Spencer's waist and giving her unprompted hand-squeezes whenever Amelia emerged in a particularly fabulous outfit. When they'd passed Cartier on the walk down to Saks, he'd even grabbed Spencer's hand and asked if she wanted to go inside—he'd buy her something. "Only if it's a platinum love ring," she teased. That had made Amelia give them both a sickened look and walk several paces ahead of them for the rest of the afternoon.

Mrs. Hastings waved at the three of them as they approached the table. Mr. Pennythistle sat on her right.

Both were dressed in opera regalia, Mr. Pennythistle in a tuxedo, and Spencer's mother in a beaded gown that clung snugly to her thin frame. An opened bottle of red wine already sat on the table, along with a platter of fried calamari. As they sat down, Mrs. Hastings made up a plate for Mr. Pennythistle. "I know you hate the ones with the tentacles," she said in a motherly voice as she placed it in front of him.

"Thank you, dear," Mr. Pennythistle said, picking up his knife and fork.

Spencer and Zach exchanged a glance, nearly bursting out laughing over the word *tentacles*. Zach covertly reached for his flask and poured some into his and Spencer's glasses of sparkling water. They both took a big sip.

"So what did you kids do today?" Mrs. Hastings dipped a piece of calamari into the bowl of marinara sauce.

"Oh, we did the New York tourist thing," Spencer said. "Saks, Bendel's, Barneys. Amelia got a lot of great clothes."

"Oh, those stores are lovely," Mrs. Hastings sighed wistfully.

Mr. Pennythistle's forehead wrinkled. "You didn't go to any museums? You didn't visit the stock exchange?"

Amelia clamped her mouth shut. Zach wilted in his seat. Mr. Pennythistle shoved a calamari into his mouth with gusto. "What about the tour of Carnegie Hall I arranged for you, Amelia? I had to pull major strings to get that."

"I'll go tomorrow, Daddy," Amelia piped up quickly. *Suck-up*.

"Good." Mr. Pennythistle nodded, then glanced at Zach. "And are you telling me you didn't meet with Douglas?"

Spencer glanced at Zach—she'd forgotten about his meeting with the Harvard admissions guy. Zach shrugged. "I didn't feel like it."

Mr. Pennythistle blinked hard. "But he was waiting for your call." He pulled out his BlackBerry. "I'll see if he can meet with you tomorrow morning . . ."

It looked like Zach was going to explode. "You know, not all of us want to go to Harvard, Dad."

Mr. Pennythistle's mouth dropped open slightly. "But . . . you'll *love* it at Harvard, Zachary. Some of my best memories are from my time there."

"It *is* a lovely school," Mrs. Hastings chimed in. Mr. Pennythistle squeezed her hand gratefully.

But Zach folded his hands on top of the table, unblinking. "I'm not *you*, Dad. Maybe I want other things."

Mr. Pennythistle looked like he was going to say something else, but Mrs. Hastings quickly interrupted. "Now, now, let's not fight!" She pushed the plate of calamari over to Zach like it was consolation. "We're all having such a nice time in New York. Let's just keep it that way."

A *ping* sounded from Mr. Pennythistle's phone. "Ah," he said, studying the screen. "Douglas can meet you at ten A.M. tomorrow. Problem solved."

A waiter approached to take their orders. Spencer turned to Zach. "Are you okay?"

Zach's jaw muscle twitched. Patches of red bloomed on his neck and cheeks. "Everything I say to him goes in one ear and out the other."

"I'm sorry."

Zach shrugged and covertly added more vodka to their waters. "Story of my life. But listen, we have some catching up to do. My dad was totally throwing his weight around."

"We need to take at least five drinks, by my count," Spencer whispered.

There were plenty more drinking opportunities after that, too. Once they ordered, the conversation turned to Mr. Pennythistle and how he was such a loyal Smith and Wollensky customer that they'd put his name on a brass plaque on the wall—*drink, drink, drink.* When the food came, Mrs. Hastings scrambled to procure steak sauce for Mr. Pennythistle's T-bone, mayo for his fries, and the wine list so he could choose another bottle—*drink, drink, drink.* Spencer was so dizzy with vodka that she barely tasted her filet—she wasn't even sure why she'd ordered it. Zach kept bursting out laughing at random intervals. Amelia stared suspiciously at them from across the table but didn't say a word. She hadn't been this wasted since . . . well, since this past summer. But she closed off that part of her mind before she could think too carefully about that.

As the dinner progressed, Zach's father and Spencer's mother moved closer and closer to each other until they were practically in each other's laps. Mr. Pennythistle fed Mrs. Hastings a bite of creamed spinach. Mrs. Hastings wiped a dab of steak juice off Mr. Pennythistle's cheek. Admittedly, Spencer hadn't seen her mom look this happy in a long time—she and Spencer's father weren't very touchy-feely. Spencer and Zach had moved closer to one another, too, their feet bumping under the table, their hands touching as they drained Zach's flask.

When the waitress brought giant slabs of cheesecake for dessert, Mr. Pennythistle clanged his fork against his glass. "Well, kids, I have an announcement to make." He looked around the table. "We meant to keep this a secret until tomorrow, but we might as well tell you now." He took Spencer's mother's hand. "I've asked Veronica to marry me. And she's said yes."

Spencer stared at her mother, who was unveiling a Tiffany jewelry box from her purse. The box creaked as it opened, revealing an enormous diamond ring. "Wow." Spencer breathed, always feeling a little cowed by diamonds. "Congratulations, Mom."

"Thanks!" Mrs. Hastings slid the ring on her finger. "We broke the news to Melissa before you guys arrived. She wants us to have the ceremony at the townhouse, but I'm thinking of something a little more fabulous."

"When are you getting married?" Zach asked tentatively.

"We think the wedding will be in a few months," Mr. Pennythistle said, his cheeks pink with pride.

"Perhaps a destination wedding, we haven't decided,"

Mrs. Hastings added. "But for now, I've asked Nicholas if he'd move into the house with us, Spencer. Amelia and Zach will be your stepsiblings pretty soon—you might as well get used to one another."

Amelia let out a note of horror, but Spencer and Zach turned to each other and drunkenly grinned. "Hey, *bro*," Spencer joked, punching Zach on the shoulder.

"Nice to meet you, *sis*," Zach said back in an utterly *un*brotherly voice. He hid his hand under the table, entwined it with Spencer's, and squeezed hard.

"This definitely calls for a toast." Mrs. Hastings flagged down the waiter. "I suppose the kids can have a glass of champagne, don't you think, Nicholas?"

"Just this once," Mr. Pennythistle demurred.

"A round of champagne for the table!" Mrs. Hastings trilled. Flutes arrived right away.

Spencer and Zach glanced at one another once more, daring the other not to laugh. "Cheers!" they both cried. They knocked their flutes together and drank them down.

Spencer's mother and Zach's father were off to the Met after dinner, so they bid their kids goodnight at the escalators at the Hudson. Amelia retreated to her room immediately, but Spencer and Zach took their time, giggling about the hotel's faux-minimalist décor and the ubiquitous techno music.

Their rooms were right next to each other, and they unlocked their doors with keycards in unison. "Holy shit,"

Spencer said when she opened her door. "It's like a Japanese sleeping pod!" A porter had brought up her stuff earlier today, so she hadn't been inside the room until now. The whole thing was the size of her family's first-floor powder room.

"A hobbit should live here," Zach called from his doorway. "Dad really pulled out all the stops for us."

Spencer joined him in his room. It was the same as hers—the bed barely fit in the tiny nook the hotel called a bedroom. "And look at the bathroom!" she cried, wedging herself into the minuscule space. "How does someone fit on this toilet?"

"At least the bed's comfy," Zach called from five feet away. He kicked off his shoes and started bouncing. "Come jump with me, *sis*."

Spencer removed her stilettos and climbed up on the bed. Manhattan blinked at them out the huge picture window. "If you call me sis one more time I'll kick your ass."

Zach kept bouncing. "You don't look like you can kick anything."

"Oh yeah?" Spencer leapt up on the bed and tackled him, pushing him to the mattress and wrapping her arms around his head. Zach pushed her off easily, flipping her around so that he was on top of her. He hovered over her for a moment, his longish hair hanging in his face, his mouth twisted into a messy grin, and then he tickled her stomach.

"No!" Spencer flailed. "Stop it! Please!"

"This is what brothers do!" Zach chanted. "Get used to it!"

"I'll kill you!" Spencer screamed, giggling uncontrollably.

"You're laughing!" Zach whooped. "That means you like it!"

But then he stopped, slumping down on the mattress and propping his head on his arm. "You are so evil," Spencer whispered, panting hard. "But I like you anyway."

"Would you like me even if I didn't go to Harvard?" Zach asked.

Spencer blew air out of her cheeks. "That school is for losers."

"Would you like me if I was gay?" Zach's long-lashed eyes were very wide.

Spencer blinked at him. "*Are* you?"

Zach's lips parted. His eyes shifted to the right. He moved closer to her without answering. All of a sudden, he was kissing her softly on the lips. Spencer shut her eyes, tasting vodka and steak sauce. But the kiss was more friendly than romantic, more drunken and hyped-up than truly lustful. Spencer thought she'd feel disappointed, but she was surprised to find she didn't care. Zach had a lot of figuring out to do. Maybe Spencer should help him through it, not confuse him even more.

They broke apart, smiling at each other without having to say a word. "Want to snuggle?" Spencer asked.

"Sure," Zach said. And then he wrapped his arms around her, pulling her tightly to him. It immediately calmed Spencer, and in moments, she fell into a deep, blissful sleep.

26

THINGS GET STEAMY AT THE POOL

Emily stroked hard, dolphin-kicking with all her might. The blurry pool wall loomed just ahead, and she lunged for the electronic timing pad on the wall. When she turned around, everyone else was still finishing their race. *Yes.* She'd won. And when she glanced at her time on the clock, she saw it was four tenths of a second faster than last year's best.

Amazing.

"Congratulations," one of the judges said as Emily climbed out. "You almost beat the course record."

Raymond, her coach, barreled over to her and gave her a big hug, not even caring that she was soaking wet. "Outstanding for your first meet back!" he whooped. "I knew you had it in you!"

Emily peeled off her goggles and cap, her muscles throbbing and her heart still thudding hard. The crowd cheered. The other competitors climbed out of the pool and glared enviously at her. Various teammates slapped her on the back as she returned to her gear and towels. "Awesome!" said a girl named Tori Barnes, who Emily had been BFF with one summer in second grade. "They ate your wake," added Jacob O'Reilly, Tori's boyfriend, who'd crushed on Emily during swim season in fourth grade and put a gumball machine diamond ring in her locker.

Emily grinned back at them, dropping her goggles by her gear bag. She'd forgotten how good it felt to win a race. But she wanted to share the special moment with someone . . . well, *special,* and the kids on the team didn't quite suffice. Rummaging through her bag, she found her phone and composed a new text to Chloe. *Just won my race! So excited to hang out tonite!* Emily couldn't wait to celebrate—non-alcoholically, of course.

"Emily?"

A man in a University of North Carolina sweatshirt wove through the knot of swimmers. He had a clean-shaven face, crinkly blue eyes, thinning brown hair, and carried a leather-bound clipboard and a video camera. Mr. Roland walked beside him. Mixed feelings instantly filled Emily. As much as she wanted to see the recruiter, she wished Mr. Roland wouldn't have come with him.

"Emily, this is Marc Lowry from the University of North Carolina," Mr. Roland said.

"Nice to meet you." Emily shook his hand.

"Nice to meet *you*," Mr. Lowry answered. "Amazing race. Great stroke. You show real promise."

"Thanks."

"Mr. Lowry has some news for you," Mr. Roland announced. "Can you talk with us in private?"

He gestured toward the small, empty room off the pool that the team used for dry land practice. Emily followed them through the doors. A Pilates machine sat in the corner, a box of medicine balls and resistance bands in another. A spilled puddle of something neon-yellow, Gatorade probably, welled by the door. An empty wrapper that had once contained a Speedo swim cap lay abandoned by the fogged-up window.

Mr. Lowry let his clipboard fall to his side and studied Emily. "Based on your times and your performance both today and the past four years, we'd like to offer you a full scholarship to our school."

Emily clapped her hands over her mouth. "*Really?*"

Mr. Lowry nodded. "It's not a done deal yet—we'll have to interview you, review your transcripts, all of that. And Henry said you took some time off last year because of the Alison DiLaurentis incident, correct?"

"That's right," Emily said. "But I'm fully committed to swimming now. I promise."

"Great." When Mr. Lowry smiled, Emily could see a gold filling in the back of his mouth. "Well, I'd better get going—I have a couple other kids in the area to speak to. We'll be in touch early this week. Definitely celebrate, though. This is huge."

"Thank you so much," Emily said, trembling with hap-

piness. Then Mr. Lowry turned on his heel and marched
back through the door. Emily expected Mr. Roland to follow him, but he didn't. His eyes were on Emily.

"Amazing, huh?" he said.

"This is truly, truly, incredible," she answered. "I don't
know how to thank you."

One of Mr. Roland's eyebrows arched. A sly smile
curled across his lips. The harsh fluorescent light made his
skin look ghoulish. Suddenly, Emily felt like one of those
animals in the wild who sensed danger before she saw
it. He inched closer to her, his breath hot on her cheek.
"Well, I have some ideas . . ." His fingers danced lightly
across the skin of her slightly damp arm.

Emily pulled away. "Mr. Roland . . ."

"It's okay," Mr. Roland murmured. His body moved
even closer to her, trapping her against the wall. He
smelled like Head & Shoulders shampoo and Tide laun-
dry detergent, such innocent scents. His fingers slipped
under the straps of her swimsuit. He made a horrible
grunting sound as he pressed against her.

"Stop, please," Emily said, wrenching away.

"What's the matter?" Mr. Roland whispered, covering
her mouth with a kiss. "You were into it on Thursday,
Emily. You kissed me. I felt it."

"But—"

She made a break for the other side of the room, but
Mr. Roland caught her wrist and pulled her back. He kept
pawing at her, kissing her neck, her lips again, her throat.

The starting gun beeped through the door, followed by the splash of swimmers. The crowd roared, oblivious, as Emily struggled to push him off once more.

"Oh my God."

Mr. Roland turned around at the figure who'd appeared in the doorway. Relief burst through Emily at the welcome interruption. But then Mr. Roland's face went eggshell-white. "Ch-Chloe?"

Emily's heart dropped to her feet. Sure enough, Chloe was standing there, a big, hand-lettered poster that said GO, EMILY! pressed against her chest. "Chloe!" Emily cried.

Mr. Roland pushed his hands into his pockets and walked to the other side of the room from Emily, as far away from her as he could get. "I didn't know you were coming, honey. But did you hear about Emily? She got the scholarship!"

Chloe let the poster drop to the tile floor. By the devastated look on her face, it was clear she'd seen everything. "I was going to surprise you," she said tonelessly to Emily. "I saw your race. I saw my dad and that recruiter take you in here to talk to you. And I thought . . ." Her eyes flickered from her father, then back to Emily again. A horrified expression crossed her face. Emily looked down. Her swimsuit strap was halfway off her shoulder. It looked like she *wanted* this.

"Chloe, no!" Emily protested, quickly pulling the strap back up. "This isn't . . . I didn't . . . *he* . . ."

But Chloe backed out of the room, shaking her head

silently. Myriad emotions washed across her face at once—disgust, betrayal, abhorrence. A half sob, half growl emerged from the back of her throat, and she turned and ran.

"Chloe, wait!" Emily cried, barreling out the office door, slipping on the wet floor. "Please!"

But it was too late. Chloe was gone.

27

AHH, VACATION MEMORIES

"Hey, guys!" a voice called softly. "I guess you got my note!"

Hanna stood motionless by the stairs of the crow's nest. Nerves snapped and crackled under her skin. Tabitha, the girl at the end of the roof deck, suddenly looked different. More Ali-like than usual. All of a sudden, she could believe it. Emily was right. It was Ali.

"Come closer, Hanna!" Ali teased, beckoning with one curled finger. "I won't bite!"

Hanna's eyes flew open. Sweat poured down the back of her neck. Her thumb was firmly between her lips. Ever since Jamaica, whenever she felt really scared, she sucked her thumb in her sleep.

She had been thinking of it again. *Dreaming* of it again.

"Hanna?" Her mother knocked on Hanna's bedroom door. "Hanna? Get up!"

Dot, Hanna's miniature Doberman, licked Hanna's face enthusiastically. Hanna peered at the digital clock next to her bed. It was 10 A.M.; normally, Hanna slept until noon on weekends. She sat up and groaned. "Mom, I don't want to do Bikram with you!" Ever since her mom had returned from Singapore last year, she'd been obsessed with doing ninety minutes of intense yoga poses in a 100-degree room on Saturday mornings.

"This isn't about Bikram." Ms. Marin sounded exasperated. "Your father's on the phone. He wants you to meet him at his office. *Now*."

The previous night zinged into Hanna's head. The weight of that stolen money in her bag as she hopped a late SEPTA into the city. Checking her phone over and over again—for a response from Mike, for a note from A—and receiving nothing. Meeting the flower seller, Pete, who had dirt under his fingernails, a tattoo on his neck, and looked at Hanna like he wanted to shove her behind the springy bouquets of tulips and have his way with her. Handing over the envelope of cash. Looking over her shoulder for A, but seeing no one suspicious.

She hadn't felt satisfied just giving the money to Pete, so she'd skulked around the train station until Patrick had shown up, accosting him and demanding that he erase the photos from his camera and hard drive *in front of her*. "Fine," Patrick sighed dramatically, pulling out his camera and laptop. Hanna watched as the photos disappeared from the folder and the camera memory. Before she left, Patrick groped her boob, and she elbowed him in the ribs.

Hopefully, she'd done the right thing. No scantily

clad images of Hanna had appeared on the Internet over-
night. She hadn't received any red-alert phone calls from
Jeremiah, telling her she'd ruined everything. With any
luck, Patrick had taken the first plane to Mexico and
Hanna would never hear from him again.

Ms. Marin shifted her weight in the doorway. "Why is
he bothering you on a weekend?" she asked suspiciously.
"Is this something about the campaign?" She said *campaign* with an eye-roll. Hanna doubted her mom would
be a Tom Marin supporter on voting day. Whenever there
was a mention of him in the paper, she sniffed disapprov-
ingly and quickly turned the page, saying that he'd better
not participate in government the same detached way he
participated in their marriage.

"I don't know," Hanna mumbled. She rose from her
bed, patted Dot's tiny, diamond-shaped head, and stared
at her reflection in the mirror. Her skin looked pale and
puffy. Her lips were cracked at the corners. Her hair was
wild and knotted around her face. Perhaps her dad *was*
summoning her to his office because of his campaign.
Maybe they were doing an impromptu brainstorming session. *Would* they do something like that on a Saturday
morning?

She threw on a pair of Citizens jeans and a Juicy
hoodie and drove to her father's office building. Some
of the campaign posters from last night's party still littered the atrium. The air reeked of catered food and men's
cologne. The elevator dinged loudly in the empty space.

When the doors slid open on the third floor, Hanna was surprised to see that her father's office was lit up like it was a regular workday. Her dad sat on the black leather couch, a mug of coffee in his hands. Hanna pushed through the double doors nervously, trying to keep her knees from knocking together.

Her father looked up when she came in. "Hey, Hanna." He didn't stand. He didn't rush over to hug her. He just sat there, staring.

"Uh, what brings you here so early?" Hanna tried to sound light and joking. "Did another focus group say they loved me?"

Mr. Marin didn't crack a smile. He took a long sip of coffee, then sighed. "There's money missing from my campaign petty cash fund. Someone stole it from my office during the party last night. Ten thousand dollars. I counted it myself."

A gasp slipped out of Hanna's mouth before she could control herself. He kept *that* good a count of the petty cash?

"I know, I know, it's terrible." Mr. Marin shook his head. "But you have to be honest with me, Hanna. Do you know anything about this?"

"No!" Hanna heard herself say. "Of course not!"

Mr. Marin set his coffee on the table next to the couch. "Someone saw you go into the stairwell at the benefit last night. Did you come up here?"

Hanna blinked. "W-who told you that?" Kate? *A?*

Her father looked away, staring out the window. The tracks that creepy car had made in the snow last night were still there. "It doesn't matter. Is it true?"

"I-I *did* come up here," Hanna said, thinking on her feet. "But that was because I saw someone else come up here first. He was acting shady. I wanted to make sure nothing was wrong."

Mr. Marin leaned toward her like he was watching the cliffhanger scene of a thriller movie. "Who did you see?"

A lump formed in Hanna's throat. This was where her whole plan either came together or crashed and burned. "Jeremiah," she whispered.

Her father sat back. Hanna licked her lips and continued, hoping he couldn't hear her heart banging in her chest. "I followed him up here. He didn't see me when he came out. Then I went in after him and looked around. But, Dad, I never imagined he'd actually *steal* from you."

"Why didn't you tell me this last night?"

"Because . . ." Hanna stared at her lap. "I'm sorry. I should have."

She covered her face with her hands. "I'm so, so sorry. I would never take anything from you, Dad. I've been so happy that I've been able to help you . . . that we've bonded. Why would I jeopardize that?"

Tears filled Hanna's eyes. It wasn't just an acting job to garner his sympathy—it was, in so many ways, the truth. In so many ways, she wished she could have just told him about Patrick and that it was an honest mistake—then they could've gone to the police and settled this the right way. But she couldn't bear to think of the disappointment on her dad's face if she told him about the photos—especially not now that she was in his good graces. It would undo everything.

Mr. Marin sighed. When Hanna dared to look, she saw a sad, conflicted expression on his face. "I'm happy we've bonded, too, Hanna," he said quietly. "We haven't done much of that lately."

Then he rose and paced around the room. "Thank you for telling me. I appreciate your honesty. Full disclosure, I found something of Jeremiah's by the safe—something potentially incriminating. He denies everything, of course, but he's no longer part of the team. This is a serious crime."

"Are you going to call the police?" Hanna asked, terrified. She'd figured her dad would just fire Jeremiah and that would be that. Did they really have to get the cops involved? What if they could trace that money to Patrick?

Mr. Marin patted Hanna's shoulder. "Leave that to me, Hanna. But you did the right thing. So thank you."

Then his phone rang, and he told Hanna he'd see her later and darted into his office to take the call. There was nothing more for Hanna to do except leave. The elevator dinged once more, and she stepped inside and slumped against the wall.

As if on cue, her phone buzzed. Hanna pulled it out

and checked the screen. She had a new text . . . and she had a horrible feeling she knew just who it was from.

The past is never far, Hannakins . . . and sometimes it's even closer than you think. –A

"Huh?" Hanna whispered, staring at the screen. Then, just as the elevator began to descend, there was a horrible screeching sound and the car bounced to a stop. She froze. There was no longer that telltale whir of the motor running and the cables moving. The elevator was as silent as a tomb.

Hanna pressed the DOOR OPEN button over and over. Nothing. The LOBBY button. Zip. She pressed every button on the keypad, including the one with the fireman's hat on it. "Hello?" she shouted, hoping that her father might hear her through the shaft. "Help! I'm stuck!"

The lights snapped off.

Hanna shrieked. Only a small stripe of light at the top of the car was visible. "Hey!" she screamed, pounding on the door panels. "Someone! Please!"

But it was the weekend; no one was in the building. Hanna pulled out her phone again and called her father's office number. The cell phone tried to dial out, but because she was in an elevator, the call couldn't connect. She tried her mother's cell, then Spencer's, then Aria's. She dialed 9-1-1. Nothing. *Call lost.*

Beads of sweat stood out on Hanna's forehead. What

if the elevator was stuck for days? What if the building caught fire and she was trapped in here? It was just like being locked in that bedroom in the Poconos when Ali had set fire to the house. Or being caught in the head-lights of Mona's car as Mona-as-A gunned forward and hit her. "Help me!" she screamed. "Help!"

And then, horrifyingly, she heard the voice.

I bet you weren't always pretty, were you?

"No!" Hanna screeched, willing it out of her brain. She couldn't think about it right now. She couldn't let the memory in.

But Tabitha's voice just got louder. *I feel like I've known you girls forever!*

All at once, Hanna could no longer resist. The memo-ries of Jamaica slipped in sideways, longways, folded up and pressed flat. The voices of her friends swarmed in her ears, and suddenly she could clearly see the hotel room at The Cliffs.

"Do you think we should go see what she wants?" Aria held up the note Tabitha had pushed under the door.

"Are you crazy?" Emily stared at her. "That's a death sentence! Ali's setting us up!"

"Em, it's not *Ali*." Aria groaned.

Everyone else shifted awkwardly. "Actually, it really *seems* like Ali," Spencer whispered. "We all think so, Aria. You're the only one who doesn't."

Hanna looked at the note again. "Maybe Aria's right,

though. If we don't go upstairs now, she'll find us another way. She'll get us alone. At least, this way, we'll all be together."

And so they went. Tabitha was waiting for them on the crow's nest, which was a smaller, higher platform atop the roof deck restaurant that was perfect for tanning and stargazing. She sat on one of the chaises, sipping a piña colada. No one else was up there. Tons of potted palms swayed around the space, making the little balcony seem private and way too secluded.

When she saw them, she leapt to her feet, smiling broadly. "Hey, guys! I guess you got my note!"

The smile on her face had been twisted, diabolical. Hanna's gaze drifted to the bracelet on her wrist—just like Emily said, it was an exact match to the one Ali had made for them after the Jenna Thing. It was frayed at the edges, just like Ali's was. And it was that perfect, lake blue they'd all thought was so pretty.

It was Ali. It had to be. All traces of Tabitha were gone, and Hanna could see Ali so clearly it hurt.

Spencer wrapped her hands around the top of an empty chaise longue almost like she was going to use it as a shield. "Why did you want us to come up here?"

"Because I was going to show you something," she said innocently.

Spencer's eyes narrowed like she didn't believe the girl for a minute. "Who *are* you?"

The girl put her hands on her hips and tilted back and

forth teasingly. "Are you drunk, Spencer? My name is Tabitha. I told you that."

"Your name isn't Tabitha," Emily said in a small, terrified voice. "You know things about us. Things no one else could know."

"Maybe I'm psychic," the girl said, shrugging. "And, okay, there's something about all of you I can't quite put my finger on. I feel like I've known you girls forever—but that's impossible, isn't it?" Her eyes sparkled mischievously. Hanna's stomach swooped.

Then the girl fixed her gaze on Hanna, who was still standing by the stairs. "You can come closer, Hanna." She beckoned, curling her finger. "I won't bite. I just want to show you the incredible view. It's amazing from up here."

Hanna clamped her mouth shut, feeling immobile. Then, the girl took a lurching step toward her, seemingly crossing the crow's nest in one step. Her drink sloshed in her glass. Her wide eyes didn't blink. In seconds, she had pinned Hanna to the low wall that surrounded the deck. Up close, she smelled like vanilla soap and rum. When she gazed into Hanna's eyes, she let out another lilting, familiar giggle. Hanna's heart banged. She thought of the times she'd heard Ali's giggle even after Ali had supposedly perished in the Poconos fire. The mornings she'd woken in a cold sweat, sure Ali was after them. Now, it was coming true.

"What do you want from us?" Hanna cried, shielding her face with her hands. "Haven't you taken enough?"

The girl stuck out her bottom lip. "Why are you so afraid of me?"

"You *know* why," Hanna whispered, staring into the girl's crazed eyes. "You're Alison DiLaurentis."

A flicker of something—maybe surprise, maybe amusement—passed across the girl's face. "The *dead* girl?" She pressed her hand to her chest. "The crazy murderer? Now why would you say something horrible like that?"

"Because of everything you've said to us!" Aria said behind Hanna. "Everything you know! A-and because of the burns on your body. Are those from the fire?"

The girl glanced at her burned arms and smiled playfully. "Maybe. But I didn't survive that fire, did I?"

"No one really knows what happened," Emily said shakily. "Everyone thought you died, but . . ."

"But what?" the girl interrupted in a teasing voice, her eyes gleaming. "But I *escaped*? Any ideas how *that* could have happened, Em?"

Emily paled and took a step back. Hanna, Spencer, and Aria glanced at her for a moment, not knowing what the girl was getting at.

Then, the girl advanced toward Hanna. Hanna shrieked and jumped away. "What's the matter?" The girl looked offended. "What do you think I'm going to do?"

"Leave me alone!" Hanna screamed, lurching back. The rough bamboo that lined the walls scraped against her skin. She sensed the open air behind her, the wall giving way to a thirty-foot drop. The ocean crashed far, far below.

"Don't touch her!" Aria ran up to the girl, grabbed her arm, and spun her around. "Didn't you hear her? She wants you to leave her alone!"

"Just tell us who you are, okay?" Spencer called behind Aria. "Just be honest."

A slow smile spread across the girl's face. "You want an honest answer? Okay. I'm Tabitha. And I'm *fabulous.*"

Everyone gasped. Hanna was pretty sure she screamed. Ali always said that.

Tabitha really was Ali.

Ali broke from Aria's grasp and turned for Hanna again. Hanna tried to press against the wall, but her ankle turned and she lost her balance. She wheeled around, face-to-face with the crashing ocean below. With just one push, she'd fall down, down, down . . .

"Help!" Hanna screamed now in the elevator just as she'd screamed then. "Someone help me!"

Suddenly, the lights snapped on again. The car bounced once, throwing Hanna to the ground. The motor began to whir, dragging the car toward the lobby.

The bell dinged. The door opened smoothly at the ground floor, as if nothing had been amiss. Hanna stepped out into the empty atrium, her heart chugging fast, her body both sweating and shivering, and the horrible memories she'd long suppressed now flying around her head like a flock of geese caught inside a shopping mall. It had happened. All of it had happened. A was right—the past was never far away.

Something off to the left caught her eye. A small, gray utilities closet stood slightly open. ELEVATOR, said a sign on the door. Levers, gauges, and switches lined the wall. It certainly hadn't been open when Hanna arrived a half hour ago. In fact, she'd never seen it open before today.

She peered into the room and sniffed. It smelled the slightest bit like vanilla soap. Someone had been in the elevator room, tampering with the controls. And Hanna knew just who it was.

Ali.

WHEN PUSH COMES TO SHOVE

That same morning, Aria pulled on her ski pants, layered on an extra pair of socks and a wooly sweater, strapped on her ski boots, and waddled out to the slopes. The Kahn boys were milling around outside the lodge, gearing up and surveying the latest snowfall. Klaudia sat alone on a green bench, strapping on her skis.

When Noel noticed Aria, a tiny, repentant smile crossed his face. "Hey."

"Hey." Aria crunched over to him.

"You sleep okay?" Noel said in a stilted, overly polite voice.

Aria nodded. "Just fine." Then she turned to Klaudia. "I want to talk to you."

Klaudia glanced at Aria for a split second, then looked away. "I busy."

Aria gritted her teeth. This was going to be harder than

she thought. But she had to talk to Klaudia. She'd come to a decision.

After she'd gone up to her room last night, she'd had horrible waking nightmares of the Kahn boys having their way with Klaudia in the tub. She'd picked up her phone a million times, daring herself to compose an *It's over* text to Noel, but she kept putting it down, something inside her not quite ready.

Then, about forty-five minutes later, she'd heard footsteps in the hallway and ran to the peephole and looked out. Noel plunged the keycard into his room across the hall. He was alone. There was no sign of his brothers or Klaudia. And then, five minutes later, a text appeared on Aria's phone: *Good night. See you tomorrow. XX, Noel.*

Nothing had happened between Noel and Klaudia. The jealousy that had been present in Aria ever since she was friends with Ali was eating her alive. It had almost destroyed her relationship with Noel once; she couldn't let it happen again. Klaudia was going to be living with the Kahns until June. If Aria ever wanted to feel comfortable at the Kahns' again—with *Noel* again—she had to make peace with her.

"Please?" Aria placed a hand on Klaudia's shoulder. "I need to apologize."

Klaudia shook her off. "I have nothing to say to you. I embarrassed and hurt." Then she skied over to one of the chairlifts and waited for the next gondola.

"Wait!" Aria cried, snapping on her own skis and sliding after her. Just as Klaudia sat down on the gondola, Aria jumped on, too.

"Idiot!" Klaudia spat, moving as far to one side of the lift as she could. "What you *doing*?"

"I need to talk to you," Aria insisted. "It's important."

"Aria?" Noel cried worriedly behind her. "Uh, you forgot your poles!" He waved two long, thin sticks in the air. "And that lift is for a double-black diamond!"

Aria hesitated. They were already twenty feet off the ground. Empty gondolas swayed back and forth behind them. Skiers zigzagged below, suddenly looking like minuscule ants.

"It's okay!" she called bravely. Hopefully she could just stay on the gondola and ride it back down.

Then Aria looked at Klaudia, who was pointedly faced the opposite direction, staring at the pines. "I owe you an apology. I shouldn't have embarrassed you last night. I didn't realize what Finland's cultural practices were. I'm sorry." Aria didn't really believe that everyone in Finland hot-tubbed naked, but it was easier just to let Klaudia believe she did for now and move on.

Klaudia didn't move a muscle. Even her skis remained motionless.

Aria sighed and continued. "I have a jealousy problem. I loved Noel when I was in sixth and seventh grades, when there was no chance of us ever hooking up. So when he was interested in me last year, I didn't exactly believe it was real. Sometimes I just let that jealousy get the best of me, and that's what I was doing with you. I . . . well, I accidentally read one of your texts to your friend Tanja. You said I was a *peikko*. A troll."

Klaudia whipped around. *That* got her attention. "You spy on me?"

"I didn't mean to," Aria said quickly. "It was just lying there, and . . . well, I'm sorry. For a while, I was really mad at you—it sounded like you wanted Noel, and it hurt that you thought I was a troll when I thought we were becoming friends. But I'm over it. Sometimes people talk behind friends' backs. That's life. But we're going to be seeing a lot of each other, so I want us to be friends again. Can we have a truce?"

A swirl of wind blew Klaudia's icy-blond hair over her face. On the slope below, someone wiped out in a cloud of white. The top of the mountain appeared over the crest. A big sign in the snow said LIFT BAR TO DISEMBARK.

Silently, Klaudia pushed the bar up, gripped her ski poles hard, and met Aria's eyes. There was a forgiving look on her face, and for a moment, Aria thought she was going to apologize and everything would go back to normal.

But then Klaudia's lips curled into a conniving smile. "Actually, Aria, I'm going to fuck your boyfriend. Tonight."

Aria stared at her. It felt like Klaudia had just punched her in the throat. "*Excuse* me?"

Klaudia scooted closer to Aria. "I'm going to fuck your

boyfriend," she said again—in textbook-perfect English. "*Tonight*. And there's nothing you can do about it."

It was like they were in a horror movie where a character suddenly became possessed by a demon. Who was this well-spoken, nerves-of-steel girl? Klaudia's face had transformed from helpless sex kitten to ruthless boyfriend stealer. And even more than that, the look in her eyes was almost *dangerous*, as though she meant Aria harm. Aria remembered the last time she'd seen that look: on Tabitha's—*Ali's*—face when she threatened Hanna on the roof deck in Jamaica.

The memory rushed in hard and fast, as though it had been patiently waiting for nearly a year to rear its ugly head. Aria hadn't believed Tabitha was Ali until Tabitha started threatening Hanna on the crow's nest. Then, suddenly, it seemed so . . . *real*. Tabitha's every gesture, her every aggressive movement was exactly like how Ali had behaved the night she'd tried to kill them in the Poconos.

All of a sudden, Aria saw what the others already knew. Ali was *here*. She'd tried to sneak back into their lives in disguise. And Aria had almost let her.

"Please!" Hanna had wailed as Ali pinned her to the wall that surrounded the balcony. "Leave me alone!"

Every protective instinct in Aria's body kicked in. She inserted herself between the two of them. "Don't touch her!"

Ali turned to Aria, looking at her like she was crazy. "What do you think I'm going to do? I just want to show her the view."

But Aria wasn't falling for that. "I *know* what you're going to do!"

Ali moved away from Hanna and lunged for Aria instead. Now it was Aria's turn to lose her balance and get a terrifying view of the crashing whitecaps below.

"Aria!" someone shrieked behind them. Glass shattered. Aria's knee banged against the low wall, scraping off skin. Ali barreled for Aria again, her arms stretched out in front of her. Aria stared into her wide, crazed eyes, clearly seeing Ali inside. She had come to kill them, just like she'd killed Courtney, Ian, and Jenna. She was going to throw them over the roof one by one.

It was unclear what had happened next. The only thing Aria remembered was feeling a burst of strength, grabbing Ali's arms, spinning her around, and pushing her hard. Ali's feet left the ground. An unnatural sound came out of her mouth. Her arms flailed desperately around her, but suddenly she seemed boneless and feather-light. Before anyone could do anything, she tipped into the black, empty space.

Someone screamed. Someone else gasped. Ali's body spilled over the low wall, first her head and shoulders disappearing, then her torso, then her butt and legs, and then her feet. She tumbled into the darkness, not even making a sound as she plunged down the face of the resort.

And then . . . *thud.* The solid slap of a body hitting sand.

The memory whizzed through Aria's brain in a split

second. When her vision focused again, she saw Klaudia's body pressed against hers. Her hands groped for her, pushing her to the side of the ski lift. She grabbed Aria's shoulders and started to shake her hard. Her face was mere inches from Aria's. The same self-preserving impulse coursed through Aria's veins once more. "Get off me!" she screamed, jerking up. She pushed Klaudia once, lightly, but Klaudia just let out an ugly laugh and covered Aria's mouth with her mittened hand. Fear and fury raged through Aria's veins. "I said, get *off* me!" she hollered, shoving Klaudia's chest.

Klaudia wheeled backward, letting out a yelp. At that exact moment, the gondola tilted down to let the skiers off the lift. Klaudia's body tilted with it. Without the bar to protect her, she slid right off the lip of the chair.

"Oh my God!" Aria grabbed for Klaudia's hand, but it was too late. Klaudia hurtled toward the ground, her hat flying off her head, her arms wheeling wildly, her skis kicking, her face a twisted mask of terror and fury. Three devastating seconds later, her body landed facedown in a pile of fresh, powdery snow.

And, just like it had been with Ali, all was silent after the fall.

29

DON'T ASK, DON'T TELL

Spencer opened her eyes. She was lying on top of silky sheets in a very, very small room in the Hudson Hotel. Soothing ocean waves from a sound machine played in her ear. Funny, she didn't remember a sound machine from last night—but then, she had been pretty wasted when she fell asleep.

When she looked over, Zach was lying next to her. He looked so different this morning. His short, brown hair was long and blond. And there were scars on his neck and arms, and a trickle of something red seeping out of his left ear. Was that . . . blood?

She shot up and looked around. This wasn't the Hudson. She was lying on a long stretch of unspoiled white sand. The sun blazed high in the sky, and there wasn't a person around for miles. The smell of salt and fish tickled her nostrils. Waves crashed on the shore. Gulls circled overhead. Behind her was a pink stucco resort with a crow's nest deck peeking out over the beach. A very *familiar* crow's nest.

"*No*," Spencer whispered. She was in Jamaica. At The Cliffs. She looked at the figure to her left once more. It was a girl. The line of scarlet blood trickled from her ear to the sand. A blue string bracelet circled her wrist. Her yellow halter dress was pushed up almost to her butt, and her legs were bent at an unnatural angle.

It wasn't Zachary. It was Tabitha. *Ali.*

"Oh my God." Spencer leapt to her feet and ran around to stare into the girl's face. Her eyes were closed tightly, her skin was a washed-out blue, like she'd been dead for hours.

"Ali." Spencer slapped the girl's cheek hard. "*Ali.*"

The girl didn't answer. Spencer felt for her pulse at her wrist. Nothing. Her head hung limply on her neck like the vertebrae had shattered into a thousand pieces. Blood pooled under her eyes.

Spencer looked around desperately for the others, but they were nowhere to be seen. They had *all* run down here after Aria pushed her, hadn't they? They'd been in it together.

"Ali, please wake up." Spencer screamed into the girl's face. She shook her shoulders hard. "*Please.* I'm sorry Aria did what she did. She was just scared. She didn't know what you were going to do to us. I would have done the same thing." And she would have. The scene on the crow's nest deck reminded her too chillingly of the last moments she'd had with Mona Vanderwaal when Mona confessed she was the first A.

Suddenly, Ali's eyes popped open. She reached forward, grabbed Spencer's collar, and pulled her so close that Spencer could smell a faint tinge of vanilla on her skin.

"I know what you did," Ali whispered hoarsely. "And pretty soon, everyone else is going to know, too."

Spencer woke up mid-scream. Sun streamed through the blinds. A kids' TV show was on the screen. This time, she really was in the Hudson. Zach was lying next to her, not Ali. But she could still smell the salt and the sand from Jamaica. Her scalp ached from where Ali pulled her hair. It felt so *real.*

Bang bang bang.

The noise was coming from the door. Spencer blinked hard at it, still caught in the dream.

Bang bang bang. "Hello?" a voice called from the hall.

Zach stirred next to her, pressing his arms above his head. "Hey," he said, giving Spencer a long, slow smile. "What's that noise?"

"Someone's knocking." Spencer swung her legs around the side of the bed.

Just then, the door burst open. "Zach?" a familiar man's voice boomed. "It's nine-thirty. Douglas is waiting to talk to you about Harvard. Get off your ass and get ready."

Spencer gasped and froze. It was Mr. Pennythistle.

He saw Spencer the same instant she saw him. The blood drained from his cheeks. Spencer quickly wrapped herself up in the bed sheet—at some point in the middle of the night, she'd kicked off her skirt and tights and was now only in her blouse and underwear. Zach shot up, too, groping for his T-shirt, which he'd also stripped off. But it was too late—Mr. Pennythistle had seen everything.

"Jesus Christ!" he screamed, his face contorting. "What the hell?"

Zach pulled his shirt over his head. "Dad, it's not . . ."

"You sick bastard." Mr. Pennythistle narrowed his eyes at his son. He yanked Zach up by the arm and slammed him hard against the wall. "She's going to be your stepsister! What the hell is wrong with you?"

"It wasn't what it looked like," Zach protested weakly. "We were just hanging out."

Mr. Pennythistle shook Zach's shoulders hard. "You just can't keep it in your pants, can you?"

"We were just sleeping!" Spencer cried. "Honest!"

Mr. Pennythistle ignored her. He shook his son again and again, making Spencer wince. "You're a twisted pervert, Zachary. A sick, disgusting pervert not worthy of anything I do for you."

"Dad, please!"

Mr. Pennythistle's hand drew back and slapped Zach's face. Zach reeled backward, struggling against his dad, but Mr. Pennythistle threw his whole body against him, holding him there. The worst part was that it looked like he'd done this many times before.

"Stop it!" Spencer screamed, wriggling into her skirt from last night and catapulting over the bed to the two of them. "Just stop it! Please!"

Mr. Pennythistle didn't seem to hear. Zach crumpled against the wall, but Mr. Pennythistle only shook him harder. "When will you listen?" he growled. "When will you understand?"

Spencer tugged Mr. Pennythistle's arm. "Please stop! It wasn't what it looked like! I swear!"

"Spencer . . ." Zach eyed her over his father's shoulder. "Just go. You don't need to see this."

"No!" Zach was Spencer's soon-to-be stepbrother, and she needed to protect him. She pulled at the back of Mr. Pennythistle's oxford shirt, tearing it. "Zach didn't touch me! He's gay!"

Mr. Pennythistle immediately let go of his son and whirled around to stare at her. "*What* did you say?"

Spencer glanced at Zach's stricken face. He shook his head desperately, like he couldn't believe what she'd said either, but what was she supposed to do, let his father whale on him some more?

Zach covered his face with his hands. His father turned back to him. "Is what she said *true*?"

A gurgling sound emerged from between Zach's lips. His dad stepped away from him as though he were toxic. Then, abruptly, he reached out his arm and punched the faux-wood wall next to Zach's head. Spencer jumped back and yelped. Mr. Pennythistle punched the wall again and again. Plaster flew everywhere. When he was finished, he bent over at the waist and placed his bloody fists on his knees. His face twisted with anguish. He looked like he was about to cry.

A small, timid knock sounded on the door. "Nicholas?" Spencer's mother called. "Is everything okay?"

No one said a word. After a moment, Mr. Pennythistle turned and stormed out of the room, slamming the door so hard that the walls shivered. Spencer could hear him talking to her mom in the hall.

She dared to peek at Zach. He looked rattled, but okay. "What the hell is wrong with you? Why did you tell him that?"

Spencer reached out to him. "I thought he was hurting you!"

Zach's lips warped into a sneer, and he took a step back from her. He looked at her with utter hatred, a look she thought she'd never see in him. "I asked you to keep it a secret, but I guess that was too much to ask of a Pretty Little Liar," he snarled. "Rot in hell, bitch."

Before Spencer could protest, he scooped up his coat, shoved on his shoes, and stormed out of the room, too. The door slammed once more. And then, silence.

Spencer sank to the mattress, knocking one of the pillows on the bed to the floor. It still had an indentation from Zach's skull. The mattress was still warm from his body.

Another chunk of plaster fell from the wall to the ground. Mr. Pennythistle's blood dripped onto the carpet from the hole he'd created. It reminded Spencer of the dream she'd had that morning: the line of blood trickling from Ali's ear. *I know what you did.*

Beep.

It was Spencer's BlackBerry, which she'd set on the nightstand before falling asleep last night. Even from across the room, she could tell that the screen said ONE NEW TEXT.

No, Spencer thought. *Please. Not now.* But she couldn't ignore it. She had to press READ.

Watch out, Spencer. Eventually, all secrets wash ashore. I think you know exactly what I mean. –A

30

SHE'S SMARTER THAN SHE LOOKS

The Lenape medical center was nothing but a squat, square building that smelled like antiseptic and cough drops. A TV in the corner silently played an infomercial about a magical potato peeler, the chair Aria was sitting on was making her butt fall asleep, and she was about to lose her mind from the constant drone of the automaton-like National Weather Service voice on the radio. Apparently, this area was due for two more feet of snow tomorrow. Not that they'd stay the extra day to ski. Not after what had happened with Klaudia.

Aria strained to listen for anything coming from the examination room—moans of pain, screams of agony, a heart monitor flat-lining. The room was deadly quiet. Eric and Christopher Kahn lounged on the couches, reading old copies of *Sports Illustrated*. Noel paced around the small space, on the phone with his mother. "Yeah, Mom . . . she just *fell*, I don't know . . . the ski patrol got her . . . we're at the med center now . . . I hope she's okay, but I don't know."

Just hearing Noel rehash the event made Aria feel shaky and sick. The last few hours had been ugly and surreal. After Klaudia fell off the lift and didn't move, several skiers stopped around her. A ski guard appeared next, and then a snowmobile with a rescue sled. Someone knelt down and felt Klaudia's pulse. They screamed in Klaudia's ear, but Aria couldn't tell if she answered—that was about the time the lift reached the top of the hill and she'd stumbled off.

Now, everyone was waiting to see what damage had been done. Apparently the ski patrol had been able to wake Klaudia up before they'd loaded her onto the rescue sled and pulled her down the mountain, but she'd been in a lot of pain. An ambulance was waiting for her at the bottom by the time Aria butt-slid down the treacherous hill, and they'd all come here. This didn't seem like a very decent trauma center, though. It looked more like a DMV.

Noel slumped back down in the plastic chair next to Aria. "My mom's beside herself. She wanted to come up here and take care of Klaudia, but I said she should wait."

"She must be so worried," Aria mumbled, closing the copy of *Ladies' Home Journal* in her lap. She'd been reading the same line of an article about how to make prize-winning cheesecake for the last twenty minutes.

Noel leaned closer. "So what happened, exactly? How did Klaudia fall?"

Aria looked at him, feeling a mix of guilt and regret. Noel had arrived on the scene a few minutes after everything happened; he hadn't seen a thing. They'd been too keyed up to talk on the drive here, but he kept gazing at Aria suspiciously, as if he sensed she'd done something awful.

"I'm not really sure." It was the truth—she hadn't *meant* to push Klaudia off the lift. Shove her away, yeah. But not hurt her.

"Were you guys fighting or something?" Noel searched Aria's face. "Did she, like, jump?"

Aria shook her head. "She just . . . slipped off. It was really weird."

Noel crossed his arms over his chest and gave her a long, discerning look that made Aria's skin prickle. He didn't believe her. But what was she supposed to do, tell him the real story? That Klaudia said *I'm going to fuck your boyfriend* in perfect English, without even an accent? That Klaudia had lunged for her, looking crazed and vengeful? Noel would just accuse Aria of being jealous again.

She turned away, fearing that if she stared at him for much longer she'd blurt out everything—and not just what happened on the lift, either. The stuff about A, too. The stuff about Jamaica. The stuff Aria couldn't block out on the lift today, the horrible thing she'd done. The horrible thing A knew about.

Then again, maybe what she did wasn't as horrific as she'd thought all these months. If A *was* Ali—and who else could it be?—then Aria's push hadn't killed her.

The door to the treatment rooms opened, and a female doctor in a crisp white coat emerged. "Ms. Huusko is resting," she said. "You can see her now."

Everyone rose and followed her to the back. The doctor parted a pink-striped curtain, and there was Klaudia, lying on a cot with a bulky white cast on her ankle. Her blond hair spilled across the pillow. Her plain cotton gown gaped at the bosom. Her lips were pink and glossy as though she'd recently applied a fresh coat of lipstick. She'd managed to look ready for sex even in the hospital.

"Oh my God, Klaudia," Aria said, feeling a rush of remorse despite Klaudia's perky appearance. "Are you okay?"

"Does it hurt?" Noel and the other boys asked too, gathering around her bed.

"I fine." Klaudia simpered at all of them, all traces of her excellent English enunciation gone. "Just a little owie."

"She has a broken ankle." A nurse bustled in and wrapped a blood pressure cuff around Klaudia's arm. "That's pretty minor, considering the accident she had. Luckily, her fall was toward the top of the slope. If it had been in the middle, she would've been in real trouble."

"Yes, is crazy!" Klaudia pretended to wipe sweat off her brow. "I never fall from lift before! Oof!"

"So what happened?" Noel perched on the edge of Klaudia's bed.

Klaudia licked her lips and eyed Aria. The only sound in the room was the nurse pumping up the blood pressure cuff. Every muscle in Aria's body tensed, waiting for the blow. Of course Klaudia was going to rat her out. She wanted to sleep with Noel—this would get Aria out of the way.

Finally, Klaudia shifted higher in her bed. "It is blur. I no remember."

"Are you sure?" Noel curled his hands over his knees. "It just seems crazy to me that you'd slip off a lift. You've been skiing for years."

Klaudia shrugged, looking faint. "I don't know," she said weakly, her eyelids fluttering closed.

Eric punched Noel's arm. "Dude, don't push her."

"Maybe she has amnesia or something," Christopher said.

Aria grabbed the bed for balance, her heart still racing. Could that be it? Had Klaudia lost her memory?

The doctor parted the curtain. "Don't overwhelm her too much, guys. Because Ms. Huusko hit her head, we want to observe her for a while to make sure she isn't showing any signs of a concussion. If she is, we'll have to airlift her to a bigger facility. If not, we can probably discharge her tomorrow morning."

Everyone nodded. "I'll book the rooms for an extra night," Noel said in a perfunctory voice, whipping out his iPhone.

"Oh." Aria looked at him. "I can't stay an extra night. I promised my dad I'd babysit Lola."

"Fine." Noel didn't even look up from his Google search. "Do you mind taking the bus home?"

Aria opened her mouth, then shut it again. She'd hoped Noel would drive her back to Rosewood himself. Couldn't the other brothers stay here with Klaudia? Couldn't he come back tomorrow to retrieve them?

But Noel didn't offer, and so Aria shrugged into her coat and dug out her phone to check Greyhound times. "What time do you think you'll be back tomorrow?" she asked Noel. "Maybe we can hang out in the evening."

Noel's head shot up. "We don't even know if Klaudia's going to be okay yet. I don't think we should make plans until we do."

"Oh." Aria backed away from him. "Right. Sorry."

"And anyway, I should probably hang out with Klaudia for the next few days." Noel glanced at Klaudia's sleeping shape. "It's the least that I can do. She's probably going to be in a lot of pain. She'll need someone to help her get around."

"O-of course." Aria fought back tears.

The next Greyhound bus to Philly was in an hour. Aria could walk to the station from the clinic, and Noel could grab the rest of her things from the hotel and bring them home tomorrow. Just as Aria was backing out of the tiny curtained-off area, something made her turn. Klaudia's eyes had opened, and she stared straight at Aria. There was a tiny, victorious smile on her face. Slowly, deliberately, she raised her small, pale hand, and gave Aria the finger.

Aria gasped. The realization was like a rush of cold air. Klaudia didn't have amnesia—she remembered everything on the ski lift with perfect clarity. And now she had exactly what she wanted. Now she had something to hold over Aria's head. Now, Klaudia had Aria in her power.

Just like A did.

31

CONGRATULATIONS, NOW EFF-OFF

Later that afternoon, Emily pulled into her driveway just as an ad blared over the radio. "*The devastating deceit. The identity twists. The lives at stake. Get the whole story tonight on the anniversary of the Poconos fire and her death.* Pretty Little Killer. *Brought to you by . . .*"

"Ugh," Emily moaned, switching it off. She couldn't wait until this day was over and the advertisements went away. *She* certainly didn't want to relive the day of Ali's death—any of them. Especially since she wasn't even sure if Real Ali was truly dead.

She got out of the car, pulled her swim gear bag over her shoulder, and walked up the snowy front path. Before she opened the door, she tried texting Chloe one more time. *I need to talk to you. It isn't my fault. I didn't know how to tell you.* She'd texted Chloe five times since the swim meet, but Chloe hadn't written back.

Sighing, she slipped her key in the door, but the knob

turned easily already. That was strange—her parents usually kept the door locked tight, afraid of intruders. "Hello?" Emily called in the foyer. No answer. That was weird, too—her parents always at least mumbled some sign of their presence, even if they were beyond pissed at her. The house seemed occupied, though—there was an unfamiliar scent in the air and a nagging sense that someone had just walked down the hall.

The hairs on Emily's arms stood on end. Various scenarios flipped through her head. What if A was *here*? What if A had hurt her family? Maybe A—*Ali*—was pulling out all the stops. Maybe this was the day everything was going down.

A horrible thought stopped her cold. Today was the day of reckoning, the anniversary of Ali's death, the day she'd tried to kill them. Naturally this was the day she'd come back to finish them off.

"H-hello?" Emily called out again, creeping down the hall toward the kitchen. A sound made her stop and turn. Was that . . . a *giggle*? Her heart banged in her chest. It was coming from the living room, which was closed off to the hall by French doors. Those doors were *never* closed.

There was the giggle again. Emily's hands started to shake. Her mouth went cottony-dry. Slowly, she pushed on the door. It gave way with a wailing *creak*. What was inside? Dead bodies? The police, here to arrest her for what she did in Jamaica? *Ali?*

"Surprise!"

Emily screamed and jumped back, bumping hard against the doorjamb. Tons of balloons were tied to the chairs, a wrapped present sat on the couch, and her mother had placed an enormous sheet cake that was in the shape of the University of North Carolina logo on the coffee table. Her parents rushed toward her, huge smiles on their faces.

"Congratulations on the scholarship!" Mr. and Mrs. Fields enveloped her in a hug, the first one they'd given her in months. "We're so, so proud of you!"

There were more people behind Emily's parents. She craned over their lumpy bodies and saw baby Grace, Mr. and Mrs. Roland . . . *and* Chloe. "Oh my God," Emily whispered, letting her arms go limp.

Mrs. Fields turned and gestured to them. "I invited the Rolands over for cake to help us celebrate! If it weren't for them, this might not have happened!"

"Yes, thank you again," Mr. Fields said, walking over to the family and pumping Mr. Roland's hand up and down.

"It was no trouble," Mr. Roland said in a stiff, fake-friendly voice. He avoided Emily's gaze, which was fine with her.

"I'm so glad it worked out for you!" Mrs. Roland gave Emily a big hug. As Emily pressed up to her thin chest, Chloe made a small, choked noise. Emily glanced at her. Her eyes blazed with hatred. The corners of her mouth didn't show a hint of a smile. To Chloe, Emily was the adulteress. The home wrecker.

Mrs. Fields cut the cake and served everyone a slice. Thankfully, the adults engaged in their own conversation, leaving Emily and Chloe alone. Emily caught Chloe's eye. "I need to talk to you."

Chloe turned away, pretending she didn't hear her. But Emily couldn't let Chloe go on believing something that wasn't true. She grabbed Chloe's arm and dragged her into the kitchen. Chloe went willingly, but she leaned against the island, crossed her arms over her chest, and pretended to be fascinated by the chicken cookie jar that sat on the counter. She wouldn't look Emily in the eye.

"I'm sorry," Emily whispered. "You have to believe me when I tell you I had no idea that was going to happen with your dad. And I didn't *want* it to happen."

"Yeah, right," Chloe hissed, her head still turned toward the cookie jar. "Were you ever really my friend? Or were you just using me to ensure you got the scholarship?"

Emily's mouth fell open. "Of course not! I would never do anything like that!"

Chloe rolled her eyes. "I *heard* my dad in that room by the pool, you know. He said you were acting like you wanted it on Thursday night. When I went to bed, drunk, did something *happen* between you guys?"

Emily turned away, biting her bottom lip hard. "He was the one who kissed me, I swear. I didn't know how to tell you."

Chloe winced, then finally stared Emily in the face.

"You knew about this for three whole days and didn't say anything to me?"

Emily ducked her head. "I didn't know how to—"

"We were supposed to be friends." Chloe placed her hands on her hips. "Friends tell friends things like that. And why should I believe that you're totally innocent, anyway? I barely *know* you. All I know, really, is that you had a baby this summer and—"

"*Shhh!*" Emily shrieked, clapping a hand over Chloe's mouth.

Chloe wrenched away, knocking against one of the kitchen chairs, which was decorated with a chicken-printed cushion. "I should tell your parents. Ruin your life like you've ruined mine."

"Please don't," Emily begged. "They'll kick me out. It will absolutely shatter them."

"So?"

Emily grabbed her hands. "I told you that secret because I felt I could trust you. I felt like we were really becoming friends. And . . . and I haven't had a real friend in so, so long, not since last year. It's been so lonely." She wiped away a tear. "I hate myself for screwing up and not telling you. I just wanted to protect you. I just wanted you to be happy. I hoped it wouldn't happen again. That it was all just a horrible mistake."

Chloe jutted her chin to the left, saying nothing. Was that good or bad? Emily couldn't tell.

"Please, *please* don't tell anyone what I told you," Emily

whispered. "I certainly won't tell anyone about your dad. I'll wipe it out of my mind completely, I promise. I wish it had never happened."

Chloe's head remained turned for a long while. The chicken-shaped clock over the stove ticked loudly. The adults murmured in the other room. Finally, she looked at Emily with cold, tired eyes and sighed. "I won't tell your secret if you leave my dad alone."

"*Thank* you," Emily said. "And of course I will."

She moved toward Chloe for a hug, but Chloe pushed her away like Emily was a rude dog nosing for table food. "That doesn't mean I want to be friends."

"What?" Emily cried. "W-why?"

"I just can't." Chloe turned on her heel and walked toward the kitchen door. "Tell my parents I got a phone call and I'm in the car, okay?" she said over her shoulder. "No offense, but I don't really want to do the 'Yay, Emily' cake thing right now."

Emily watched as Chloe yanked on the kitchen door and then slammed it shut again. It felt like someone had just scooped out her heart and run it through a potato masher. Everything was ruined. Sure she had a scholarship, sure her future was set, but it felt like she'd won it at too great a cost.

Squeak.

Emily turned around, squinting in the blinding sunlight that poured through the windows. What was that? She scanned the cabinets and the floors, then noticed a thin sheet of paper at the foot of the door Chloe had just passed through. Her heart kicked in her chest. She ran to the window and stared outside, searching for whoever had put it there. Was that a shape disappearing through the trees? What was that movement in the cornfield?

She opened the back door, letting the cold air rush in. "Ali?" she screamed. "Ali!" But no one answered. "Chloe?" she called next, thinking Chloe might have seen something. But Chloe didn't answer, either.

The adults laughed at something in the other room. Grace let out a happy cry. Trembling, Emily picked up the piece of paper and unfolded it. Spiky handwriting blurred before her eyes.

She may not tell, but I can't make the same promise—about ANY of your secrets. Sorry! –A

32

ALI, THE CUNNING CAT

"Um, excuse me?"

Hanna looked down from the elliptical trainer she was chugging away on and saw a petite girl with big doe eyes and a size 23 waist staring up at her. "There's a thirty-minute limit on these machines," the girl complained. "And, like, you've been on for *sixty-three*."

"Too bad," Hanna snapped back, wheeling faster. Let the gym police kick her off.

It was later that Saturday afternoon–the anniversary of Alison DiLaurentis's death, all the news channels blared, not that Hanna could ever forget–and Hanna was at the Rosewood Country Club's state-of-the-art gym. The room smelled like ylang-ylang candles, MTV appeared on every TV mounted over the machines, and a very hyper Zumba instructor was screaming so loudly in the fitness room that Hanna could hear her over the hip-hop music blaring on her iPod. She'd hoped the elliptical would exorcise the memories of Tabitha, Jamaica, the elevator incident, and especially A, but it wasn't really working. She kept feeling Tabitha's—*Ali's*—hands on her shoulders, ready to push her off the roof. She kept hearing her friends' screams. And then Aria had stepped in, and everything moved so fast . . .

At first, Hanna had been relieved that Aria pushed Ali over the side. She'd killed so many people, getting rid of her felt like a good deed for all humanity. But then she realized what they'd done. A life was still a life. They weren't murderers.

Hanna and her friends ran down to the beach, taking the stairs two at a time. They banged out the back door onto the sand and looked around. The moon cast a silvery stripe down the beach. The ocean roared. Hanna stared at her pale feet below, hoping she wouldn't bump into Ali's limp, twisted body. Surely she'd died on impact, right?

"Do you see her?" Aria's voice called from a distance.

"Not yet," Spencer answered. "Keep looking!"

They ran up and down the shore, splashing through the warm water, searching the dunes, even looping around and checking out the coves and cliffs. But there was no body anywhere.

"What the hell?" Aria stopped, out of breath. "Where did she go?"

Hanna looked around frantically. It wasn't possible. Ali couldn't just disappear. Aria had *pushed her*. She had fallen hard. They'd heard her hit the sand. They'd looked over the rail and, in the fuzzy darkness, they'd sworn they'd seen a body. *Hadn't* they?

"The tide must have picked her up." Spencer gestured to the sea. "She's probably washed away by now."

"What happens if she washes back up?" Aria whispered.

"It's not as if anyone can prove we did it." Spencer looked around, checking the beach again. It was still empty. No one was watching. "And Aria, it—it was self-defense—Ali could have killed us."

"We don't know that for sure." Aria's eyes were wide and scared. "Maybe we misunderstood her up there. Maybe I shouldn't have—"

"You *should* have," Spencer said sharply. "If you wouldn't have pushed her, we might not be standing here right now."

Everyone was silent for a moment. Emily stared at the round moon above them. "What if Ali didn't wash away?" she whispered. "What if she survived the fall and crawled away to find help?"

Hanna's stomach swirled. She'd been thinking the same exact thing.

Spencer kicked at a clump of sand. "There's no way. She couldn't have survived that fall."

"She survived a fire," Emily reminded her. "We don't know who we're dealing with. She's, like, *bionic.*"

Spencer's eyes blazed. "Just let it go, okay? She washed out to sea. She's *dead.*"

Now, Hanna noticed something across the gym. Jeremiah stood in the doorway near the check-in desk, glaring right at her.

Hanna jumped off the elliptical and toweled off her face. She could feel her racing pulse even in her lips. As Jeremiah approached, she gave him a big, innocent smile. "Uh, do you go to this gym?"

"As a matter of fact, I do," Jeremiah snapped. His face was purple with fury. "Or I should say I *did*. Your father got me a complimentary membership. But now that's been revoked."

"Oh," Hanna said quietly.

"Oh? That's all you can say? *Oh?*" Jeremiah was so angry he was shaking. "I hope you're happy, Hanna. This is all because of *you*."

A shockwave rippled through Hanna's skin, but she stood her ground. "I didn't do anything wrong. I just told my dad that I saw you go upstairs."

"You didn't *see* anything, and you know it." He leaned closer to her, his breath smelling sour and unclean. "You had something to do with this, didn't you?"

Hanna turned her head away. The girl who'd wanted her elliptical glanced over at them, her brow furrowed. "I don't know what you're talking about."

Jeremiah pointed a finger at her. "You've ruined my career. And I have a feeling you're going to find a way to ruin your father's campaign. Remember that anonymous note I got, saying you were hiding something? I'm going to look into it, Hanna. And you're going down."

Hanna let out a terrified squeak. Jeremiah remained in Hanna's face for a moment longer, then wheeled around and marched back through the room.

"Are you okay?" the elliptical girl asked, pausing on the treadmill. "He seemed pretty . . . intense."

Hanna ran her hand over her sweaty hair and murmured a noncommittal reply. She definitely wasn't okay. How serious was Jeremiah? What had she gotten herself into?

And then, out of nowhere, a high-pitched, lilting giggle, floated out from the vents. She stared around the room. *Ali?*

The laugh persisted. Hanna shut her eyes, thinking about that empty beach again. For so long, Hanna had suppressed the thought that Ali had survived, but now she knew Emily was right.

Ali was here. Maybe not here at this gym right now, but she was here in Rosewood, following them, watching them, ready to ruin their lives for the third and final time. Ali was like a cat with nine lives: She'd survived the fire in Spencer's woods, then she'd survived the fire in the Poconos, and now she'd survived that impossible fall off the crow's nest. She'd crawled away, nursed her wounds, got healthy again, and was *back*. Maybe she wouldn't die until she got exactly what she wanted: to get rid of them, once and for all.

There was only one thing Hanna could do: go to the

police. Ali had to be stopped. If it meant admitting what happened in Jamaica, then so be it. It had been in self-defense, after all. They'd done it to stop Ali's evil cycle of murders—who knew who else she'd killed after she survived the fire. Besides, it wasn't as if they'd actually *killed* Ali—she was still alive. Hanna would even take the blame for her friends, even if it meant falling out of favor with her dad. There was no way she could let Ali do this to them again.

When Hanna's phone buzzed against her hip, she jumped. *Mike*, she hoped—he could only freeze her out for so long. She reached into her pocket, pulled it out, and stared at the screen. TEXT FROM ANONYMOUS. With a shudder, she opened it and read the message.

Turn on the news, sweetie. I have a surprise for you. Kisses!

—A

33

THE NEWS THEY HAVEN'T BEEN WAITING FOR

The Acela bullet train back to Rosewood shuddered into Penn Station, and Spencer, her mother, and the Pennythistles boarded silently. Mr. Pennythistle sank rigidly into his seat, looking like he was about to burst a blood vessel in his brain. Mrs. Hastings was next to him, shooting him overwrought glances, staring anxiously out the window, or glaring at Spencer and shaking her head. Spencer wondered what he'd told her about this morning. Had he included the part about shoving Zach around? Had he included the part about how he was a homophobe?

Amelia kept twisting around and eyeing everyone, certain that something was up but not privy to what it was. Zach hunched by the window, iPod headphones in his ears. He threw his coat and bag on the adjacent seat so Spencer wouldn't be able to sit there. She'd tried to apologize to him again and again, but it did no good—he wouldn't even look at her.

They passed Newark, then Trenton. Spencer's phone rang—CALL FROM HANNA MARIN. But she didn't want to talk to Hanna right now. She didn't want to talk to anyone.

Spencer pressed her forehead against the cool glass windowpane and stared at the trees and houses rushing past. The sky was a perfect blue today and nearly cloudless. It reminded her, suddenly, of the plane ride home from Jamaica a year ago. When they'd lifted off from the runway and circled the airport, she'd spied the endless, empty beach and crashing blue ocean below. From the high vantage, she was sure she'd see Ali's body bobbing in the waves, a speck of yellow fabric among so much blue, but she didn't see anything.

The days following Ali's death had been awful: They'd kept up the guise of happy, vacationing teenagers, especially because Noel and Mike were there. They snorkeled and swam, ocean kayaked and jumped off the cliffs a dozen more times. Hanna got a massage, and Aria took a couple of yoga classes. But the secret weighed on each of them. They barely ate. They were slow to smile. They drank a lot, but the drinks made them tense and combative instead of happy or relaxed. Sometimes Spencer heard Hanna, with whom she was sharing a room, rise from her bed in the middle of the night, shut the bathroom door, and spend hours in there. What was she doing? Asking her reflection what she'd helped do? Reliving the whole horrible thing?

Spencer always pretended she was asleep when Hanna

emerged from the bathroom, never wanting to talk about it. The distance between them had already begun to grow. They didn't want to look at each other for fear someone would burst out crying.

Every morning, Spencer woke up, padded to her balcony, and looked out to the shoreline; sure Ali's body would be lying there, bloated and blue. But it never was. It was like it never happened. No Jamaican policemen knocked on the doors to their rooms, asking questions. No members of the hotel staff stood in a tight huddle, discussing a missing guest. It seemed no one even noticed she was missing. And it appeared that no one, no one at all, had seen what Spencer and the others had done that awful night.

On the plane ride home, Emily touched Spencer's hand. Her skin was waxy, and her hair looked greasy and unwashed. "I can't stop thinking. What if the ocean didn't wash her away? What if she didn't die on impact? What if she's *suffering* somewhere?"

"That's crazy," Spencer snapped, hardly believing Emily was bringing this up in such a public place. "We scoured every inch of that beach. She couldn't have crawled anywhere that fast."

"But . . ." Emily fiddled with the plastic cup she'd received from the refreshment cart. "It just seems strange the tide didn't bring her in."

"It's *good* the tide didn't bring her in," Spencer whispered, tearing her cocktail napkin into tiny pieces. "The

292 ♦ SARA SHEPARD

universe is looking out for us—and everyone *else* she would have murdered. She was crazy, Emily. We did the best thing possible. The only thing."

But now, Spencer doubted that Ali had drifted out to sea. She stared at the latest note A had sent: *All secrets wash ashore . . . eventually.* Emily was right. Ali never washed ashore because she didn't die in the fall.

Finally, the train pulled into the Rosewood station, and everyone disembarked. They threw their bags into the back of Mr. Pennythistle's Range Rover and started for home. The drive back from the train station was equally silent and awkward, although the conservative news channel Mr. Pennythistle had on at least provided some welcome noise. Spencer had never been so grateful to see her house in her entire life. As she opened her door, Mr. Pennythistle swiveled around and stared at her. "Say goodbye to Zachary, Spencer. This is the last you'll ever see of him."

Spencer almost dropped her duffel onto the slushy street. "What?" Hadn't they just said the Pennythistle family was moving into the Hastings house last night?

"He's going to military school in upstate New York," Mr. Pennythistle said in a bloodless, perfunctory voice he probably used when firing employees. "It's all set. I made the call this morning."

Amelia gasped—this, apparently, was the first she heard of it, too. Spencer eyed Mr. Pennythistle pleadingly. "Are you sure that's necessary?"

"Spencer." Mrs. Hastings pulled her away from the vehicle. "This isn't our concern."

Spencer slid back into the car anyway. She was about to apologize once more when hyped-up breaking-news music blared on the radio. "This just in," a reporter said excitedly. "We just received reports that the remains of a teenage girl have washed up in Jamaica."

The hair on the back of Spencer's neck rose. She pulled away from Zach and stared at the speaker in the backseat. *What* did the reporter just say? But before she could lurch forward and turn up the dial, Mrs. Hastings yanked her out of the car. "Come on." She slammed the door and gave Mr. Pennythistle a morose wave. They both watched as the red taillights disappeared down the street and rounded the turn.

Remains of a teenage girl . . . Jamaica. Spencer reached for her phone just as Hanna was calling again. Spencer answered. "Is there something going on in Jamaica?"

"I've been calling you for over an hour," Hanna whispered. "Spencer, oh my God."

"Get over here," Spencer said, running toward her house, heart pounding. "Get over here, *now*."

34

THE GIRL ON THE BEACH

When Aria pulled up to Spencer's, every light was on in the house. Hanna's Prius and Emily's Volvo wagon were also parked at the curb. As Aria cut the Subaru's engine, she saw them delicately walking up the slippery driveway. She joined them at the door. "What's this all about?" When Spencer had called her, Aria was just getting off the bus from New York. All Spencer would say was that she had to come over right away.

Hanna and Emily turned to her, wide-eyed. Before they could say anything, Spencer whipped the door open. Her face was drawn and pale. "Come with me."

She led them through the hall to the family den. Aria looked around; she hadn't been in this room in at least a year, but the same school pictures of Melissa and Spencer lined the walls. The television was on, the volume turned up loud. She saw the CNN logo in the bottom right-hand corner. A large yellow banner ran across the screen:

FISHERMAN FINDS REMAINS OF MISSING GIRL IN JAMAICA.

"Jamaica?" Aria whispered, staggering backward. She looked at the others. Emily covered her mouth. Hanna had a hand on her stomach like she was about to puke. And Spencer couldn't tear her eyes away from the screen, which showed a robin's-egg blue ocean and a smooth, tan shore. A rusty-looking fishing boat sat on the sand, and about a zillion reporters and officials gathered around it, taking pictures.

Hanna's eyes shifted back and forth. "This doesn't mean anything. It could be anyone."

"It's not anyone," Spencer said in a shaky voice. "Just *watch*."

A blond reporter wearing a green CNN-logo polo popped up on the screen. "What we're seeing below is the ongoing police investigation of the discovered remains on the shore earlier this morning," she explained, her hair whipping across her face. "According to the fisherman, who wishes to remain anonymous, he found the remains in a cove about six miles south of Negril."

"Negril?" Hanna stared around the others, her lower lip trembling. "You guys . . ."

"*Shh*." Spencer waved her hands to silence her. The newscaster was speaking again. "Judging by the condition of the remains, experts say the girl was about seventeen. From the level of decay, they believe she died about a year ago. Forensic experts are working very diligently to identify who this victim might be."

"Oh my God." Aria slumped down in the chair. "You guys, is this . . . Ali?"

"How is that possible?" Hanna held up her phone. "Isn't she the one sending us the texts? Isn't she the one who *saw* what we did?"

"What are the odds that another seventeen-year-old girl died near The Cliffs?" Spencer barked, her mouth a wobbly rectangle. "This is her, you guys. And when the cops identify her and figure out that *we* were there around that time, they'll put two and two together."

"They don't have any proof it was us!" Hanna said.

"They *will*." Spencer squeezed the bridge of her nose. "A is going to tell them."

Aria looked around the room, as though the school pictures on the wall might give her some solace. Everything suddenly felt turned on its head. So Ali really *did* die in the fall? Had the ocean swept her away that quickly, before they could even find her on the beach? Why had it taken her a whole year to turn up in a cove only six miles away?

And, the biggest question of all: Who was A, if not Ali?

"I'm just getting some new information!" the newscaster shouted, making the girls' heads snap up. The camera wobbled, first showing the knot of people on the beach, then focusing on the newscaster's feet, then righting itself on her face once more. The newscaster pressed her finger to her ear, listening to someone's voice through an earpiece. "They've identified the body," she said. "We have a match."

Hanna gasped. Aria grabbed Emily's hand and squeezed. *Alison DiLaurentis*, Aria waited for the reporter to say slowly. A look of confusion would surely wash over her face. She'd worry that she hadn't gotten that name quite right. Wasn't Alison DiLaurentis dead? she'd think. Or was this a girl by the same name, a cruel coincidence?

Suddenly, a photograph filled the screen, and the girls screamed. There was Ali in her latest incarnation, with her straight blond hair, slightly pointier chin, higher cheekbones, and thinner lips. It was exactly the girl they'd met on the roof deck after dinner that horrible night. Exactly the girl who'd teased them with eerie secrets only Ali knew, lured them up to the roof, and almost pushed Hanna off. It was almost a relief to Aria to finally see her again, though. At least they knew she was really dead.

"The parents have just identified the deceased by three pins in her ankle bone from an old accident," the newscaster explained, the photo of Ali minimizing to the corner of the screen. "They've released this photograph of what she looked like just before she disappeared. Her name was Tabitha Clark from New Jersey."

For a moment, Aria thought her brain had malfunctioned. She swung around and stared at Spencer at the exact same time Spencer turned to look at her. Emily leapt to her feet. Hanna tipped closer to the TV, as if she didn't believe it. "Wait a minute, *what* did she just say?" Hanna said.

"Her name was Tabitha Clark," Spencer repeated in monotone, looking stunned. "From New Jersey."

"But . . . *no!*" Aria's head started to spin. "Her name wasn't Tabitha! It was Alison! *Our* Alison!"

Spencer whipped around and pointed at Emily. "You were sure of it! You looked at her and said '*That's Ali*'!"

"She knew things only Ali knew!" Emily cried. "You guys believed it, too!"

"We all did," Aria whispered, staring dazedly ahead.

The newscaster continued. The girls turned back to the screen. "According to her parents, Tabitha had run away from home about a year ago. She was always a troubled child, first suffering from a near-fatal house fire when she was thirteen years old, then undergoing agonizing reconstructive surgeries to deal with the burns. Her parents knew she'd been in Jamaica, but they didn't realize anything was wrong until five months ago, when she didn't check in with them as usual. They tracked down her friends, who said they hadn't heard from Tabitha in more than a year."

The newscaster paused and sadly shook her head. "I'm just getting word that Mr. and Mrs. Clark have been looking for her for months to no avail. It's heartbreaking that their long search for their daughter had to end in such tragedy."

Another image appeared on the screen. It was a picture

of Tabitha in a cheerleading uniform, surrounded by girls Aria had never seen before. Then, there was a photo of Tabitha standing in front of a stadium, wearing an oversized New Jersey Devils T-shirt and giving a thumbs-up. Ali *never* would have worn something as garish as a New Jersey Devils T-shirt.

Hanna clutched the side of her head. "You guys . . . what's *happening*?"

Aria's heart thumped so fast she was sure it was going to burst out of her chest. The worst possible thought clanged in her head. By the looks on her friends' faces, she was sure they were thinking the exact same thing.

She took in a deep breath and said the scariest thing she could even imagine out loud: "Guys, Tabitha wasn't Ali. We killed an innocent girl."

35

DON'T CLOSE YOUR EYES . . .

Emily sank to the floor, the awful truth swarming in her head like a hive of bees. *Tabitha wasn't Ali. Tabitha was innocent. We killed an innocent girl.*

It didn't seem possible, and yet there it was on the screen. Tabitha had a whole life that was nothing like Ali's. She had parents. A home. Her burns had been from a house fire when she was young, not an explosion in the Poconos. Whatever she was doing to them in Jamaica must have been a silly ruse, a dare she'd wagered with herself, a game of chicken she didn't want to lose.

"M-maybe she just heard about us on the news or something," Aria said out loud, echoing everyone's thoughts. "Maybe she followed the tabloid websites, all those news reports . . ."

"There might have been sites that told more about us than we realized," Spencer murmured faintly, her eyes glazed and unblinking. "Maybe she was, like, obsessed. And when she saw us . . ."

". . . she thought she'd fuck with us," Hanna finished, placing her head in her hands and rocking her body side to side. "You guys, I was about to go to the police about this. I was going to tell them about A, and Ali, and even what we did in Jamaica."

"Jesus," Spencer whispered. "Thank God you didn't."

Tears pricked Hanna's eyes. "Oh God. Oh *God*. What have we done? They're going to trace the murder back to us!"

"A sent that picture of me and Tabitha dancing," Emily whispered. "It's proof we knew her. What if A sent that photo to Tabitha's parents, maybe? Or the cops?"

"Wait a minute." Aria pointed at the screen.

The reporter was pressing her finger into her ear again, clearly receiving a new set of information. "The sheriff is deeming this death an accident," she said. "Given the proximity to the The Cliffs resort, which is notorious for underage drinking and partying, investigators hypothesize that Ms. Clark had too much to drink one night and died in a tragic accident."

The camera cut to a shot of the sheriff, a tall Jamaican in a shiny blue uniform. He stood on a makeshift platform right behind the dilapidated fishing boat that had exhumed Tabitha's bones. "Our guess is that Ms. Clark decided to go swimming while intoxicated," he said into a series of microphones. "The Cliffs resort has had trouble with underage drinking, and it's time to put a stop to it. As of today, the resort is shut down indefinitely."

Flashbulbs popped. Reporters lobbed questions. Emily sat back in her chair, feeling numb. Spencer blinked. Aria pulled her knees up to her chest. Hanna shook her head and burst into tears again. Emily knew she should feel relieved, but the feeling didn't come. She knew the truth. It hadn't been an accident. Tabitha's blood was on their hands.

The fireplace snapped and crackled. The sharp, woodsy smell reminded Emily of so many things at once—like the campfire they'd sat around in the woods the summer after the Jenna Thing. By dying firelight, Ali had presented them with their string bracelets, making them promise never to tell what they'd done until the day they died. The bracelet on Tabitha's wrist had been eerily identical to the ones Ali had made for them, three different colors of blue string wound together to make the colors of a clear, clean lake.

But it must have been a coincidence. And now, they had a new secret they had to keep until the day they died. One that was way, way worse than the last.

The smoky smell reminded Emily of something else, too: the charred, blazing Poconos cabin the day Ali set fire to it, hoping to kill them all. For a brief moment, Emily allowed herself to revisit the memory of when she'd raced toward the kitchen door, desperate to get free. Ali had been there, too, grappling to get out before the others so she could barricade them inside. But Emily caught Ali's arm and spun her around.

"How could you do this?" she demanded.

Ali's eyes blazed. A small smile appeared on her lips. "You bitches ruined my life."

"But . . . I *loved* you," Emily cried.

Ali giggled. "You're *such* a loser, Emily."

Emily squeezed Ali's shoulders hard. And then, a loud boom filled the air. The next thing Emily knew, she was lying on the ground by the door. As she scrambled for safety, she knocked something to the floor. It was an orange tassel that had hung over the doorknob ever since she could remember. Every time Emily entered the Poconos house, giggling with Ali, ready for a fun weekend, she'd run her fingers through the tassel's silky threads. It made her feel like she was home.

Not knowing quite why, Emily slipped the tassel into her pocket. Then, she glanced over her shoulder one more time. She saw something she would never tell another soul, partly because she wasn't sure it was true or something she'd hallucinated after inhaling too much smoke, partly because she knew her friends wouldn't believe her, and partly because it was too scary and awful to even utter out loud.

When she'd looked back through the open doorway into the about-to-explode house, Ali wasn't anywhere. Had she been surrounded by too much smoke? Had she simply crawled farther into the kitchen and resigned herself to death?

Or maybe, just maybe, she was trying desperately to get out of the house, too. What Emily did next she would never forget. Instead of slamming the door hard, even shoving an Adirondack chair in front of it to make sure Ali wouldn't escape, she'd left the door unlatched and ajar. One weak push, and Ali would be out. Safe. Free. Emily just couldn't let her die in there. Even if Ali had said all those horrible things, even if Ali had broken Emily's heart in a million different ways, she couldn't do that.

Now, in Spencer's den, Emily reached into her pocket and touched the silky orange tassel once more. That horrible scene in Jamaica flashed before her eyes. *Everyone thought you died in the fire*, Emily had said to the girl they all swore was Ali. *But—*

But what? The girl interrupted. *But I escaped? Any ideas how* that *could have happened, Em?* Then she'd pointedly glanced at Emily's pocket as though she had X-ray vision and could see the orange tassel Emily had carried everywhere even then, the tassel that hung on the very door that had allowed for Ali's escape.

Tabitha knew what Emily had done. But . . . *how?*

When Emily's phone beeped in her bag, shrill and loud in the silent room, she nearly jumped out of her skin. Moments later, Spencer's cell phone buzzed. Aria's let out a car honk. Hanna's made a bird-tweet. The noises cycled once more, the ringing and buzzing a cacophony of wails. The girls stared at one another, terrified. If Tabitha wasn't Ali, and Tabitha had died that night, then who was doing this to them? Ali *still* could have survived the fire. Was A *still* Ali, tormenting them with the juiciest, most heinous secret of their lives?

Slowly, Spencer reached for her phone. So did Aria, then Hanna. Emily pulled her own phone out of her bag and stared at the screen. ONE NEW TEXT. From anonymous. Of course.

You think that's all I know, bitches? It's only the tip of the iceberg . . . and I'm just getting warmed up. –A

WHAT HAPPENS NEXT . . .

Did you *really* think it was over? Please. As long as these girls are misbehaving, I'll be watching. And boy, have they been bad. Shall we recap?

Hanna's boob nearly made Page Six. And, sure, she paid off Patrick, but she's about to find out that there's more than one way to kill Daddy's campaign.

Emily shattered Chloe's family. Last time I checked, that's *not* what friends are for. Perhaps Chloe should return the favor and tell Mrs. Fields exactly how Emily spent her summer break . . . or maybe I'll do it for her.

When push came to shove, Aria became pretty . . . *vicious*. Now, Klaudia's leg isn't the only thing that's broken. Can Aria and Noel's relationship survive Hurricane Klaudia? As they say in Finland: *Ja* right.

And finally we come to naughty, naughty Spencer. Think Zach is the only person whose life she's ruined? Think again. She pulled some *very* dirty tricks to get into her dream school—and someone got trampled in the process.

But here's the question that's on all of our minds: Just how long will Hanna, Emily, Aria, and Spencer be able to keep what they did in Jamaica under wraps? Or I guess the real question is: How long will I let them?

Stick with me, kids. It's about to get so good . . .

—A

ACKNOWLEDGMENTS

First off, let me say how thrilled I am that the Pretty Little Liars saga continues. As soon as I wrote the very first sentence of this book, I felt so . . . right, so thrilled and privileged to delve into the twisted lives of Spencer, Aria, Emily, and Hanna once more. As always, I owe a ton of gratitude to the smart, lovely people who helped create the new web of lies and threats for our Liars to face: Les Morgenstein, Josh Bank, Sara Shandler, and Lanie Davis at Alloy. It's been such a pleasure working with all of you on this series—there is truly something magical that happens whenever we convene.

Also big thanks to the amazing people on the other side of the country who have made Pretty Little Liars a success on the small screen—namely, Marlene King, Oliver Goldstick, Bob Levy, and Lisa Cochran-Neilan; the fabulous actresses Lucy Hale, Ashley Benson, Troian Bellisario, and Shay Mitchell, and all the rest of the cast; the wonderful writers for understanding the series so completely and giving it your own cheeky, spooky, excitingly different spin; and everyone else who works on the project, even in the smallest role. Thanks so much, too, to Farrin Jacobs and Kari Sutherland at HarperTeen, who always have amazing insight (and good memories) about the series, and much love to Kristin Marang and Allison Levin at Alloy for your awesome work on all things PLL online—including keeping the blog fresh and funny and interesting! A huge shout-out to Andy McNicol and Jennifer Rudolph-Walsh at William Morris for making PLL 9–12 a reality. I'm probably forgetting tons of other people in the amazing PLL process—the list keeps on growing!

As usual, much love to my family and husband, Joel, who is always there with forensic advice. But mostly, I want to dedicate this book to all of the readers of the series, from the very first girls who decided to give the hardcover of *Pretty Little Liars* a try back at my very virgin reading in Carle Place, New York, to the many fans I met in the sweltering heat in Fort Myers, Florida, to the lovely girls and librarians at the Jewish Library in Montreal, to everyone at events in between, as well as all the readers I've met on Twitter and Facebook and in chats and Skype talks. Without your unflagging enthusiasm and love for the series, *Twisted* wouldn't exist. I value each and every last one of you more than words can say.

SARA SHEPARD is the author of two *New York Times* bestselling series, Pretty Little Liars and The Lying Game. She graduated from New York University and has an MFA from Brooklyn College. Sara's Pretty Little Liars novels were inspired by her upbringing in Philadelphia's Main Line, where she lives today.

For exclusive information
on your favorite authors and artists,
visit www.authortracker.com.

READ ON FOR A PREVIEW OF
PRETTY LITTLE LIARS BOOK TEN,

Ruthless

1

Even though it was almost 10:30 P.M. on July 31 in Rosewood, Pennsylvania, a wealthy, bucolic suburb twenty miles outside Philadelphia, the air was still muggy, oppressively hot, and full of mosquitoes. The flawlessly manicured lawns had turned a dry, dull brown, the flowers in the beds had withered, and many of the leaves on the trees had shriveled up and fallen to the ground. Residents swam languidly in their lime-rocked pools, gobbled up homemade peach ice cream from the open-till-midnight local organic farmstand, or retreated indoors to lie in front of their air conditioners and pretend it was February. It was one of the few times all year the town didn't look like a picture-perfect postcard.

Aria Montgomery sat on her back porch, slowly dragging an ice cube across the back of her neck and contemplating going to bed. Her mother, Ella, was next to her, balancing a glass of white wine between her knees. "Aren't you thrilled about going back to Iceland in a few days?" Ella asked.

Aria tried to muster up enthusiasm, but deep down,

she felt a niggling sense of unrest. She adored Iceland—she'd lived there from eighth to eleventh grade—but she was returning with her boyfriend, Noel Kahn, her brother, Mike, and her old friend Hanna Marin. The last time Aria had traveled with all of them—and her two close friends Spencer Hastings and Emily Fields—was when they'd gone to Jamaica on spring break. Something awful had happened there. Something Aria would never be able to forget.

At the very same time, Hanna Marin was in her bedroom packing for the trip to Iceland. Was a country full of weird, pale Vikings who were all related to one another worthy of her Elizabeth and James high-heeled booties? She threw in a pair of Toms slip-ons instead; as they landed in the bottom of the suitcase, a sharp scent of coconut sunscreen wafted out from the lining, conjuring up images of a sun-drenched beach, rocky cliffs, and a cerulean Jamaican sea. Just like Aria, Hanna was also transported back to the fateful spring break trip she'd taken with her old best friends. *Don't think about it*, a voice inside her urged. *Don't* ever *think about it again.*

The heat in Center City Philadelphia was no less punishing. The dormitories on the Temple University campus were shoddily air-conditioned, and summer students propped up box fans in their dorm windows and submerged themselves in the fountain in the middle of the quad, even though there was a rumor that drunken junior and senior boys peed in it regularly.

Emily Fields unlocked her sister's dorm room, where

she was hiding out for the summer. She dropped her keys in the STANFORD SWIMMING mug on the counter and stripped off a sweaty, fried-food-smelling T-shirt, rumpled black pants, and a pirate's hat she'd worn to her waitress job at Poseidon's, a gimmicky seafood restaurant on Penn's Landing. All Emily wanted to do was to lie on her sister's bed and take a few long, deep breaths, but the lock turned in the door almost as soon as she'd shut it. Carolyn swept into the room, her arms full of textbooks. Even though there was no hiding her pregnancy anymore, Emily covered her bare stomach with her T-shirt. Carolyn's gaze automatically went to it anyway. A disgusted look settled over her features, and Emily turned away in shame.

A half mile away, near the University of Pennsylvania campus, Spencer Hastings staggered into a small room in the local police precinct. A thin trickle of sweat dripped down her spine. When she ran her hand through her dirty-blond hair, she felt greasy, snarled strands. She caught a glimpse of her reflection in the window in the door, and a gaunt girl with hollowed-out, lusterless eyes and a turned-down mouth stared back. She looked like a dirty corpse. When had she last showered?

A tall, sandy-haired cop entered the room behind Spencer, pulled the door closed, and glared at her menacingly. "You're in Penn's summer program, aren't you?"

Spencer nodded. She was afraid if she spoke, she'd burst into tears.

The cop pulled an unmarked bottle of pills from his

pocket and shook it in Spencer's face. "I'm going to ask you one more time. Is this yours?"

The bottle blurred before Spencer's eyes. As the cop leaned close, she caught a whiff of Polo cologne. It made her think, suddenly, about how her old best friend Alison DiLaurentis's brother, Jason, went through a Polo phase when he was in high school, drenching himself in the stuff before he went to parties. "Ugh, I've been *Polo'd*," Ali would always groan when Jason passed by, and Spencer and her old best friends Aria, Hanna, and Emily would burst into giggles.

"You think this is funny?" the cop growled now. "Because I assure you, you are *not* going to be laughing when we're done with you."

Spencer pressed her lips together, realizing she'd been smirking. "I'm sorry," she whispered. How could she think about her dead friend Ali—aka Courtney, Ali's secret twin—at a time like this? Next she'd be thinking about the *real* Alison DiLaurentis, a girl Spencer had never been friends with, a girl who'd returned to Rosewood from a mental hospital and murdered her own twin sister, Ian Thomas, Jenna Cavanaugh, and almost Spencer, too.

Surely these scattered thoughts were a side effect of the pill she'd swallowed an hour before. It was just kicking in, and her mind was speeding at a million miles a minute. Her eyes darted all over the place, and her hands twitched. *You got the Easy A shakes!* her friend Kelsey would say, if she and Spencer were in Kelsey's dorm room at Penn instead of locked in two separate interrogation cells in this dingy station. And Spencer would laugh, swat Kelsey with her notebook, and then return to cramming nine months' worth of AP Chemistry III information into her already jam-packed head.

When it was clear Spencer wasn't going to own up to the pills, the cop sighed and slipped the bottle back into his pocket. "Just so you know, your friend's been talking up a storm," he said, his voice hard. "She says it was all your idea—that she was just along for the ride."

Spencer gasped. "She said what?"

A knock sounded on the door. "Stay here," he growled. "I'll be back."

He exited the cell. Spencer looked around the tiny room. The cinder-block walls had been painted puke-green. Suspicious yellowish-brown stains marred the beige carpet, and the overhead lights gave off a high-pitched hum that made her teeth hurt. Footsteps sounded out-side the door, and she sat very still, listening. Was the cop taking Kelsey's statement right now? And what exactly was Kelsey saying about Spencer? It wasn't like they'd rehearsed what they'd say if they got caught. They never thought they *would* get caught. That police car had come out of nowhere. . . .

Spencer shut her eyes, thinking about what had hap-pened in the last hour. Picking up the pills from South Philly. Peeling out of that scary neighborhood. Hearing the sirens scream behind them. She dreaded what the next hours would bring. The calls to her parents. The disappointed looks and quiet tears. Rosewood Day would probably expel her, and Spencer would have to finish high school at Rosewood Public. Or else she'd go to juvie. After that, it would be a one-way trip to community college—or worse, working as a hoagie-maker at the local Wawa or as a sandwich board–wearer at the Rosewood Federal Credit Union, advertising the new mortgage rates to all the drivers on Lancaster Avenue.

Spencer touched the laminated ID card for the University of Pennsylvania Summer Program in her pocket. She thought of the graded papers and tests she'd received this week, the bright 98s and 100s at the top of each and every one. Things were going so well. She just needed to get through the rest of this summer program, ace the four APs she was taking, and she'd be at the top of the Rosewood Day pyramid again. She deserved a reprieve after her horrible ordeal with Real Ali. How much torment and bad luck did one girl have to endure?

Feeling for her iPhone in the pocket of her denim shorts, she pressed the PHONE button and dialed Aria's number. It rang once, twice . . .

Aria's own iPhone bleated in the peaceful Rosewood darkness. When she saw Spencer's name on the Caller ID, she flinched. "Hey," she answered cautiously. Aria hadn't heard from Spencer in a while, not since their fight at Noel Kahn's party.

"Aria." Spencer's voice was tremulous, like a violin

string stretched taut. "I need your help. I'm in trouble. It's serious."

Aria quickly slipped through the sliding glass door and padded up to her bedroom. "What happened? Are you okay?"

Spencer swallowed hard. "It's me and Kelsey. We got caught."

Aria paused on the stairs. "Because of the pills?"

Spencer whimpered.

Aria didn't say anything. *I warned you*, she thought. *And you lashed out at me.*

Spencer sighed, sensing the reason for Aria's silence. "Look, I'm sorry for what I said to you at Noel's party, okay? I . . . I wasn't in my right mind, and I didn't mean it." She glanced at the window in the door again. "But this is serious, Aria. My whole future could be ruined. My whole *life*."

Aria pinched the skin between her eyes. "There's nothing I can do. I'm not messing with the police—especially not after Jamaica. I'm sorry. I can't help." With a heavy heart, she hung up.

"Aria!" Spencer cried into the receiver, but the CALL ENDED message was already flashing.

Unbelievable. How could Aria do this to her, after all they'd been through?

Someone coughed outside Spencer's holding room. Spencer turned to her phone again and quickly dialed Emily's number. She pressed her ear to the receiver, listening to the *brrt-brrt-brrt* of the ringing line. "Pick up, pick *up*," she pleaded.

The lights in Carolyn's room were already off when Emily's phone started to beep. Emily glanced at Spencer's name on the screen and felt a wave of dread. Spencer probably wanted to invite her to a get-together at Penn. Emily always said she was too tired, but really it was because she hadn't told Spencer or any of her other friends that she was pregnant. The idea of explaining it to them terrified her.

But as the screen flashed, she felt an eerie premonition. What if Spencer was in trouble? The last time she'd seen Spencer, she'd seemed so scared and desperate. Maybe she needed Emily's help. Maybe they could help each other.

Emily's fingers inched toward the phone, but then Carolyn rolled over in bed and groaned. "You're not going to get that, are you? *Some* of us have class in the morning."

Emily pressed IGNORE and flopped back down to the mattress, biting back tears. She knew it was a burden for Carolyn to let her stay here—the futon took up nearly all the floor space, Emily constantly interrupted her sister's studying schedule, and she was asking Carolyn to keep a huge secret from their parents. But did she have to be so mean about it?

Spencer hung up without leaving Emily a message. There was one person left to call. Spencer pressed Hanna's name in her contacts list.

Hanna was zipping her suitcase closed when the phone

rang. "Mike?" she answered without looking at the screen. All day, her boyfriend had been calling her with random trivia about Iceland—*Did you know there's a museum about sex there? I am so taking you.*

"Hanna," Spencer blurted on the other end. "I need you."

Hanna sat back. "Are you okay?" She'd barely heard from Spencer all summer, not since she began an intensive summer program at Penn. The last time she'd seen her was at Noel Kahn's party, when Spencer's friend Kelsey came along, too. What a weird night *that* had been.

Spencer burst into tears. Her words came out in choppy bursts, and Hanna only caught bits of sentences: "The police . . . pills . . . I tried to get rid of them . . . I am *so* dead unless you . . ."

Hanna rose and paced around the room. "Slow down. Let me get this straight. So . . . you're in trouble? Because of the drugs?"

"Yes, and I need you to do something for me." Spencer clutched the phone with both hands.

"How can *I* help?" Hanna whispered. She thought about the times she'd been dragged to the police station— for stealing a bracelet from Tiffany, and later for wrecking her then-boyfriend Sean's car. Surely Spencer wasn't asking Hanna to cozy up to the cop that arrested her, as Hanna's mother had done.

"Do you still have those pills I gave you at Noel's party?" Spencer said.

"Uh, yeah." Hanna shifted uncomfortably.

"I need you to get them and drive them to Penn's campus. Go to the Friedman dorm. There's a door around the back that's always propped open—you can get in that way. Go to the fourth floor, room four-thirteen. There's a keypad combination to get into the room—five-nine-two-oh. When you get in, put the pills under the pillow. Or in the drawer. Somewhere kind of hidden but also kind of obvious."

"Wait, whose room is this?"

Spencer curled her toes. She was hoping Hanna wouldn't ask that. "It's . . . Kelsey's," she admitted. "*Please* don't judge me right now, Hanna. I don't think I can take it. She's going to ruin me, okay? I need you to put those pills in Kelsey's room and then call the cops and say that she's a known dealer at Penn. You also need to say she has a sketchy past—she's trouble. That will make the cops search her room."

"*Is* Kelsey really a dealer?" Hanna asked.

"Well, no. I don't think so."

"So basically you're asking me to frame Kelsey for something you both did?"

Spencer shut her eyes. "I guarantee you Kelsey's in the interrogation room right now, blaming me. I have to try to save myself."

"But I'm going to Iceland in two days!" Hanna protested. "I'd rather not go through customs with a warrant out for my arrest."

"You won't get caught," Spencer reassured her. "I

promise. And . . . think about Jamaica. Think about how we *all* would have been screwed if we hadn't stuck together."

Hanna's stomach swirled. She'd tried her hardest to erase the Jamaica incident from her mind, avoiding her friends for the rest of the school year so as not to relive or rehash the awful events. The same thing had happened to the four of them after their best friend, Alison DiLaurentis—really Courtney, Ali's secret twin sister—disappeared on the last day of seventh grade. Sometimes, a tragedy brought friends together. Other times, it tore them apart.

But Spencer needed her now, just like Hanna had needed her friends in Jamaica. They had saved her life. She stood up and slipped on a pair of Havaiana flip-flops. "Okay," she whispered. "I'll do it."

"*Thank* you," Spencer said. When she hung up, relief settled over her like a cool, misty rain.

The door burst open, and the phone almost slid from Spencer's hand. The same wiry cop strode into the room. When he noticed Spencer's phone, his cheeks reddened. "What are you doing with that?"

Spencer dropped it to the table. "No one asked me to hand it in."

The cop grabbed the phone and slipped it into his pocket. Then he gripped Spencer's hand and roughly pulled her to her feet. "Come on."

"Where are you taking me?"

The cop nudged Spencer into the hall. The odor of

rancid takeout burned her nostrils. "We're going to have a discussion."

"I told you, I don't know anything," Spencer protested. "What did Kelsey say?"

The cop smirked. "Let's see if your stories match."

Spencer stiffened. She pictured her new friend in the interrogation room, preserving her own future and wrecking Spencer's. Then she thought of Hanna getting into her car and setting the GPS to Penn's campus. The idea of blaming Kelsey made her stomach churn, but what other choice did she have?

The cop pushed open a second door, and pointed for Spencer to sit down in an office chair. "You have a lot of explaining to do, Miss Hastings."

That's what you think, Spencer thought, rolling back her shoulders. Her decision was a good one. She had to look out for herself. And with Hanna on her way, she'd get away with this scot-free.

It was only later, after Hanna had planted the drugs, after her call came into the central switchboard, and after Spencer overheard two cops talking about going to the Friedman dorm to search room 413, that Spencer found out the truth: Kelsey hadn't said a single word to implicate either herself or Spencer for the crimes they'd been accused of. Spencer wished she could undo everything, but it was too late—admitting she'd lied would get her into worse trouble. It was better to keep quiet. There was no way to trace what the cops had found back to her.

Shortly after that, the cops let Spencer go with a warning. As she was leaving the holding room, two officers marched Kelsey through the hall, their meaty hands gripping her arm like she was in big, big trouble. Kelsey glanced at Spencer fearfully as she passed. *What's going on?* her eyes said. *What do they have on me?* Spencer had shrugged like she had absolutely no clue, then walked into the night, her future intact.

Her life went on. She took her APs and aced every single one. She returned to Rosewood Day at the top of her class. She got into Princeton early decision. As the weeks and months flew by, the nightmarish evening faded and she rested easy, knowing her secret was safe. Only Hanna knew the truth. No one else—not her parents, not the Princeton admissions board, not Kelsey—would ever find out.

Until the following winter. When someone discovered everything.

   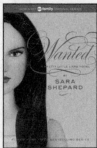
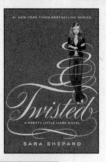  

PRETTY GIRLS DON'T PLAY
BY THE RULES...

THEY MAKE THEM.

DON'T MISS THE LYING GAME,
A KILLER SERIES FROM SARA SHEPARD